W9-CTZ-349

ROCK
WAGRAM

A NOVEL BY

WILLIAM SAROYAN

1951

DOUBLEDAY & COMPANY, INC.

GARDEN CITY, NEW YORK

c.1

ROCK WAGRAM

 Chapter I

THE FATHER

Every man is a good man in a bad world. *No man changes the world. Every man himself changes from good to bad or from bad to good, back and forth, all his life, and then dies. But no matter how or why or when a man changes, he remains a good man in a bad world, as he himself knows. All his life a man fights death, and then at last loses the fight, always having known he would. Loneliness is every man's portion, and failure. The man who seeks to escape from loneliness is a lunatic. The man who does not know that all is failure is a fool. The man who does not laugh at these things is a bore. But the lunatic is a good man, and so is the fool, and so is the bore, as each of them knows. Every man is inno-*

cent, and in the end a lonely lunatic, a lonely fool, or a lonely bore.

But there is meaning to a man. There is meaning to the life every man lives. It is a secret meaning, and pathetic if it weren't for the lies of art.

ONE day in September he found that he was in Amarillo, Texas, on his way to San Francisco in his new Cadillac, a man named Rock Wagram, thirty-three years old. It was seven o'clock in the morning, and he was up from three hours of sleep, eager to get going again but hushed in heart by the haunting of death.

The end—the good end, the bad end, the great end, the miserable end—death—had haunted him from the beginning, and yet he *had* lived, he had stayed alive, he had had fun, he had been lucky with women, he had laughed a lot, he had worked, and he had done all right.

He had been tending bar at Fat Aram's in Fresno, twenty-five years old, when a man from Hollywood standing at the bar turned out to be the Vice-President in Charge of Production at U.S. Pictures. This man noticed only those who didn't notice him.

Rock Wagram (or as he was then known Arak Vagramian) was noticed by this man as Rock told jokes to the boys at the end of the bar.

The U.S. Pictures' man watched and listened an hour, then handed Rock his card and asked that Rock go and see him at his office at ten the following morning. Paul Key meant his office at U.S. Pictures in Hollywood, two hundred miles away. That was the way he did things. The bartender glanced at the card, at the sharp little man with the hard face, winked, almost smiled, put the card in the pocket of his white coat, and went back to the laughing boys at the end of the bar.

Two days later a fat man named Sam Schwartz stepped up to the bar and said to Rock, "Are you the man P.K. gave his card to day before yesterday?"

Rock didn't even know who P.K. was.

Even so, he and Schwartz sat in an airplane two hours later, and that night Rock had dinner with P.K. at Romanoff's.

"What are you?" Paul Key said.

"I'm a bartender," Rock said.

"What nationality?"

"American Indian."

"Are you a Turk?"

"I'm an Armenian," Rock said. "I hate the Turks."

"How much do you hate them?" Paul Key said.

"Not enough," Rock said. "I was born in Fresno. To hate them enough you've got to be born where my father and mother were born, in Armenia. All the Armenian hoodlums of Fresno call themselves American Indians."

"Why do you call them hoodlums?"

"We call *ourselves* hoodlums."

"Why?"

"Because that's what our parents call us in Armenian."

"Why do they call you that?"

"Because that's what we are."

"How do you mean?" Paul Key said.

"We don't hate the Turks enough," Rock said. "We're Americans. How can we hate them? How can we hate anybody? Most of us are dark and look like Indians anyway, so we've made a joke of calling ourselves American Indians. Besides, we've recognized a couple of pals from Fresno play-

3

ing Indians in the movies. They look more like Indians in the movies than Indians do. Most of the Indians you see around Fresno are Tule and don't look very Indian, anyway. First of all, their bodies are small, something's the matter with their faces, and they aren't dark the way we are. Most of our noses stand out better, too. Bull Bedikian played Chief Rapaport of the Cherokee Tribe in *The Indian Fighter* and was a sensation in Fresno."

"Rapaport?" Paul Key said.

"Another joke," Rock said. "I've forgotten the name of the Chief in the movie, and any time we forget a name we put in a funny one."

"Why?"

"For the fun of it."

"I'm Jewish," Paul Key said.

"Is that so?" Rock said.

"Are you anti-semitic?"

"What's that?"

"Well, let me put it this way," Paul Key said. "Do you put in a name like Rapaport because you don't like Jews?"

"No," Rock said, "we put in a name like Rapaport because we think it's a funny name. We like everybody, but especially busy people like Armenians, Syrians, and Jews. The only people we don't like are Turks, but we don't dislike them enough."

"What do you mean by *busy?*"

"Funny."

"I don't believe I get it," Paul Key said.

"Well," Rock said, "people with a lot to do who are glad to be doing it and haven't got time to bother too much about anything else."

4

"You like such people?"

"They're the people who make you laugh," Rock said. "Jews from the big cities in the East have been coming to Fresno every summer for years and we've gotten to know them, working in their packing houses. I used to drive for one of the best of them, a fellow from Brooklyn who'd changed his name to Murphy."

"Drive?"

"I was fifteen," Rock said. "Drove his Cadillac all over the valley. Everything he ever said was funny. Sometimes I used to drive off the highway and stop the car, so I could get out and laugh."

"Jews are supposed to be the saddest people in the world," Paul Key said.

"Is that so?" Rock said.

"Yes," Paul Key said. "Being one, I believe they *are*."

"They weren't in Fresno," Rock said. "Not even when they went broke. Murphy went broke. They all went broke. The saddest ones were the Irish when they went broke. They were the most generous, too, but it was because they were so sad."

"Then, when you put in a Jewish name it's not to belittle the Jews?" Paul Key said.

"No," Rock said. "There was never any politeness between the Jews from the East and the hoodlums of Fresno, but they were pals. The only time I ever saw Murphy slow down was when a polite man who was riding with us to Bakersfield, an Erie railroad man named Fickett, told Murphy he had always admired the Jews. Murphy didn't route any of his cars over the Erie after that."

"Maybe the railroad man meant what he said," Paul Key said.

5

"No," Rock said. "He was a phony."

"How do you know?"

"I call tell a phony."

"How about you?" Paul Key said. "Are you a phony?"

"Not on purpose," Rock said. "If I am, I didn't mean it to happen."

"Am I?" Paul Key said.

"Why ask me?" Rock said. "You ought to know."

"What would *you* say?"

"I'd say I don't know."

"How about the business with the card?" Paul Key said.

"A lot of guys come to Fat Aram's and leave their cards, so I'll know them the next time they come in," Rock said. "Everybody likes to know a bartender."

"I didn't leave my card so you'd know me the next time I came in," Paul Key said. "You know that isn't why I left it. I asked you to be at my office at ten the following morning."

"You were drunk," Rock said.

"I don't like to be told I was drunk," Paul Key said.

"I don't like to be told how to talk," Rock said.

The film man, a man of fifty-two who had lived a hard and bitter life, looked around the room. No one in the film-making business could speak to Paul Key as this man had just spoken to him, but then of course this man was not in the film-making business. He was a bartender at Fat Aram's in Fresno. Was the man an imbecile? Or was it just that Paul Key had dealt with hypocrites for so long he'd become fond of them and couldn't abide anybody who wasn't one? There was still a great deal to find out about the bartender, and he owed it to himself and to the studio to go on, but he was not going to let the crack go without at least half a minute of critical silence.

6

"Then, you don't feel that the business with the card was phony?" Paul Key said at last.

"I haven't thought about it one way or another," Rock said. "Didn't Schwartz say your wife was coming, and a friend of hers?"

"They'll be along in a minute," Paul Key said. "What's a phony?"

"A phony, that's all."

"How can you tell one?"

"You just know."

"How far did you go in school?"

"I didn't finish high school."

"Why not?"

"Didn't want to."

"What do you want?" Paul Key said. "I know you want something. You've given it a lot of thought. What do you want?"

"Fun. Wife. Kids. Money," Rock said.

"In that order?"

"For the time being," Rock said. "Wife. Fun. Kids. Money. Later on."

"How much money?"

"Enough."

"How much would be enough?"

"What I make at Fat Aram's."

"What do you make?"

"Seventy-five a week."

"Tips?"

"I don't allow tips," Rock said. "Most of the boys I tend bar for are pals. If somebody slides a quarter or half a buck across the bar and goes off before I can slide it back, I put it in a cup and the next day put everything in the cup on a horse."

7

"Do you win?"

"No."

"Why do you bet?" Paul Key said.

"A pal of mine runs the book," Rock said. "He's got a family."

"What else do you want?" Paul Key said.

"I want whatever I've got coming," Rock said. "I like to read, and I like to write."

"I don't understand," Paul Key said. "You say you like to read and *write?*"

"Yes."

"What do you write?"

"Poems."

"What kind of poems?"

"Well, not dirty, if that's what you mean," Rock said. "Funny, I guess, if you know what *I* mean."

"I'm beginning to get an idea," Paul Key said. "What made you want to write poems?"

"My father wrote poems," Rock said. "We took poems for granted in our family."

"Do you know why you're here?" Paul Key said.

"Schwartz said you wanted to talk to me," Rock said.

"But why did I want to talk to you?"

"Because you've got an idea I can act."

"Can you?"

"I can act natural," Rock said. "And it's natural for me to act a lot of different ways."

"Yes," Paul Key said. "The girls will be here in a minute. Schwartz has set you up at the Beverly Wilshire. Well, I want a test made of you tomorrow morning. At ten. Come to my office. I mean, be there at half past nine, so I can tell you

8

a few things. If nothing comes of it, you'll be paid for your time and trouble. If something comes of it, we'll have to do something about your name. What's Arak mean?"

"Swift."

"What's the other name mean?"

"Nothing. It's just a name. Vagramian. It means me."

"Have you boxed?"

"No. Just street fights."

"Is your nose broken?"

"Yes, but I want it to stay that way."

"Why not straighten it out?" Paul Key said.

"My father broke it when I was sixteen and thought I was big stuff," Rock said. "I want it to stay the way it is."

"You mean you had a fight with your father?"

"Yes."

"Over money?"

"No."

"Girls?"

"Yes."

"Arak Vagramian, is that it?"

"That's right."

"How did you happen to become a bartender?"

"One of those things. A cool place in a hot town. A good place to stand and talk, pass the time, get paid for it."

"You don't look like an Armenian," Paul Key said.

"Nobody looks like an Armenian," Rock said.

The girls arrived and sat down. Vida, the film-maker's wife, was a quiet, dark woman in her middle forties who couldn't take her eyes away from her husband. She kept waiting for him to look back at her so their eyes could embrace. The other girl was a famous actress named Selena Hope who hadn't

9

had a job in more than a year and was beginning to worry. She was probably in her early thirties.

It was from her house somewhere near the ocean that Rock Wagram set out the following morning for Paul Key's office.

Now, the same man, seven years later, in Amarillo, Texas, sat at the counter of the hotel coffee shop and had a cup of black coffee, glancing at the morning paper. After coffee, he settled with the desk, got into his car, and began to go, but a mile from the heart of town, he saw a girl with long blonde hair walking swiftly, just up from sleep, wearing a red cotton dress. He turned the car around, drove past the girl, turned it around again, slowed down to have a last look at her, and then sent the car plunging out of town.

No man's life means more than another's, as each man himself knows. The luckiest man is the one who enjoys his portion, but no man is very lucky, for every man's portion is equally poor, and putting up with it is painful. Most of his experience cannot be enjoyed. Most of it hurts, and some of it kills, or inflicts the wound that stops him in his tracks.

Every man is an animal. He is the animal all men are, but after that he is also his own kind of animal. He is a small and lonely thing, not unlike all of his breed, all alive at the same time.

He is his own poor friend, his own proud stranger, his own cunning enemy, watching with sharp eyes his mother's own son, and he knows more than he is ever able to tell. Whatever the acts of his life, his own cunning friend and his own forgiving enemy watches and mocks or comforts him, and a man lives out his time in secret, leaving behind no word of what he was or did or knew. Or leaving half a word, mixed with laugh-

*ter, or half an act of dancing mixed with love, in the warm
light, along the bright floor of his own mother's kitchen when
he was five and she was his girl, baking bread for him.*

*No man's portion is good, there is no man unwounded, but
the wounds of some heal slowly, the wounds of others never
at all.*

*The wounds of Paul Key never healed. He carried them
all in the hard eyes that were somehow full of understanding,
tenderness, and hate.*

IT was not Paul Key's habit to step into insignificant little
bars in insignificant little towns, but J.B. had told him to fly to
Fresno and find out what was eating the company on location:
they were taking too long. Paul Key had found out that the
reason they were taking so long was that they were getting the
job done the only way they knew how to get it done—that
is, slowly and stupidly—so before telephoning J.B., he thought
he would get out of the heat, cool off at a bar, and listen to
whoever might be talking in the place.

The bar was on a corner, called Fat Aram's, and it would
do. There were seven dark men at the end of the bar, men
somewhere between twenty and thirty, although one of them
was older. The bartender was telling them a story, he had
them by the tail, talking easily, taking his time, letting them
know they would never guess what the prize of comedy would
be this time. He glanced at Paul Key and went right on telling
the story.

The end of the story came a long time later. Perhaps it was
three minutes, perhaps five. At any rate, there had been plenty
of time for Paul Key to leave and go to another place. He had
not done so.

The end came in a strange language. It came clearly and cleanly, and the men received it as if they had been waiting for it all their lives, two of them falling to the floor, three of them running out the side door, the others walking around in a kind of preposterous immortality brought about by humor, while the man who was soon to become Rock Wagram stood where he was, watching them, but not even smiling.

At last he went to where Paul Key was standing, and waited for him to speak.

If this had happened at Romanoff's or Chasen's, the bartender would have been fired. Or didn't they fire them any more? At any rate, it wouldn't have happened. Paul Key had planned to say to the bartender, "I'm glad you and your friends are enjoying yourselves, but if you don't mind I'd like a Pimm's Number One." This was just the drink for a hot day and although only the boys at 21 in New York knew how to make it and serve it, he often had it on hot days at one or another of the places in Hollywood or Beverly Hills.

Now, however, he knew he was not going to say any such thing, and he knew he was not going to ask for any Pimms.

"Scotch over ice with a water chaser," he said. He would have specified Black Label, but that wouldn't do either.

The bartender was swift, once he decided he was ready to oblige you. He was *that*, at any rate. Paul Key swallowed the first one straight.

"Another, please," he said quickly because he was afraid the bartender would walk off and never come back. He put a fifty-dollar bill beside the water chaser, but the bartender let it lie. He poured the second drink and placed the bottle on the bar, as if to say that if he didn't happen to get back in time to pour the third one, not to stop on that account.

"God damn you, Rock," one of the dark men said. "I'm going to tell that one to my wife tonight."

"You and your wife," Rock said. "What business you got marrying a foreigner? A girl from Van? You're from Bitlis." He then said something in a language Paul Key didn't know, and everybody laughed. But he knew one thing: this bartender, this happy and arrogant hooligan the others called Rock, *was* an actor.

It was three o'clock in the afternoon. He had been out in the country near Kerman with the company on location since ten in the morning. He'd had lunch with the director and the two stars, the man and the woman simultaneously flirting and fighting, and the whole thing—his whole life, that is—had once again overwhelmed him as an absurd, hopeless, and wretched thing. If he had to put up with such imbeciles, his life was dirt. He *did* have to put up with them, and his life *was* dirt.

The heat was intense, but there was a kind of dry exhilaration in it. He felt alive in a way he couldn't remember ever before having felt, and here he was very nearly fifty-three, a man whose height was five feet six, whose weight was never above 140 pounds, whose thick black hair had been gray at the temples since he was twenty. A man whose hands and feet were small, whose head was small, whose eyes and nose and mouth were big. A man whose physical appearance repulsed most women and amused all men.

"Paul Key?" he had once overheard a famous actor say to an ambitious girl. "See him by all means if you can stand the sight of him. He may make you want to vomit, but he won't make a pass at you. He loves his wife, and he's devoted to his kids, two boys and a girl. Don't be cute with him. He's got the sharpest eye in town, and maybe if you keep your pretty mouth shut long enough and let him do all the talking, he'll think you're intelligent. He *is*. But what a face!"

Paul Key listened to the bartender an hour. There was nothing wrong with the fellow going right on being a bartender the rest of his life, but there was something wrong with Paul Key not finding out what made the bartender the way he was. It couldn't be only his youth, for even at twenty-five Paul Key had been no different from Paul Key at fifty-two.

Rock Wagram drove along Highway 66, the roadster top down, the radio on, the hot sun overhead, the desert all around, the four wheels rolling swiftly and smoothly, murmuring the haunting theme of death, the good enemy inside listening and speaking.

"Who are you, Rock? Everybody knows who Rock Wagram is, but do *you* know? Are you Arak Vagramian? Is that who you are? Well, he was never much, either, Rock. All he ever was was a kid who drove for Murphy two summers, tended bar at Fat Aram's for three years. What about it, Rock? Who are you, and what do you want?"

Rock let the forgiving enemy talk, himself singing *Cool Water* with the cowboys on the radio.

The Cadillac plunged forward as if it were not on wheels at all, as if it were flying.

"What about it, Rock?"

"Shut up," Rock said. "You know I'm looking for my wife. You know I'm looking for the mother of my kids. You know what I want, so shut up."

A man lives his life in ignorance, never knowing the true meaning of any experience, never knowing the great truth about himself. He lives all of his life instantly every minute

*he is up and abroad, doing, or down and out in his bed, asleep,
or turning in sleeplessness, or standing alone in nightmare. A
man is suddenly instantaneously alive and out of touch with a
secret. He is suddenly an instantaneous thing, and he does not
stop being this thing until he is in touch again with the lost
secret, and then it is that a man is dead. As long as he lives a
man seeks the instantaneous woman, hoping to find in her the
everlasting secret. But the man and the women together do
not find the secret. Even if they become father and mother
of son and daughter, they do not find the secret, they are not
healed of their aloneness, and they see their son instantaneously
himself and alone, and their daughter also. A man's own are
not his own, for a man himself does not belong to his own
instantaneous self. His wife is not his own, nor is his son his
own, nor his daughter.*

*In an instant a man is, in an instant he is not. He never knew
who he was. The nearer he came to finding out, the more hopeless finding out became.*

AT thirty-three Rock Wagram was no wiser than he'd
been the instant he reached out and took from his small
brother's hand the peach his brother had been eating, and himself ate it: no wiser than he'd been the instant a half hour later
he took the boy a *bigger* peach and said to him, "You eat it."

His brother's name was Haig. He came along when Rock
was three, a man who smiled all his life. Rock's taking of the
peach was memorable because Haig didn't do what he was
supposed to do about it. He didn't fight, cry, or complain. He
smiled. Rock ate the peach slowly, looking back at the strange
man who was his brother. After that Rock loved him, took
him everywhere he went, and explained everything to him.

But Haig didn't love Rock. Had he loved Rock, he wouldn't have died.

He couldn't have loved *any of them* to have done that.

"I don't understand," Rock's father said. "He was stronger than any of the rest of us. He had the best manners. But when he smiled, he broke my heart. I loved his mother, and he was born out of that love. Why did he forgive me by smiling? What did I do?"

"You've got to live," Rock said. "A man has got to keep himself alive. The rudest thing a man can do is die. It's rude to his mother and father, to his unborn son and daughter. A man's got to drive his car carefully and stay alive."

When he came to Vega, he stopped the car in front of a restaurant called Charley's and went in. He sat and talked with Charley a half hour, then got up to go.

"Anybody ever tell you you look like Rock Wagram?" Charley said.

"I *am* Rock Wagram."

"I *thought* you were," Charley said, "but a fellow ought to be able to go any place he likes and not be recognized. I'd be awful mad if I couldn't go to Amarillo every Saturday night and not have a soul know who I am."

"You're Charley, aren't you?" Rock said.

"I am," Charley said, "but that ain't the half of it. There's more to me than just Charley, only I'm going to keep it to myself, the same as ever. I knew you the minute you stepped in here. Anybody would know you. The broken nose for one thing. I kept my mouth shut until you were ready to go, so you could sit in peace and enjoy your coffee. No man ought to be recognized everywhere he goes. It ain't good for him. Take it easy now."

"O.K.," Rock said.

He got back into his car and drove off.

"You're famous all right," the cunning friend said. "Charley of Vega knows you. He's seen you in the movies. Well, what do you want, Rock? You've had your coffee, so what do you want *now?*"

"I just want to drive to San Francisco and see Mama," Rock said. "I just want to hear Mama talk in Armenian. I just want to hear the news about all of us from Mama."

No man cares about anyone but himself. No man loves anyone but himself. A woman is grateful to the man who plunges her into a passion for herself, and so it is with a man. Together they come to fine or ferocious feelings about themselves, and call it love. But it is actually only another way for them to forget for a moment the nagging truth that it is meaningless to live.

ONE day in February he was drinking at a place on Sunset Boulevard called Dirty Dan's, an after-hours place, when Eddie Lucas stood beside him at the bar and said, "Let's sit down a minute. I want to talk to you."

They took a table in a corner.

"What's the matter now?" Rock said.

"It's this girl I married last month in Mexico," Eddie said. "She's driving me crazy."

"The usual way?"

"No, that was the one before this one," Eddie said. "This one's stupid. I think she's feeble-minded. I've got to have somebody around I can say something more than *ugh* to, don't I?"

"Do you?"

"Listen, Rock. I'm not in this dive at three in the morning because I know what I'm doing. I'm here because I'm desperate. This is my fourth wife. We're just married. She wants a baby. She claims she's pregnant. I want to get rid of her before it's too late. I don't want to be the father of an imbecile."

"She's very pretty," Rock said. "Why should she be intelligent, too?"

"I can't stand a stupid girl," Eddie said.

"Sure you can. She's just the girl for you. You'll be crazy about the baby."

"I hate babies."

"What's the matter?" Rock said.

"I'm in love with another girl," Eddie said.

"When did you meet her?"

"Last night, here."

"She *must* be intelligent."

"Most intelligent piece I ever ran into."

"What seems to be the trouble?"

"I feel guilty," Eddie said. "I feel silly about all this trouble I keep getting into all the time. You know all the jokes about me and my wives. Hell, I'm a serious man. It's no joke with me. I had dinner at Chasen's tonight with Paul Key. I'm doing the songs for *The Great Lover*. I began to tell him about this wife of mine, and he listened all night. So did Vida. They went home. I came here because she's going to meet me here in a half hour. She's out with that jerk millionaire with the oil wells who's in town to buy a movie studio. Her mother thinks she's the kind of girl who *ought* to marry a rich man, but she's coming here to meet me the minute she gets rid of him, which she said would be around half past three, most likely."

"You feel guilty about *what?*" Rock said.

"About the way I haven't been working for almost a year," Eddie said. "I'm nothing if I'm not a song-writer, and every-body's noticed that my songs are lousy lately. I can't even steal a decent melody any more. I haven't got time to hunt them out. I'm crazy about this girl from New York, though. I want to marry her."

"I think you *ought* to have two wives," Rock said.

"No. This is serious. I mean, as soon as I can get rid of the one I'm married to now. What do you think she said this morning?"

"What?"

"Good morning."

"What a stupid woman," Rock said.

"It was the stupidest remark I ever heard," Eddie said. "I thought I must be in a whorehouse somewhere, and this was one of the day girls coming with a cup of coffee for a drunk who'd passed out early in the morning. She was carrying a tray with breakfast on it for me."

"Anything else?" Rock said.

"Yes," Eddie said. "Will you telephone her and tell her I had to fly to San Francisco?"

"Your wife?"

"No, this other girl. I'm scared to death. I don't want to see her for a couple of days. I want to find out if I'm really in love with her before I get a divorce."

"Why don't you wait until she gets here and just tell her you're scared to death?"

"She doesn't know I'm married."

"Well, if she's intelligent, she's not very well informed. I won't phone her, but if you'll tell me what she's like, when she gets here I'll tell her you waited until three-thirty and then went home."

"She's blonde, she's seventeen, she's got everything," Eddie said. "You'll know her the minute you see her. You agree that I ought to stay out of trouble, don't you?"

"Not necessarily," Rock said. "Tell me more."

"I made a pass at her last night," Eddie said. "I even asked her to marry me. I don't want to fool around any more. I'm tired. I've got to write some decent songs for a change. I'm drunk all the time. My wife drives me crazy. I can't be fooling around this way forever. I'm thirty-six years old."

"Now you're talking," Rock said. "What else?"

"She knows I'm married," Eddie said. "I *did* try to get a fast lay out of her last night, but I didn't mind not making it. She asked if I knew you. I said we were old pals. I promised to have you here at three-thirty in case she comes by. You know how these things are. I wasn't sure I'd remember any of it. But I *did* try to reach you at your home around midnight. And I came here myself, not expecting to see you, not even expecting her to show up. In case she did, though, I could tell her you couldn't make it tonight, and maybe try one time more."

"Anything else?" Rock said.

"No," Eddie said. "That's it. I don't know if you ought to meet her."

"Why not?" Rock said.

"Well, for one thing she's stupid," Eddie said. "She's a blonde. She can talk about anything, but she's a blonde. For another, she's probably a little crazy. I mean she sounds as if she expects a lot of big things to happen to her just because she's seventeen and blonde. I don't think you ought to meet her."

"She may not show up," Rock said. "I want to have a couple more before I go, anyway."

They sat and talked a half hour longer, and then the song-writer said, "There she is. That's that millionaire with her. I'll bring them over."

It was thus that Rock Wagram met Ann Ford.

Every man is a liar, a crook, a hoodlum, or a bore, and yet no man is any of these things on purpose, or eagerly, or especially, or to the exclusion of other and perhaps nicer things, and he is innocent, he is forever innocent. A man is a liar by accident. The more intense his search for truth the more apt he is to become a bigger liar than ever. He is a crook by accident, too, receiving, for instance, when he gives. He is a thief who does not know when he has stolen, or from whom, or what. His cheating is unknown to him, whether he cheats others or himself.

A man is a man by accident. He might have been an ape.

But a man hangs onto his illusion, living and dying a lie that must amuse worms. A man seizes his portion, however paltry it is, and jumps for joy.

"Yes," he says, "this is truly myself. I have all this hair and all these teeth. Yes, this is the one I am, and how unfortunate are the others with so much less."

But a man also laughs at his vanity, and winks at his death.

AFTER Vega would be Endee and after Endee Tucumcari. The road map was on the seat beside him, and every now and then he glanced at it as he drove. There was no hurry, except the hurry that is always in a man to get somewhere: to keep a mysterious schedule, to enter into a mystic rhythm that might just somehow bring wonderful things to pass.

He had plenty of time, but he was letting the car fly: Montoya, Newkirk, Santa Rosa, Moriarty, Albuquerque. One by one they were to be reached.

He would see his mother in two or three days. They would sit and talk in Armenian. She would tell him some new things about herself, and then she would ask if he had found the girl to be his wife, the mother of his children.

He would tell her about Ann Ford.

I was standing at the bar remembering Haig and the fight I had with my father when I was sixteen and how you said shame, *and I walked until morning, ashamed, but angry at him for wanting me to be better than I am, angry at* you *for wanting me to sing at the Armenian Church, angry at Haig for dying—I'll never forgive him for that—and lonely for all the things a man is always lonely for, when a song-writer I know came up and said he wanted to talk to me. We sat down and he talked two languages at once, one with words and the other without them and I understood both and neither, but it was no matter because I was thinking about other things anyway. He talked about this girl, the way they talk about them there, and then at half past three in the morning I saw her, a girl something like the* Match Girl *dressed up and something like* Queen Evil *herself, and all I wanted to do was get to her because that's all I've ever known to do, the way they are, the way I know they are, the way I am and know I am, angry because I would like to find one to love, to love truly, but at the same time not wanting to take the time to let her be the one to love truly. I saw her and wanted her because the way she'd got her body was something I know you'll understand, a way a girl* ought *to get it, a way that seems to have to do*

22

*with roses and snow, a lonely and arrogant way, a way few
get them, and fewer keep them, the eyes enormous and staring,
the hair thick and warm and young and the color of honey
that comes from mountains with snow on them, the hands like
damned little birds. I was drunk of course but I never got into
trouble from being drunk and nobody who ever saw me drunk
ever knew I was drunk. I wanted to get to her so badly I
didn't look at her or talk to her but talked to the man she was
with, a good man who talked softly and never laughed, while
everybody else shouted and laughed, especially this girl. They
sat only a few minutes and then went along, and the song-writer
said, Here's her phone number, she asked me to give it to you,
so I guess you're in. That was in February, and here it is September. If she's a lot of things I'm not sure about just now
she's at least the best yet and she says she loves me. You know
that doesn't mean anything, but she cries when she says it, but
you know that doesn't mean anything, either. Getting to her
means something, but you know that doesn't mean very much,
either, but it means something, and she's the best yet unless you
count the ones that are older and love you but can't say much
about it out of pride, the ones that love you when you love
them, unless you count the ones that can't say they love you
but do love you when you love them, she's the best, and I'm
so old myself I ought to see that my children get a young
mother, a beautiful one, a good place to start. But I don't know,
I don't know if she ought to be the mother, they're stuck with
their father, I'm the only father they can have, and you know
what I am, so I've got to be careful about the mother, I've got
to find them the best one I can, don't I? They'll get good
bodies from both of us, most likely, and bodies ought to be
good, they'll get heads that are well-shaped, and they'll be*

handsome and sound, but you know what I am, and she's a liar. She's a young liar but everything she says is a lie, and I know she doesn't love me, she loves the idea of being married to me, she loves to say my name, she says she wants to become an Armenian, she says she wants to learn to speak to you in Armenian, she wants to teach our children Armenian, she wants to have nine of them because I told her I wanted nine of them, but she's a liar, I know she's a liar, and the worst of it is it's so good getting to her, it must be just as good for children to get out of her, and that's something, so I don't mind that she's thinking of something else when she says she loves me and all the other things she says.

THE racing automobile came to Endee. It was suddenly a street with buildings and people, alive in the desert. When Endee was gone the enemy spoke again.

"What do you want, Rock?"

"I want *this*," Rock said. "To sit in my car and go. To be alone in my car and go and look. I want to look at the desert that will *never* be gone, that will grow its grass and cactus when I'm gone and everybody I ever loved or ever will love will be gone. There, over there. I see *that*, and that is what I want. To *see* it. I want to see."

"What do you see, Rock?" the enemy said.

"Look over there," Rock said.

The enemy looked. He saw the bones of a steer rubbed white by sand and wind. "For God's sake," he said, "turn on the radio."

Rock turned on the radio, *against* blindness, absence, loss, farewell, and death: and *for* the girl in New York, for the daughter of her, for all women, for all the daughters of them, kissing the men goodbye.

A man is forever involved in a dream of cities, money, love, danger, oceans, ships, railroads, and highways. But in all of his sleep, in all of his travel, a man knows his true destination. He knows everywhere else he goes is a detour. But a man cherishes his detours, for they take time.

AFTER Endee, long after it, came Tucumcari, but where was Tucumcari? Vega was in Texas, Endee was in New Mexico, but where was Tucumcari? It was in the dream, in his sleep, no less than New York, London, Paris, Berlin, Rome, Athens, and Moscow.

"Go to Dublin," the enemy said. "It's a good city. Go there."

"I went there," Rock said.

That was in the summer of 1939. On O'Connell Street a boy in a ragged coat stepped up to him and said, "Aren't you Rock Wagram?"

"Yes, I am," Rock said.

"You may wonder how I recognized you," the Dubliner said. "I have your books. They are two, are they not? *Winery,* and *Eye.*"

"My books?" Rock said. "But they were published privately. How did they ever reach you?"

"An American came through here three years ago and gave me the first," the Dubliner said. "I sent for the second. I am also a poet, Brian O'Brian."

"Let's have a drink," Rock said, for he was astonished and delighted.

Brian guided him to a bar, to the backroom there, and they sat and talked.

"I know your poems well," Brian said, "although I don't understand the titles."

"*Winery* is for a house," Rock said. "*Eye* is for a street. I was born in a house on Winery Street. I stood and talked on Eye Street. I worked in a saloon on Eye Street. I must get *your* books."

"There are none," Brian O'Brian said. "I write and recite my poems. They are not published in books. I have had a half dozen or so in small magazines in England. I hope to do plays some day. What are you doing here?"

"Visiting."

"Friends?"

"Dublin itself," Rock said. "I'm amazed and pleased that you know me from two privately printed books of bad poetry."

"Not altogether bad," Brian said. "Hard, careless, arrogant, yet gentle, so personal as to be impersonal, and full of a kind of comforting hatred."

"Not love?" Rock said.

"Perhaps," Brian said. "I have spoken of the good things, but the bad things are *very* bad. Man, you cannot think of life as a contest between yourself and the world."

"What can I think?" Rock said.

"The truth, man," Brian said. "Your good luck in being who you are was an accident. You had nothing to do with it. How can you forget the man whose luck was bad?"

"Who is *that* man?"

"All of us," Brian said. "Myself. *Yourself*, even. The best luck goes bad. To live is not a personal thing, man. One has one's brothers. The contest must always be on behalf of one's brothers. What are your plans?"

"I shall think about it," Rock said.

"I don't mean *that*," Brian said. "What are your plans for Dublin? For the rest of this day and night?"

"Anything you say," Rock said.

"Then come with me to the house of a friend in Killiney," Brian said. "There will be some people there at a singing party."

They drank until they were drunk, then took a bus, then another, then walked, and came at length to a house not surrounded by other houses, somewhat back of the road, almost in a meadow, and beyond the meadow he saw lakes and streams. They were late, so that when they entered the house everyone was there, and Rock Wagram called out to a girl he saw across the room, "I love *you!*"

A man shouted, "Ho, now!" And a woman with a sharp musical voice said, "It's Brian O'Brian himself at last with another drunk. This time an American one. *Who* is it he loves? Myself, did he say? The good-for-nothing!"

"Not yourself at all," somebody said, "but Rose here, Harry Madigan's girl, fighting mad at him but already *married* to him, drunk as he is."

"Who is it, Brian?" the woman with the musical voice said.

"Rock Wagram," Brian said. "Who *would* it be? All alone in Dublin for no reason?"

"No reason?" somebody said. "He's here to find his girl, isn't he?"

"Here, you two," a man said. "Just take a glass, and on with the singing."

Rock went to the girl.

27

"Go on, now!" she said. "Go on over there and sing!"

"Is it Rose Madigan?" Rock said.

"It is, but go on over there and sing," Rose Madigan said.

The singing began, but Rock stayed beside her and sang.

The party and afterwards fell away into something like a dream, himself and Rose in the back seat of a car racing about the countryside while the men up front, Brian O'Brian and the other two, sang.

The next morning her own brother came to the hotel, who had been at the party, who had been the last to say goodnight.

"Bad?" he said.

"Yes," Rock said.

"Some coffee, then?"

"Yes. Did I get very much out of line?"

"Not at all," the brother said. "Who *didn't*, at any rate? Brian's up at Rose's, sleeping on the couch. He has his own place, but when he's drunk he must stay where somebody can watch over him. Do you know his poetry?"

"Not yet," Rock said. "Where's Rose? I mean, where does she live? I want to send her some flowers."

"Flowers, man?" the brother said. "Don't waste your money. She lives across the Park there."

It was raining when he got to the Park. There was no telling which was the house in which she lived, for her brother had not given him the number, and he had not asked again. He began to walk around the Park. And then, far ahead, coming toward him, he saw a girl, knew it was Rose Madigan, and began to walk faster. When they reached one another, they did not speak, but stood a long time looking at one another, then kissed, but still did not speak, standing in the rain a long time. Then they went to her rooms. The others were there.

They dried their clothes, drank coffee, laughed and sang, and only he and she knew.

He was in Dublin three days longer, and saw her every day.

"It was like this," he said. "I was afraid of the Church. She wasn't. She loved it. Her father loved it, too. Her brother didn't, but she and her father did. The Church scared me. It always did. A man has to marry too much when he marries the Church. I may have been a fool, but I thought I could go back."

"You can *still* go back," the enemy said.

"No, it's too late," Rock said. "May my children forgive me."

A man's needs are few, his desires many, but one need and one desire are the same, love. But love like money is a dangerous thing and the possession of it does peculiar things to a man, as the want of it does terrible. For want of love a man may invent a religion, take to drink, or to the belittling of poets.

To be loved is to be accepted. To love is to accept. It is probably good but probably impossible to accept. To reject is probably bad but probably natural, for the achievement of truth itself is the rejection of beauty, and the rejection of beauty is the rejection of all. Man is not beautiful, but his yearning for beauty is beautiful, and man's true beauty, which is unrejectable, is failure, extreme and absolute. His effort to love is a comic and terrible thing. His failure to love is supposed to be a tragic thing and perhaps is, but a man's longing to accept and to be accepted is basically only comic. The acts of a man who is seeking to love and be loved are strange, for he will become expert at all manner of things, solely in the hope of attracting love. Everything a man does is for love, therefore hopeless and futile, and therefore beautiful and comic.

A man is supposed to be blessed if he is meek, but this may not be so. A man may be only partly blessed if he is meek, for a man is not completely anything. The only thing he is completely is alive, a business of which he is mainly ignorant. And it may not be important or possible for a man to be blessed, or no more important than it is for him to be irritated or discontented, angry or tired, indifferent or bored. The only other thing a man can be completely is dead. A man cannot be meekly dead or righteously dead or nobly dead. He can only be totally dead. This may or may not be the tiresome thing it seems to be to so many men, for it is past a man's own experience, even though it is his most private one, after birth.

A man knows something of both of these secret experiences when the life in him is in the act of seeking to give life to another, when he is with a woman, in the act of love. It is here that he knows all he is ever apt to know, and be able to remember, about birth, about death, for here it is that the vitalest part of him returns to the place from whence all of him came, and it is here, in this tender and violent home-going that he, in the act of giving life, tastes a little of the death that is altogether his only end. Dead is the man who was meek, who was proud, who was good, who was wicked. Proud and dead is the man who was meek. Good and dead is the man who was wicked. Dead is the man who was not dead.

"LOOK over there," Rock said. "That's her at that corner table."

He was in the Cub Room at the Stork Club with Myra

Clewes who wanted to have Rock in a play she was excited about called *The Indestructibles.*

"*Who,* for God's sake?" she said.

"That girl," Rock said.

"What girl?"

"That I've been thinking about all night."

"What a nice compliment to me, you dog!" Myra said. "I had no idea you've been thinking about a girl all night. I thought you were thinking about *me.* I thought you were thinking about *The Indestructibles* and the part in it for you. Is that her there? All that dazzling white I see over there?"

"Yes," Rock said.

"Well, let me look a moment," Myra said. "Yes. I see. But do you see who she's *with?*"

"Who?" Rock said.

"Well, let me put it this way," Myra said. "By the time you go to the Stork Club with *him,* it is understood by everybody —certainly everybody in New York—that you have gone the distance and no longer care who knows it."

"Why?" Rock said.

"Because he pays," Myra said. "Sometimes in diamonds, sometimes in furs, sometimes in promises, sometimes in what he thinks is most precious of all, his charm. That girl's a child, isn't she?"

"Yes of course," Rock said. "She probably doesn't know very much about him except that he's rich, whoever he is. Who *is* he?"

"Andrew Joseph Blanca," Myra said, "but everybody calls him Junk. He's fifty-five."

"She's seventeen," Rock said.

"How nice."

"What do you think of her?"

"Another blonde."

"Is that all?"

"That's all, my boy," Myra said. "Now let's talk about this play by Patrick Kerry."

"How can you be so sure?" Rock said. "You don't even know the girl."

"If it's Ann Ford," Myra said, "I know her. It *is* Ann Ford, isn't it?"

"Yes," Rock said. "Do you know her?"

"Yes."

"Tell me about her."

"Why?"

"I took her out a couple of times in Hollywood," Rock said. "I've done a lot of thinking about her ever since."

"What sort of thinking?"

"The sort that has to do with children."

"Not *really?*"

"Yes."

"Well, *you* tell me something first," Myra said. "What do you know about her?"

"I know she says things to make me laugh that *do* make me laugh," Rock said.

"Anything else?" Myra said.

"I'm half in love with her," Rock said.

"In that case, good luck to you."

"Tell me about her."

"Let me put it this way," Myra said. "Get rid of that half-portion of love. She's not for you. Now, let's talk about the play."

They drank and talked. The girl passed before their table on her way to the Powder Room but didn't stop to say hello.

She walked swiftly, with a kind of shyness she was eager to conceal, as if she felt it was out of order for her to be dressed up the way she was, to be where she was, and so glad and excited about it. As if she weren't at all what she seemed to be, but didn't want anybody to suspect for a moment that she wasn't. He saw her on her way back, too, and it was still the same, but when the waiter brought him his fourth drink he handed Rock a small piece of folded paper, on which Rock read:

Don't you dare believe a word of the truth. Don't you ever dare *believe your own eyes. It's bad for you. Everything is different and better than what it really is.*

There was no name, and even though he had never before seen her handwriting, he recognized it instantly. He burst into laughter. The writing was swift, joyous, sophisticated, and yet child-like. He handed the slip of paper to Myra Clewes, who read it quickly and handed it back.

"Treasure it," she said.

"She's delightful," Rock said. "She didn't nod or smile or say hello, yet she knew all along."

"Knew *what?*" Myra said.

"Knew I had been thinking of her."

"She's a lovely girl."

"No," Rock said. "What is it? Tell me."

"Good God, Rock," Myra said. "Are all Armenians as naïve as you are?"

"I don't know all of them," Rock said.

"She's a lovely girl," Myra said. "She's yours to marry any time you're ready. And yours *alone* to marry, I might say. The others are not so naïve."

"O.K., I won't marry her," Rock said. "I get it, whatever it is you're trying to tell me. I won't do any more thinking that involves children."

"Don't do any more that involves *her*," Myra said.

"O.K., if you say so," Rock said. "It's nothing. I just happen to remember her in a way that I have never before remembered anybody else. She's got feet that make me laugh every time I see them. Her hands seem to be the washed hands of a dirty little girl who sneaks through Woolworth's stealing jewelry and valentines. She goes after life with a kind of wicked skill that is terribly innocent."

"You *have* got it bad, haven't you?" Myra said.

"Not at all," Rock said. "But I've got to find a wife and start a family. I'm thirty-three and my father had two kids when he was thirty."

"How many did he have when he was forty?" Myra said.

"He was dead when he was forty," Rock said. "He'd had three when he was thirty-seven, but that's when he died, and five years before that his last-born died, my brother Haig. My father and my brother are dead in Fresno."

"Is your mother still there?" Myra said.

"No," Rock said. "She asked me to move her to San Francisco three years ago, so she could be near her daughter, my sister Vava. Her grandkids visit her all the time. She subscribes to all the Armenian newspapers and magazines, and I send her all the Armenian books I can find."

"Family means a lot to you, doesn't it?"

"Yes."

"Well, family means nothing to Ann Ford, and never will," Myra said.

"I suppose not," Rock said.

They went back to talking about the play by Patrick Kerry. Rock promised to read it that night and telephone her around three the following day, a Sunday. It was almost two in the morning, so they got up and left. Rock took Myra to the Sherry-Netherlands, walked up Fifth Avenue a mile or so, then back to his room at the Pierre. He was reading the play when Ann Ford telephoned.

"Don't ask me how I found out where you're stopping," she said. "Just get up and come and see me because my parents and the servants are gone for the weekend."

Her hands and her feet *were* beautiful to behold, and beholding them Rock Wagram believed in his health. He believed in his humor too. He believed in the exemption of his unborn children from pain.

"Where'd you get them?" Rock said.

"These?" Ann said.

"Yes, and the feet, too," Rock said.

"Do you like them?"

"More than I could ever say."

"What do they do?" Ann said.

"They twinkle, wink, and laugh," Rock said. "Where'd you get them?"

"God gave them to me," Ann said.

He drove on, staring at the twinkling, winking desert, kissing her goodbye.

A man and his friends are liars to one another. They are friends only of one another's best. Let one among them show his worst, and the friends are gone. Let one among them speak the truth, and the others are gone. Let one among them ask of another the truth, and the others will be gone. For a man lives for himself, and is righteous in this. The man who goes abroad to do good unto others also lives for himself, and is righteous in this, and a liar. So it is with the man who goes abroad to do mischief. He, too, is righteous, and a liar. A man is not a guilty thing, he is an innocent thing, as he himself knows.

PAUL KEY was at his desk when Rock Wagram stepped into his office.

"You've had *little* sleep," Paul said. "I expected as much. All the better. Everything is set. I'll have you taken to the sound stage at the proper moment. I don't want you to be there beforehand, standing around. For your own sake, in case this turns out the way I believe it will, let me tell you a few things, which you can take or leave, as you please. When you stand before the camera, let the muscles of your face relax in final sorrow. When the girl speaks to you, notice her as if she were already dead. Say what you are to say with a voice that does not wish to be heard, with lips that do not wish to move. When she draws close to you and her eyes offer herself to you, pity her. Pity her, and then accept her. That is all I want to say about *that* part of it. That's the art. Now for the real. Yourself. You are a friend. It's your nature. You regard every man as your friend until he has proven himself your enemy. That's all right for Fresno, for your friends there, the hoodlums and hooligans, as you call them. Here, for the time being, be no man's friend. Friendship will be offered to you from all sides—if all goes well, as I believe it will. But it will not be friendship. It will not be friendship for *you*, that is. It will be each man's friendship for himself. I have brought here to this studio in twenty years only two others, as I have brought you here. I was not mistaken about

36

either of them, although one went off after only a year, to become, in my opinion, a great man. The other is one of the most famous names in the world of the theatre, but his name is no matter. I did not bring them here because of friendship. I brought them here because that is part of my work, although it is a part that I myself invented. I will not watch you work. Your director is an offensive bore who will wish to humiliate and destroy you at the outset. I insisted on him. It is good to make a test that will *be* a test. The girl will be much the same as the one you had dinner with last night, except that she will be under twenty and more difficult to be near. You will be told when your work is finished. It may take no more than five minutes in front of the camera, but it may take hours before you will be permitted to be in front of the camera. I insisted on that, too, although I myself do not know how long the director will choose to take. Your name is Rock Wagram. The pronunciation and accent is that of your own language. That is, Vah-GRAM. Did you sleep at all?"

"No," Rock said. "We talked until it was time to go."

"That's just right," Paul Key said. "The way you spoke those words. Now. Who are you?"

"Rock Wagram."

"That's just right, too," Paul Key said. "Are you the bartender from Fresno Paul Key thinks is an actor?"

"Who's Paul Key?" Rock said.

"That's just right, too, away from the camera," Paul Key said. "This one's for the camera. What happened last night?"

"I don't talk about things like that," Rock said.

"That's perfect, for the camera," Paul Key said. "What happened?"

"I don't know what you're talking about," Rock said.

"That's perfect, too, away from the camera," Paul Key said. "The minute you're told your work is finished, no matter when that is, come here."

It was more than three hours before Rock got back to Paul Key's office.

"Well?" Paul Key said.

"It was pretty much like you said," Rock said. "I did pretty much like you said, too, except for one thing."

"What's that?"

"Before I left I spoke to the director."

"What did you tell him?"

"What do *you* think?"

"What did *he* say?" Paul Key said.

"He laughed," Rock said. "He was laughing when I left."

"He wasn't angry?"

"No."

"Why not?"

"I wasn't," Rock said.

"Yes," Paul Key said. "Still, unless he had a better reason than that, he would have gotten angry. Perhaps it's turning out all right. If it isn't, though, will going back to Fresno make much difference?"

"No," Rock said.

"How about dinner tonight?" Paul Key said. "The same four? Or would you rather it were the girl you just worked with?"

"No," Rock said. "The same four."

"What do you make of Selena Hope?"

"I like her."

"She telephoned my wife this morning."

"I don't understand."

38

"It's all right," Paul Key said. "*She* doesn't know, but *you* may as well know, I *had* to do it. I'm thinking of putting her to work here. Everybody else is finished with her. What did you talk about?"

"None of your business," Rock said.

"I'm not your friend, *either*, you see," Paul Key said. "It's all right, though, because telling you so makes me more nearly your friend than anybody else you'll ever run into around here. Besides, I may be just a little mistaken. Perhaps I *am* your friend. We won't know about the test until day after tomorrow. In the meantime, I'd like you to read a story I'm thinking of shooting. Are you still angry?"

"I wasn't angry in the first place," Rock said. "I just said it's none of your business because it isn't. As a matter of fact, we talked about ourselves. I told her some stories."

"Did she laugh?"

"Yes."

"She hasn't laughed in a year," Paul Key said. He handed Rock a manuscript. "This is the story," he said. "Take your time. I'll send the car for you around seven-thirty."

"No," Rock said. "I'll be wherever we're going to be, whenever we're supposed to be there."

"Chasen's, at eight?"

"O.K."

"How about a car to get you to your hotel?"

"No."

"I understand," Paul Key said.

"You *think* you do," Rock said.

"You want to walk."

"Yes."

"You didn't think I knew, did you?"

39

"No, I didn't."

"Well, it's a two-hour walk," Paul Key said.

"I've got a lot of time."

"Do you know what direction to take?"

"I'll find out," Rock said.

He was an hour and a half getting to the hotel. He had a little thinking to do, and he wanted to walk as he did it.

When he got to his room he sat down and read the story. It was called *To Remember Harry*. Harry tried to hold-up a bank in a small town, got caught, and was sent to the penitentiary. He tried to escape, was shot, and died at the age of twenty-five. He was remembered by his mother, his eighteen-year-old brother, his girl, a teacher of grammar school, and a pal who had tried to get him to stay out of trouble.

At dinner Vida Key said, "Did you like the story?"

"I just handed it to him this afternoon," Paul Key said to his wife. "He hasn't had time to read it."

"I liked it," Rock said.

"He *has* had time," Paul Key said.

It was an inexpensive picture, shot in twenty-two days, and six months later his pals in Fresno saw Rock in *To Remember Harry*, and began to remember him as if he had died.

A man himself is junk, and all his life he clutters the earth with it. He carries junk around with him wherever he goes, and wherever he stops he accumulates it. He lives in it. He loves it. He worships it. He collects it and stands guard over it.

ROCK loved his car. He'd ordered it in October, and he'd gotten it in June.

He went to Paul Key.

"I just got my car," he said. "I want to take it for a drive."

"O.K.," Paul Key said.

"To New York," Rock said.

"Oh."

"I don't want to do the new picture," Rock said.

"Don't you like the story?"

"I'll be thirty-three in a couple of months," Rock said. "I'll be in the Army before the year's out."

"No, you won't," Paul Key said.

"Yes, I will."

"I can get you a commission."

"No thanks."

"Let's have dinner at Romanoff's," Paul Key said. "I want to have a long talk with you. I don't want you to do anything foolish."

"I wouldn't be in a hurry," Rock said, "except that my car was delivered this morning, and I haven't got much time."

"Let's have dinner," Paul Key said. "You've got dependents. You've got your mother."

"I've sent her most of the money I haven't spent or gambled," Rock said. "She's all right."

"You've been here almost seven years," Paul Key said. "You just can't let yourself get drafted into the Army. It's silly."

"No sillier than if I was tending bar at Fat Aram's in Fresno," Rock said. He began to go.

"Wait a minute, Rock."

"I've got to go," Rock said.

"All right," Paul Key said. "Start driving to New York. Forget about pictures. We'll see what happens. Your draft board has got to call you yet. You've got to take your medical. You may not pass. Where *is* your draft board?"

"In San Francisco," Rock said.

"In San Francisco?"

"Yes," Rock said. "I've got an apartment in the house I built there for my mother. I was visiting her when it was time to register. I got a card from the board last week saying they'll send for me to take my physical sometime soon. If they send for me while I'm in New York, I'll take it there. If I pass and it's time to go, I'll go from there."

"Why go to New York?" Paul Key said.

"I want to drive across the country."

"All right, Rock. Take care of yourself."

Months later Paul Key telephoned Rock from Hollywood. It was about two in the morning. They talked three or four minutes, then Paul Key said, "Rock, you shouldn't have said the things you said to the newspapermen when you were getting your physical."

"Why not?" Rock said.

"They'll *have* to take you now."

"That's good."

"No, it's not, Rock."

"They'd take me anyway."

"Do you want me to name three or four dozen they're not going to take?" Paul Key said.

"No."

"They're essential. They're going to entertain troops. What's wrong with that?"

"Nothing," Rock said.

"You should have kept your mouth shut," Paul Key said. "If you'll keep your mouth shut now, I'll look into things and see what I can do."

Paul Key waited for Rock to speak.

"Hello," he said. "Hello. Rock?"

"Yes?" Rock said.

"What happened?"

"I was keeping my mouth shut," Rock said.

"I can straighten things out, Rock."

"I won't have to keep my mouth shut in the Army."

"I can straighten them out, anyway," Paul Key said. "You can tell *me* the truth, and keep your mouth shut when you talk to others, can't you? Isn't that what everybody in the world has to do?"

"It's not what I have to do," Rock said.

"You don't understand," Paul Key said. "This hasn't got anything to do with your contract. I'm talking to you as a friend. I'll fly to New York and straighten things out."

"There's nothing to straighten out," Rock said.

"I'll fly and we'll have a drink."

"I've gotten a postponement," Rock said, "so I can drive back to San Francisco. I'm leaving early in the morning."

"You mean you're going to be inducted?" Paul Key said.

"In about two weeks," Rock said.

"On your way to San Francisco, come and see me," Paul Key said.

"Sure," Rock said.

He was west now, but he wouldn't be stopping in Hollywood to see Paul Key. He'd arranged with his landlord in Hollywood to pack the stuff he'd left in his apartment and ship it to San Francisco. It was all junk, but he wanted it.

All his life everything a man does he seems to have done before. He is forever kissing the same mouth, embracing the same woman, looking into the same eyes which will not yield their secret.

43

Is a man himself therefore or is he the race itself? Is every woman her own race, but never herself? Each woman the same but older now, or younger, weeping now and desolate, or laughing and contemptuous of desolation?

A man wears the same face all his life, but sees a stranger every time he shaves. He inhabits the same body all his life, but himself is never the same in it. Everywhere he goes is a place he knows and does not know, home and nowhere, his own place and nobody's at all.

He comes to birth and goes to death. He comes to desire and goes to despair. For every man is too much for himself. Every man is too many men to contain and control, as he himself knows.

If at thirty-three, in the year 1942, in late September, driving his own car through New Mexico, he comes to noon in Montoya, he has been to noon before, to Montoya before, and if he stops there a moment to stand on his feet, look around, walk, sit down and eat, he has done it all before.

"HAM on rye and a bottle of beer," Rock said.

"Yes, sir," the girl in Montoya said, and then smiled.

Was the smile for himself, or was it for the actor she'd seen in one of the fooling fables, fooling *her?* Was the smile for the truth, or for the lie?

"How's your mother?" Rock said.

"All right, I guess," the girl said.

"How's your father?"

"All right, too, I guess."

"Is your brother all right?"

"Yes."

"Is your sister happy?"

44

"I guess so."

"I know *you* feel fine," Rock said.

"Do you always talk to people like that?" the girl said.

"Only when I like them," Rock said.

"Why do you like *me?*" the girl said.

"I *like* to like you."

"Why, though?"

"I'm glad you're here."

"I used to be at Cobb's, around the corner," the girl said.

"I don't mean in this restaurant," Rock said.

"I was born in Montoya."

"I don't mean Montoya, either," Rock said. "I'm glad you were born."

"Do you always talk like that?" the girl said.

"No. Sometimes I don't talk at all."

"What are *you* doing here?" the girl said.

"I *live* here," Rock said.

"You don't."

"I was born here," Rock said.

"You weren't."

"I'm here," Rock said.

"I know, but why?"

"It's on the highway."

"Where you going?" the girl said.

"Home."

"Where's home?"

"Fresno."

"Where's that?"

"California."

"Got a job there?"

"Yes."

"What do you do?"

"Tend bar."

"Bet you make the boys laugh, talking the way you do."

"They talk the way I do, too," Rock said.

"I never heard anybody talk the way you do," the girl said. "How's your mother? How's your father? How's your brother? How's your sister? Do *they* talk that way, too?"

"Yes."

"Everybody in that town talks that way?" the girl said.

"More or less."

"Bet it must be some town."

"Bet Montoya must be some town, too," Rock said.

"Why?"

"Because you're here."

"You don't know anything about me," the girl said.

"I *see* you," Rock said. "You're seventeen, aren't you?"

"Be eighteen in November, though," the girl said.

"What day?"

"Twenty-seventh."

"A holy day."

"You don't even know my name."

"No, I don't."

"Bet you can't guess."

"Bet I can."

"What is it?" the girl said.

"Well," he thought, "if I say Ann and her name *is* Ann, I'll know I must marry Ann Ford."

"Ann," he said.

"No," the girl said.

"Well," he thought, "I'll think about it."

"Desdemona," he said.

46

"Desdemona?" the girl said. "How'd you happen to go from Ann to Desdemona?"

"She was a lot like you."

"Who?"

"Othello's Desdemona," Rock said. "Light and quiet."

"Othello?" the girl said.

"Fellow in Fresno. Desdemona's husband."

"Are they happy?"

"No."

"Wish they were."

"So do I."

"I like to see married people happy," the girl said. "Why aren't they?"

"Well," Rock said, "Othello's dark, darker than I am, and she's light, almost as light as you are. He's neurotic, and she's not."

"What's that?" the girl said.

"He wants to know the truth all the time."

"Well, *doesn't* he?"

"Of course not," Rock said. "Nobody does."

"Are you married?" the girl said.

"No," Rock said.

"Are you what you said means you want to know the truth all the time?"

"Worse than he is," Rock said.

"It doesn't seem so bad," the girl said.

"It gets bad when you're married and jealous."

"Is she cheating on him?"

"No, but he's suspicious."

"Do you want some apple pie?" the girl said.

"No," Rock said.

"Coffee?"

"No."

"Anything else?"

"I'd like to know your name."

"Christine."

"Christine," he said.

"Christine Halverson," the girl said. "It's Norwegian."

"Christine Halverson," Rock said.

"What's yours?" the girl said.

"Arak Vagramian," Rock said. "It's Armenian. Give my love to your family."

"All right," the girl said. "Give mine to yours."

"I will," Rock said. "So long."

"So long," the girl said.

He was ten minutes at lunch. When he got into his car, around the corner, he wrote her name on the back of his hotel bill.

He drove on to Newkirk, Santa Rosa, Moriarty.

"Whoever she is," he said, "I've known her all my life, love her deeply, miss her painfully, and will never see her again."

But in Moriarty he saw another one crossing the street in front of his car that he'd known all his life, too.

"You love them all," the enemy said.

A man thinks he wants one thing but actually wants another, or wants both, or wants neither but can't think of something else to want, or is too young to stop wanting at all, or too old, or too far from a particular place he thinks he longs for, or his liver's enlarged, or his bile isn't flowing properly, or his intestines are clogged, or his heart is murmuring,

*or cancer's gotten a start somewhere, or the tissues of his brain
are deteriorating, or something else mysterious and unaccount-
able is happening to him.*

*He thinks he wants a watermelon to eat in the evening, but
what he really wants is to feel as alive as he once felt when he
ate a watermelon in the evening. He thinks he wants shoes,
but what he really wants is to be admired. Or he thinks he
doesn't want to be admired. He thinks he wants to be left
alone, so he can keep his unhappiness to himself, but by the
time he is alone, it's no longer to keep his unhappiness to himself, it's because he's gotten used to wanting to be alone and
now wants to keep his happiness (which used to be his unhappiness) to himself.*

*He thinks he knows when he's happy and when he's not
happy, but he never knows, because most of the time he's
bored when he's happy and bored when he's unhappy, and he
doesn't want to be bored. But if he stopped being bored and
thought he wanted to be something else, he would be mistaken.
He wouldn't want to be something else at all.*

*A man simply doesn't know. He doesn't know anything.
A man simply does not live, he is lived, and not simply. He is
lived foolishly and in everlasting indefiniteness and confusion.
He is lived as a tiger is, or a shark, or a hawk, or he is lived as
each thing that lives is lived, by turns, now a tiger, now a hawk.
Still, he is always a man, a thing in shoes, a better worshipper
of shoes than of God, a pale hairless thing of anxious ill-
health, made of poisons and dreams, quivering fear and roister-
ing delusions.*

*Ho for tomorrow! is the cry of his heart, or, Ah for yester-
day! Now is always his time of pain, torment, and torture.
Today is the terrible time. This moment is hell. He is an in-*

stantaneous thing which liveth in the insect's instant, an instant at a time until it is the last instant and the loneliest. Ho for tomorrow! but tomorrow never comes. Ah for yesterday! but yesterday is always gone and always a lie. He is a son of a bitch, whoever he is, and the name of his family is no help. He is a born crook, and the calling he follows is no help. But every one of him is innocent, as he himself knows. Every one of him is alone in his innocence. Every one of him is righteous. For a moment at a time, every one of him is a comedian and maketh the others to laugh. That moment is the best he knows. The comic's moment is a man's greatest moment. When he maketh to laugh, a man is his own boy, and a hell of a fellow.

AFTER dinner the night of the dinner at Romanoff's, when they were at home, Vida Key said to her husband, "Has he got *something?*"

"You saw him," Paul Key said. "You tell *me*. I'm not sure I know."

"Is he laughing?" the woman said.

"I don't know," the man said. "Perhaps he is."

"Still," Vida said, "I didn't feel that he was laughing at us, or at anybody else."

"His face hardly ever smiles," Paul Key said, "not even his eyes, and yet you get the feeling he's laughing all the time."

"Is it the way he speaks?" Vida said.

"The things he leaves unsaid?" Paul said. "Is that what you mean, Vida?"

"Yes," the woman said. "He *does* leave a great deal unsaid that comes across, doesn't he? Will that happen in front of a camera?"

"I don't know," the man said, "but we'll soon know. My

50

guess is that it will. If he were to read a dozen names out of the phone book, I think it would mean something more than if anybody else I know read Shakespeare. In fact, it might just mean a great deal that very little else has ever been able to mean."

"Is he sad?" Vida said. "I mean, we seemed to be laughing all the time, but weren't, and it was better than actually laughing. Is he as sad as all that?"

"They're supposed to be a sad people," Paul said, "but I don't know. The drinkers at the bar where I found him weren't sad. They laughed so much it was annoying. 'The laughing lunatics,' I said to myself. I am always jealous of those who laugh. It's because I want to, too. He had them killing themselves with laughter. I could never do that. I mean, I could never laugh that way. The sound I'd make wouldn't be anything like the sounds they made. Still, he's had me laughing all night. That's something I've always wanted to do. The professional comics have never made me laugh, outside or inside. They've annoyed me, or made me cry. I don't know when I've felt better. I think it's because——"

He stopped suddenly to see if he could get it straight.

"Is it because he's on the level?" the woman said.

"Yes, that's part of it, I suppose," the man said. "He has no defenses and doesn't want any. What does this do to others? They come out from behind *their* defenses. Selena liked him, didn't she?"

"*I* liked him," Vida said. "You talked about yourself as if you *weren't* talking about yourself. I never saw you do that before."

"You don't do that with anybody," Paul said. "He pays *attention* to whoever he's with, and whoever he's with always

51

turns out to be somebody *worth* paying attention to. Do you think he liked Selena? I mean, *enough?*"

"Enough for what?" Vida said.

"You don't think I had Selena there for nothing?" Paul said.

"Oh," Vida said. "Well, of course he liked her. I think he likes *people*. You didn't feel he was working on you because you can do him some good, the way everybody else does, did you? I know I didn't, and I'm very sensitive to that. I'd feel it instantly. I don't think he cares very much for things like that. I mean, he's not respectful of your power, he likes you, but it wouldn't matter if he never saw you again. He'd see somebody else. Of course he liked Selena. She's a beautiful girl."

"I was thinking she ought to be put to work again," Paul said. "Do you know what just occurred to me?"

"What?"

"If he's got something, how long can it last?"

"I don't know," Vida said, "but I don't think it's anything like that. I think we like him because as we go along we learn how like him we are."

"In what?" Paul said.

"In being able to be so unimportant as to be more important than ever, for one thing," Vida said.

"Oh," Paul said.

"In being able to be so sad or so glad and at the same time so unimportantly at ease about it as to feel that we are laughing," Vida said.

"He'll change," Paul said. "But I wish he wouldn't. I'll know a lot more about him tomorrow after he makes the test."

Paul Key took the test home when it was ready and he and Vida looked at it together in their private projection room.

"Well?" the husband said.

"There it is," the wife said.

"Will it last?" Paul said.

"A lot of it won't," Vida said, "but who knows? It may change to something even better. What did you tell him?"

"Before or after the test?" Paul said.

"What did you tell him to do?" Vida said.

"I said a few silly things."

"Did he do them?"

"No," Paul said. "Well, perhaps he did. I don't know. But whatever he did, what I was hoping would come across *has* come across."

"What is it?" Vida said.

"Shall we run it again?" Paul said. "Now, you know the lines we gave him to say are foolish. See if you can see for yourself what it is that comes across."

After they had looked at it again, five minutes of film, Vida said, "I've got it."

"What is it?" Paul said.

"He's carrying a torch," Vida said.

"For who?" Paul said.

"For *me*," Vida said. "For any woman. What is it for you?"

"He's *myself*," Paul said. "He's Paul Key himself."

"What do they think up front?" Vida said.

"Slow and easy," Paul said. "That's the slogan. They're scared to death he'll lose it. It's a week now and he's talked to nobody but me. That's part of the plan, too. We're going to get him for nothing of course. He doesn't have an agent and doesn't want one. We're going to give him the usual cut-rate, seven-year contract."

"Oh, Paul."

"I'll do what I can. He'll start at two hundred and fifty a week."

"Paul, you couldn't."

"I'll think of something."

"I'm going to talk to him myself," the woman said. "I won't let you do a thing like that."

"I'm giving it a lot of thought," the man said. "I'm thinking of him."

"Yes you are."

"I am."

"Start him at a thousand at least," Vida said. "Give him two-fifty for himself and put the rest aside for him, or something."

"I'll think of something," Paul said.

A week later Paul Key said, "He doesn't want a contract. He says he'll work for two-fifty a week as long as we want him, or as long as he feels like it."

"Did you tell him to do that?" Vida said.

"No."

"I had hoped you had. Who did?"

"Nobody," Paul said. "Everybody up front's delighted, but at the same time they're scared to death. One picture and you know what he'll be worth."

"Do you want him to sign?" Vida said.

"Of course."

"How high will they go?"

"A thousand a week, seven years," Paul said. "Or two-fifty the first year, five the second, seven-fifty the third, a thousand the fourth, and fifteen hundred thereafter, seven years."

"Has he been told?"

"Not yet."

THE FATHER

"Shall I tell him?" Vida said.

"I wish you would, at dinner tomorrow," Paul said. "Tell him to take the second schedule. It's the best for him."

A man is nonsense all his life, the impractical joke of unknown enemies and beloved friends, a fraud who only now and then suspects. He would be different, but truth will not permit it. He feeds his soul on the smiles of others for themselves, which he believes are for himself. He decorates it with shoes, hats, ties, shirts, trousers, jackets. He comforts it with numbers: numbers of money, numbers of women loved, numbers of friends, good things done, good times known, schedules effectively kept, accidents with pleasure in them. He asks his soul to be thankful for him, for having provided it with so much, so much more than it might have received, so much more than any other man in the world ever gave his soul. He carries his gifts and his losses to his soul and asks that they be noticed, cherished, treasured. He goes into the arena where his soul lies like a tiger to amaze it with his fearlessness and love. He goes as a child, a boy, a man, astonishing and loving. Or he is rude to his soul, passing it in a crowd and not even nodding. He is a lifetime joke, his borrowed soul a patient witness, but also a joke. He is nonsense, as he himself knows. His soul is nonsense, as he himself knows.

HE drove through mountains now, on his way to Albuquerque, the sun dropping to evening. He had counted and remembered for many miles the number and nature of his girls: his mother's mother; his father's mother; his mother; his sister; his father's and mother's brother's and sister's daughters; the girls he knew as a child; the ones he knew as a boy; the ones he knew as a young man, the Fresno street girls, the ones who came late at night to Fat Aram's, the working girls who were purified by their work, by failure and folly; the ones of the world, the named and famed ones, of Hollywood and New York, of London and Paris, Vienna and Moscow, and he showed them one by one to his soul, saying, "They had beauty when I saw them, did they not?"

He was glad about them, remembering the beauty of each of them, his mother's mother a beauty as a girl in Bitlis, a woman of eighty-one now, but still in love with her husband, still in love with man, the smell of him, the innocence and inferiority and charm of him.

But now that he saw the sun far off over the mountains and felt the earth cooling and the light giving way, he put aside the business of numbering these things, and began to number the hours, days, months, and years of loneliness, of discontent, of boredom and anger, of desperation and despair.

"It was murder," he said. "It was always murder, and it still is."

He would spend the night in Albuquerque, he thought. He would go to his room and bathe, put on fresh clothes, have a drink, go for a walk, stop someplace for supper, look around. Around ten he would telephone Ann Ford in New York. It would be past midnight in New York and perhaps she would be home, finished for the night, or about to go out. He would hear her voice.

But it was night when he came to Albuquerque and he was terrified. An unnamed terror told him he must not stop, that he would be too alone, too cut off from speed, too far from too many things.

He sat in his speeding car, thirty-three years old, without

wife, without son, without daughter, without house, without vineyard, without all the things he had always longed for. And now it was getting late. He just hadn't found her, that's all. He had found the others, but not her, not the one who was *his*. Not the one who was all of them held together in his own wife.

He drove through the city, looking at it, terrified by its night loneliness and despair, and he thanked God for his car, by which to hurry and leave it. He would drive all night. He wouldn't stop until he got to Fresno, until he reached his birthplace. He would stop there a moment, lie down and sleep in the arms of his desolate past. A thousand miles away or more, it was where he'd been born, and he wouldn't stop until he'd reached it again, for the haunting of death was intense now, and he wanted to be back where he began.

Every man is afraid. He is afraid of many things or of everything, but in the end they are all himself, as he himself knows. A man is afraid all his life, for every man is death given a face, eyes, ears, nose, mouth, body, and limbs, and every man is death given life, as he himself knows.

THE night was terrifying. Highway 66 was death's own highway. Haydn on the radio hummed death's own song. The car slipped in deathly silence through the night and Rock's own dream of life, which had always been a dream of death also. It was the Surprise Symphony, the symphony he had always liked so much, and still liked, but it wasn't now what it had been before. The car and Haydn rolled along together, rolling over one another, and over and through Rock's dream. He was hours and symphonies getting to Gallup where he had two cups of coffee while his car was attended to. And he was long hours of silence reaching and leaving Sanders, Navajo, Holbrook, Winslow, Winona, Flagstaff, Parks, Williams, Ashfork, Seligman, Hackberry, Kingman, Oatman, and Topock where he came at last to morning.

He crossed the Colorado into California, into Needles, and began the tiring, tedious but magnificent drive through miles of winding mountain roads.

Then he escaped from the hills into the California desert, smooth, clean, and hot.

He came at length, as a man in a car must, to Ludlow, in the middle of the desert, to noonday itself, and to the very end of tiredness.

During the night, tailing the car in front of him, he stared at the orange license plate and saw its black numbers expand in open-eyed sleep into a painting of men working in sunlight as bright and dazzling as if the painter had stared straight into the sun. Several times he fell into actual sleep, dreaming of rest, of falling asleep, the car flying away from him as he was being lured by his weariness into flying away from wakefulness, but always he caught the car and the memory of fact in time, shaking his head, holding his eyes away from the dazzling and golden painting.

He got out of the car at the gas station in Ludlow and looked around.

He telephoned one of his cousins in Fresno, the one named Haig, after his own brother, a boy of nineteen, his mother's younger brother's son.

"Rock?" Haig said. "Where the hell are you?"

"Ludlow."

"What are you doing in Ludlow?"

"On my way to Fresno."

"What are you coming to Fresno for?"

"Coming home."

"What's the matter? You sound tired."

"Been driving two days and two nights except for three hours of sleep in Amarillo."

"Why don't you go to sleep somewhere?"

"Don't want to sleep until I get home."

"Where *is* Ludlow?"

"On the way to Barstow."

"Hell, man, you're five hundred miles from Fresno. You better get some sleep."

"Sleep when I get to Fresno," Rock said. "How's your father?"

"Well, I got away from him at last," Haig said. "I got drafted. I'm in the Army. *Been* in three months. M.P. at Hammer Field. Motorcycle. I'm supposed to be on duty now. It's only an accident I was home. You want to talk to Pop?"

"Let me say hello to him, but don't go away," Rock said.

The boy's father came to the phone and spoke in Armenian, calling him Arak, and then the son came back and Rock said, "How's the old lady on Winery Street?"

"I visited her last night and she bawled the hell out of me," Haig said.

"What for?"

"She claims if I had loved my mother she wouldn't be dead. She can't get over that."

"Hell no. You go see her. Let her bawl you out. It's all right."

"I sit on the front porch with her half an hour almost every night. If I miss a night she nearly kills me the next time

59

I show up. What's going on with you? What's all the stuff in the paper about the Army and all that?"

"I'm going in," Rock said.

"They'll never take you," Haig said.

"They've *taken* me."

"You mean you passed your physical?"

"Sure. I'm in great shape."

"You're kidding."

"No, that's why I'm coming to Fresno, then to San Francisco, to see my mother before I go."

"You mean you're in?"

"Sure."

"Wait a minute," the boy said. "Hey, Pop!" he hollered. "Rock's in the Army, too." Rock heard the boy laugh. "Couldn't you get out of it, Rock?" he said.

"No. Didn't feel like it, anyway."

"Listen, Rock," Haig said. "I've got this damned Indian. It's the fastest motorcycle in the world. You get some sleep somewhere and telephone here again in a couple of hours. I'll pay somebody five bucks to go on duty in my place and I'll come where you are and drive for you the rest of the way."

"Don't want to sleep," Rock said. "Go over to your grandmother's on Winery Street and tell her I'll be home pretty soon to spend the night."

"O.K.," Haig said. "Listen, Rock. I'll ride to Bakersfield and meet you halfway. Leave your car at the Standard Station next door to the El Tejon Hotel and go in there for a steak or a drink in case I'm not there, but I'll be there."

"You want to do that?" Rock said.

"Sure," Haig said. "I haven't seen you years. Drive carefully. Stay awake. I'll see you in Bakersfield."

"O.K."

"I want to ask you a lot of questions," Haig said. "Is that Marcy Miller as hot as she looks on the screen?"

"She's O.K."

"Did you tear any of that away from her?"

"Shut up."

"See you in Bakersfield, Rock."

"O.K."

Every man needs his family, his own brothers and sisters in this family, the variations of himself, out of the same breathing and blood, in others, a father's sister's daughter, a mother's brother's son. Every man waits for the arrival of the variation of himself out of his own poor stuff, on foot, on horseback, on motorcycle.

STANDING in front of the El Tejon Hotel in Bakersfield where he'd had a shower, a steak, and a drink, and therefore felt new and well, Rock saw the boy ride up on the roaring wheel and stop.

"How do you like it?" Haig said.

"Come on in and have a drink," Rock said.

"Been waiting long?" the boy said.

"I got in about an hour and a half ago," Rock said. "Needed a shower and a steak anyway."

"I barely got away," Haig said. "I told the old lady. She's fixed your bed. It's nine now. We'll be there around eleven-thirty. She's staying up."

They went to the bar and had two each.

"You don't look as tired as you sounded," Haig said.

"The shower and the meat," Rock said. "I'm tired, though. Who's died?"

"Nobody in the family," Haig said. "Bart Holigian got killed in a highway accident. You knew him, I think. About your age. Showing off. Had a white girl in his car, both of them drunk. She was killed, too. Her parents are suing his father. Bart was one of the boys around Fat Aram's when you were there, wasn't he?"

"Yes. What happened?"

"Head on with a truck in the middle lane. No damage to the truck. You should have been at the funeral."

"When was it?" Rock said.

"Day before yesterday," Haig said. "All the boys were there. No preacher wanted to say anything good about him, so Tag Tatarian got up and said, 'One thing you got to give Bart credit for, he always did things fast and clean, the same as the way he got killed.' Well, he was damn near bawling, but the other boys were damn near laughing because it was fast all right, but not clean, the way he did things or the way he got killed, but Tag was his pal. 'If there was three bucks to bet, Bart always bet 'em, he didn't bet two and keep one for emergencies.' He talked ten minutes. Let's see if I can remember any more of it. 'Bart was a good boy, not like some good boys, but taken all in all just because he swore a lot and like that doesn't mean Bart was no good or ain't going to a better place.' Avak Boxcar says in his deep voice, 'He's going to Ararat, Tag, why don't you shut up?' It was the best funeral I ever went to, and you should have seen the pall-bearers with their white girls hanging around in the background, broken-hearted because their boys were carrying the casket of a pal."

"Who was the girl?" Rock said.

"Some working girl."

"Working girl? And her parents are suing his father?"

"Working girls don't stop being their parents' daughters, do they?"

"Who else?" Rock said.

"A lot of the old people," Haig said. "Pop goes to *their* funerals, comes home and stands around and looks at everything, especially the vines. He planted them, you know."

"Yes, and you, too."

"He's scared to death I'm going to get killed."

"That's understandable," Rock said.

"No," Haig said. "On the motorcycle. He knows I'm not going to get killed in the War. He's just scared of the motorcycle."

"Shall we go?" Rock said. "We'll tie it in the trunk compartment, and you drive."

"O.K."

They were on their way in a few minutes.

"How are the vines?" Rock said.

"They're fine," Haig said. "Listen to this. Alek Ohanian worked for Pop last year, bringing in the crop, foreman over seven men. A quiet man, after your time, but a little before mine. Everything's finished. He drives to the vineyard in the loading truck, stops it, looks around at the vines. I'm sitting there beside him. He stands up and says, 'I want to thank each and every one of you muscat vines for faithful service and hard work. Because of you 1941 has been a jumbo year, but I know each and every one of you are going to fight on to greater and greater victories, firmer stems, larger berries, greater sugar content, and, God helping, better color. Let's all work together and make 1942 another jumbo year. Farewell, then, until next summer when we shall meet again.' Ever hear anything like that? Didn't crack a smile. Jumbo."

"How *was* the crop?" Rock said.

"Great," Haig said. "Pop's loaded."

"I thought farmers' boys were considered essential."

"They are."

"What are you doing in, then?"

"That draft board said Pop's forty acres isn't enough to require my help. Besides, everybody knows I never did any work on the place. I could have stayed out if I wanted to bad enough, though."

"Why didn't you?"

"It's embarrassing to work on a thing like that," Haig said. "I'd rather be in. But what's the matter with you? Have you flipped your lid or something?"

"It's just as embarrassing for me," Rock said.

"But you're sixty-six years old, aren't you?"

"Thirty-three."

"Is that a kid?"

"I feel a little tired just now, but thirty-three's not so old."

"Besides, you're spoiled," Haig said. "You're used to a lot of—— How *is* that Marcy Miller?"

"I don't know her very well," Rock said. "Seems like a real nice girl, though."

"You don't know what it's like," Haig said. "It's not going to be very much fun. When do you go in?"

"Three or four days."

"That's the induction, isn't it?"

"Yes."

"Well, they give you a furlough of two weeks."

"They do?"

"Yes," Haig said. "You're inducted, you're in, but they give you two weeks."

"Well, that's something," Rock said.

At last they drew up in front of the house on Winery Street. The lights in every room were on. The old lady came out on the porch and waited. He went up and took her in his arms, one of his first girls. The boy got his bike out of the trunk compartment and after a few minutes went off in a roar. Rock sat at the kitchen table with his mother's mother. There was tea, flat bread, white cheese, black olives, parsley, mint, and sliced sun-dried beef. They talked an hour, then he went to his bed, and was home.

He slept and dreamed, awoke, fell back, and then at last slept on in the peace of his family and his home. It was noon when he woke up, and the old lady was sitting on the front porch.

"You ride with me to San Francisco," he said. "You come to San Francisco with me and see your daughter."

"Yes," the old lady said.

Chapter II

THE MOTHER

There is meaning to a man. There is meaning to the life every man lives. It is a secret meaning, but it is also simple and silly. It is something like this:

God knows I am nothing. Something winks and I am born. Something winks and I am dead.

A man builds a house and something winks. He finds a wife and something winks. A son is born to the man and his wife and something winks.

It is also something like this:

I didn't know any better, but I knew something was always winking. I never tried, but at the same time I never let things happen by themselves, either, and something always winked.

67

When I did poorly, something winked, and when I did well, something winked. When I did nothing or thought I did nothing, something winked. When I winked, something winked back. I winked every day and something winked back. I winked at my ignorance and something winked back. I winked at my hope and something winked back. I stopped winking and prayed, but still something winked back.

A man is meanings which come to nothing because something winks. A man who does not know that something is forever winking is a fool. A man who does not wink is a fool. But every man is a good man in a bad world, living his meaning alone, and winking, or being winked.

A man's secret meaning is something like this:

Last night I knew something I do not know this morning. This morning I knew something I do not know this afternoon. This afternoon I knew something I do not know tonight. Tonight I know nothing and something winks. Last year I knew something I do not know this year. The year before last I knew something I did not know last year. I do not know what it was I knew last night or last year, but I know I am dying, and I know something winks.

A man's secret is something like this:

I am mud that winks. I am weeds that wink. I am glue that winks.

A man's name is a wink. A man's fame is a wink. The life of a man is a circle made of winks. A wink is a smile going in a circle, from nothing to nothing. A wink swallows a man and his winking, his start and his finish. It swallows everything in the laughing circle. A wink is nothing. It is an eye circling around what it sees, bringing it to a laughing end. A man puts on his hat and the hat winks. It winks at the ceiling, the ceiling winks at the window, the window at the sun, the sun at the stars, the stars at one another. Time winks at space and space winks at light. The tree winks at the bird, the bird at the cat, the cat at the dog, the dog at the horse, the horse at the cow, the cow at the hen, the hen at the cock, the cock stamps on the hen and winks, then crows. The sand of the desert winks at the horned-toad, the horned-toad at the cactus blossom, the blossom at the sun, the sun at the moon, the moon at the vine, the vine at grapes, the grapes at wine. Numbers wink at symbols, symbols at measures, measures at music, music at statues, statues at men, and men at women. Art winks at art, language winks at lies, and lies wink at truth. The truth winks and weeps. It is the only wink that does not laugh. A wink is nothing, but a man is something. What is he?

He is a fool. He is a lunatic. He is a crook. He is a bore. He is a lie winking the truth which weeps. He is a tired lie which is tired of winking and sick of the truth which winks and weeps. A man is a sanitary thing. It is not often that syphilis winks in him. It is not often that rot in his brain winks at what he thinks. For all that, a man has fun winking and dying. He has a time.

"FOR God's sake," his grandmother Lula said, "grow a moustache and look like a man. Look like your father, the way you were meant to look. Look like my husband Manuk, the way all men were meant to look. Why do you go about with your moustache shaved?"

"In my work the moustache has not been required lately," Rock said.

"Do you call that work? Having your picture taken as you kiss one girl after another? What kind of work is that?"

69

"Acting."

"Is it honorable to stand there having your picture taken as you kiss tender girls? Where is your father's moustache that I saw on your face when you were not more than eighteen?"

"This is not the country of moustaches. Not my father's kind, nor mine, at any rate."

"What country is this?" Lula said.

"The country of fine, delicate, slight moustaches," Rock said.

"Is it against the law of this country for a man to put his father's moustache on his face?"

"Against the custom."

"Ignore the custom. With your lip naked you can never be the man you are. You are a false man with your lip naked. Why do you permit yourself to be a false man? Is it to stand there kissing them one after another?"

"You have been to the movies?" Rock said.

"I have been to the ones in which you have stood there kissing them. I have been to every one of them. One or another of my grandchildren has taken me. I sit there and marvel at their delicate white beauty, a new one in every picture, sometimes two or three, or three or four, and yourself forever a false man, with no moustache, a man with a naked lip, kissing them. Is that work?"

"It is."

"It is false work," the old lady said. "You are a false man. Grow a moustache and be a true man like your father, like your grandfather Manuk."

"I cannot grow it *now*," Rock said.

"*Begin* now," the old lady said. "You can do *that*. You are shaving. Do not shave your upper lip. I do not shave mine. My own moustache is there for all to see, a better one than those of most men. It is proudly there. I am old and have a moustache. I am a true woman. As I grow nearer to Manuk, to the man he was, I grow truer and prouder. Age takes a woman away from herself to her man. Before I die I will be Manuk himself, for that is what a woman's love for a man is, not yourself standing there kissing them, but not one of them *your* own woman, not one of them pregnant. We kissed and put ourselves together for children. Where do you think *you* came from? Where is your wife? Where is your woman, pregnant from your kissing of one another?"

"I haven't found her yet," Rock said.

"You haven't found her yet!" the old lady said. "She's not to be found. She's to be *created*. A man creates his woman. She is not found standing somewhere. She is created by you, and you cannot create her while you are a false man, with a naked lip. Grow your moustache and create your woman. Where are your sons? Where are your daughters?"

"I know a beautiful liar who says she loves me," Rock said. "I am thinking of making her my woman, and through her to see my sons and my daughters."

"She's a liar, you say?"

"Yes."

"She's beautiful, you say?"

"Yes."

"You're sure?"

"Yes."

"Make her your woman."

"I don't like liars."

"*You* are a liar. You are a false man, a man with a naked lip. Be a true man, and your woman will not lie to you but

71

will give you your children. She will give your children their place to stand and look at things. What do you want for breakfast?"

"Anything," Rock said.

"I'll sit and eat with you," the old lady said. "I have wanted to talk to you for years. When will we drive to San Francisco?"

"After breakfast?" Rock asked.

"You do not wish to visit your family here?" the old lady said. "You have almost everyone here but my daughter in San Francisco and your sister Vava and her children. Go to the telephone. Ask them to come here, one by one. This is your home. You were born here. In this very house. Tell them one by one to come here, and look at them again. They are dying. Look at them again before they are dead."

"Do they have moustaches?" Rock said.

"Only the women," Lula said. "Even the old men have naked lips. They say it is out of style to have moustaches. They say it is not American. Call them here. Stay in this house another night. I want to talk to you. Now, at this work that you do, why do you never speak in your own tongue, or in Kurdish or Turkish, so that I can understand what it is you say to them when you kiss them?"

"The people who see the pictures don't understand those languages," Rock said.

"Are there no longer Kurds or Turks in the world?"

"There are, but the pictures are made for people who speak and understand English."

"English," Lula said. "Is English the only language you speak? Is English the only language in the world? What do you say to them?"

72

"The same thing each time. I say that I love them."

"You're a liar," Lula said. "If you loved them, you would have your own woman, your sons and daughters. You've not shaved your lip?"

"No."

"Let me see," she said. "Yes. In three days you will begin to look like yourself again instead of like a lie of a man, like all of the men of this country. You will let your moustache grow?"

"Yes."

"It will make a great difference. What brought you here, at last?"

"I came to see you, to be at home, to sleep in my bed, to speak to you."

"Why did you wait so long?"

"I am a false man."

"Why did you begin to be a true man suddenly?"

"I am dying."

"That's a lie."

"No."

"Do you mean you are getting born?" the old lady said. "The way the man at the church says it is written? Is that what you mean?"

"No, I am dying."

"Then, tell me, how old are you now?"

"Thirty-three."

"Yes," she said, "that is the year. It happened to Manuk when he came to that year. That whole thirty-third year he went about dying, and then began to be born again, as the man at the church says it is written. A dying man, as I re-member it, is a greater man than ever if he was great in the first place—but a difficult man to love. You remember Bitlis, of course."

"I was born here, in this house," Rock said. "How could I remember Bitlis?"

"I mean in your travels you surely went to Bitlis," the old lady said, "and saw where we lived, the houses surely standing there together, being made of stone, standing on the mountainside where they've stood so many years, the stream passing beside them from which we fetched our water.

"I mean you saw how Bitlis was when you went there," she said. "When winter came we were kept in our houses five months waiting for the snows to melt. Those five months that year were the most terrible I have ever known, for he would not be loved and said, 'Go to America, this is no place to live, this is a place to die.' He said many things, but I understood only that my man was dying. He was mad of course, but all great men are. He spoke madly in three languages, and everything he said had a second meaning. He was too proud, dying, to ask me to love him, but I was his woman, whom he had created. I had put myself to him when I was twelve. I had given him his sons and daughters. I therefore understood the second meaning of everything he said. If you want to know how a woman is created by a true man, plain or mad, listen to this.

"It was the third month of winter and madness," the old lady said.

" 'Go to the cellar,' he said, 'and look among the melons there for the one that is the best. Bring it to me to eat.'

"I went to the cellar, knowing there was only one melon left, the poorest one of the lot we had put aside, but I stayed in the cellar the time it takes to look among two dozen melons or more. I took him the melon and put it before him. He looked at it, a dying man, a mad man, a great man, a man of great manners, and he looked at me, the woman he had created. I did not speak. I knew when not to speak.

" 'No,' he said.

"He had long ago stopped saying my name, but we had not become strangers, for he had created me *his* woman, and plain or mad, I remained his woman.

" 'No,' he said. 'This is not the melon I want. Take it back and bring me the best melon.'

"I took the melon back to the cellar and stayed there the time it takes to examine a dozen or more melons carefully again, and then I took him the melon. Again he looked at it, and at me, his woman.

" 'This is a better melon,' he said, 'but it is not the one. Bring me the best melon there, the one I want.'

"I went to the cellar nine times, do you hear? Do you want to know how a real man creates his woman? I went there nine times and each time returned with the same melon. I did not say, 'Man, you are mad. Man, this is the only melon in the cellar, as you yourself know. Man, do not torment the one who loves you.' I neither frowned nor smiled, for he had created me out of *all* of his nature. In the cellar I wanted to throw myself upon the earth and weep, but I did not permit myself to fly from him because he was mad. Nine times I brought my man the same inferior melon and on the ninth time he looked at the melon again, and at me, and he said, 'My woman, my lovely Lula, *this* is the melon.' And he sat and ate it. Now, sit at this table and eat *this* melon. Eat it and know how a real man creates his woman. It's not the poor melon he ate, but a sweet ripe melon fifty years later, for his grandson.

Then go to the telephone and call them one by one to come here before they die."

Rock sat across the table from his grandmother and began to eat the melon.

"Why was he mad?" he said.

"It is necessary for a great man to be mad," Lula said. "It is necessary for the woman he has created to love him, plain *or* mad. Do you like the melon?"

"Very much."

"Why are you dying?"

"It is necessary to die, too."

"Is your sleep fighting you?"

"Yes."

"What hunger and thirst do you have there?"

"Hunger for bread and thirst for water."

"They are yourself. What do you seek there?"

"A home."

"Your woman," the old lady said. "What word is written or spoken there, by yourself, or by others?"

"The word *more*."

"Your sons and daughters. Any other word?"

"Now and then the word *again*."

"Yourself in your children," the old lady said. "It is a decent fight, a fight to be born, as the man says it is written. The thirty-third year is the year of dying, of madness, of being born, one or the other, or all together. As you have hungered for bread and thirsted for water, begin now to be born. Here before you is new bread which I made yesterday when your cousin Haig came and said you would soon be here. Here in this clay pitcher is cool water. And here you are at a table, awake, but, for all that, as deeply asleep as when you dream of

76

bread and water. Take the bread and break it. Pour water out of the clay pitcher into the clay cup. Eat the bread, drink the water. Satisfy your sleep and fight with it no more, or fight another fight. Go to the girl who tells lies, and create her into your woman, and again satisfy your sleep. Love the truth into her and behold your son and daughter, and satisfy your sleep. Grow your moustache and be the man you are. You are dying of falseness, your very own, which out of youth and luck and laziness you have permitted. It is time to die of falseness. It is time to begin again. To live is not a jolly thing. It is mad. It is a joke, but for a real man, a man with his moustache, it is an *enormous* joke. Eat more of that bread, drink more of that water. You are not dreaming, you are the dream itself, healthy with death and madness."

The old woman got up and walked in her bare feet to the front door, passing air in the parlor as she went, and something winked.

There *is* meaning to a man. It *is* a secret meaning. It is something like this:

A man's best meaning means nothing, therefore it is good to wink and laugh.

The luckiest man is the one whose half-words and half-acts, left in half-places at half-times, one by one grow whole, wink-ing. He is luckiest who winks as he himself is winked, winking half to half and whole to hell and says to himself, "I didn't know then, but I know now," but winks at this, too, knowing he does not know, did not know then, does not know now. But he is no luckier than the unluckiest man, the man who is winked but does not wink. He is no luckier than that man, for there is no experience, winked or not, that is without mad-

77

ness from the time a man is born to the time he dies, and the
madness of every man is enormous.

HE went to the telephone and called them one by one, and
one by one, winking, they came: the men and the women and
the children, who were his family, the eyes of the men laughing and winking, the women losing their breath with the gladness of seeing Arak Vagramian in his own house again, with his
own grandmother, the boys and girls as arrogant as himself,
as easy to take or leave.

Haig came by on his motorcycle with his father hanging on.

The cars piled up on Winery Street.

The family overflowed out of the house into the front and
back yards, men and boys, and women and girls.

Two small girls.

"What is it?"

"It's the war. He's come home before he goes."

"Isn't he famous any more? Does he look famous to you?"

"He's tired of it. He doesn't want to be famous any more.
He sat at the table in the kitchen and ate bread and water for
breakfast. They say he's looking for a wife."

"Who'd have him? Just because he knows all those actresses.
I hear they sleep with everybody, and one another, too. What
do they call them?"

"I don't know."

"What's the name of that city in Portugal?"

"Lisbon."

"Something like that is what they call them."

"What do you mean?"

"Two women."

"What do they do?"

"Fool around, I guess. How should I know what they do? But that's what they say most of those famous actresses are."

"*What?*"

"Lisbons. That's why he never married any of them."

"Can't they have babies?"

"They don't want them. They're too busy fooling around to have babies."

"Some of them have them."

"I wouldn't have *him*."

"He's your cousin and you're eleven."

"*You're* thirteen. Would *you* have him?"

"For a husband?"

"If you weren't his cousin, would you?"

"If he was nice."

"Isn't he nice?"

"I mean to *me*. Not just nice to be nice, but nice to *me*. I'd have him."

"Would *you*, not for a husband? You know."

"Would you?"

"I'd be scared."

"I would, too. Somebody'd find out. My father would kill me."

"Mine, too."

Two small boys.

"What is it?"

"He's taking her to San Francisco with him. He's going home to visit his mother."

"Isn't he going to act any more?"

"He's going into the Army."

"Who said so?"

"My father. I'd go with him if I could. Do you know how old he is? Thirty-three."

"I'm twelve. I read in the paper where a fellow somewhere went into the Marines, twelve years old. They put him out and gave his mother a ribbon."

"What for?"

"I don't know."

"Do you want to wrestle on the lawn?"

"You're only nine. You're not old enough to wrestle *me*."

"I'm *big* enough, though."

"I'm almost as big as Rock is, but I'm not thirty-three, and I can't wrestle *him*."

"You're *not* as big as he is. You're just a little bigger than I am. Do you want to wrestle?"

"All right, but I'll use only one arm."

"Use them both."

A husband and a wife.

"What is it?"

"It's nothing, woman. He wanted to see his family."

"He's your own dead brother's son. Why don't you go inside and speak to him about the government?"

"I don't know anything about the government."

"Find out what *he* knows. He may know something. Go in and speak to him."

"No."

"Speak to your own nephew. Ask him intelligent questions. You know the water level of the whole San Joaquin Valley has been falling for years. What are we going to do for water ten years from now? Ask him about that."

"No, woman."

"Is he too good to hear of our troubles?"

"There's plenty of water."

"It's falling every year. I read about it in *The Asbarez*. Go back inside and sit down like a man and ask him about Roosevelt."

"He doesn't know Roosevelt."

"Of course he knows Roosevelt. Everybody famous knows Roosevelt. Why do you wish to remain ignorant all your life? Here is an opportunity to learn something. The neighbors are going to ask us what he said. What are you going to tell them?"

"I'm going to tell them the truth."

"What did he say?"

"He said what all of us say when we meet, what we've been saying all our lives. No intelligent questions and no intelligent answers. I embraced my brother's son and kissed his cheek, and he said my name. He said I was looking well."

"You've been ill. You've aged a great deal."

"It's polite not to notice such things, certainly not in company. Just because he's an actor doesn't mean he's no longer polite."

"Take me back in and *I'll* ask him some questions."

"What will you ask him?"

"I'll ask him if they're immoral."

"Who?"

"Actors and actresses."

"You will not ask any such question."

"I've heard they are."

"Suppose they are? What business is it of yours? Perhaps I'll speak of my brother."

"Well, speak of *something*."

It was an old house, occupied by an old woman, overflow-

81

ing with a family, the house winking, the old woman going around to instruct and criticize every member of the family, winking and passing wind as she went.

A man lives instantly. He may take a lifetime to go home again, but when he is finally there, he is instantly there, and even though everything has changed, and he himself has changed, everything is instantly the same, and he is instantly the same. Some of those he knew are gone, others are come. The places are changed, yet the same, as the house on Winery Street was changed and the same.

HERE again was his father's brother, one of three, the farmer in Reedley, with his four sons and his large, loud-voiced daughter of seventeen, the boys married, each with a child or two of his own, the girl violent with cheerful power and shy boisterousness.

They had already greeted one another, and the man had gone off with his wife, a little dark woman with a sharp nose, a stranger among them, but here they were back again, and the man wanted to say something.

"Arak," the man said. "You are your father again, my own brother."

"Yes," the woman said. "I said so myself just now in the yard. 'Isn't it astonishing,' I said, 'how exactly like his father he is?' Didn't I?"

"That makes me very happy," Rock said to the woman. "You're looking well. Younger than ever, I think, and your children are all looking so well."

"Our life is a life of work and worry," the woman said. "The water level is falling."

Her husband looked at her, then at his nephew.

"There is plenty of water," he said softly.

"The boys picked their own wives," the woman said. "Each of them picked his own, not the way it was done in the old country, the parents of the boy and the girl coming together to discuss the matter intelligently. But at least they picked Armenian girls, girls who know a thing or two about cooking and housekeeping. Have you found a nice Armenian girl to marry?"

"Woman," the husband said softly.

"Do you know one?" Rock said.

"*One?*" the woman said. "There are hundreds, and most of them are here in Fresno. *Girls* are not lacking. To marry a stranger is perhaps an adventure, but the question is, Can the daughter of people who do not understand us be a true wife to one of our sons? Isn't the eye of the stranger's daughter forever out? Is it fitting for one of our sons to marry the daughter of a stranger?"

"Who is that talking?" Lula called out from the kitchen. She stepped into the dining room to look, and then said, "The Armenian girl is also the daughter of a stranger. When a man takes his woman, she becomes *his* woman if he is a true man. If he is an Armenian, she becomes an Armenian, if he is a Turk, she becomes a Turk. His mother was a Vagramian who married a Vagramian, and that's enough of that."

"I have heard they were not related, however," the woman said. "The father's grandfather having become a Vagramian through adoption." She turned to her husband. "Is that not so?"

"It was said," the man replied.

"I was not a Vagramian when I married my husband," Lula

said. "I was a stranger's daughter. Anybody he marries will be a stranger's daughter. Whoever wants to eat, come to the kitchen."

The man took his wife by the arm and said, "Let us have a piece of bread and cheese."

"I am not hungry," the woman said. The man went off to the kitchen alone. The woman was about to ask another question when Haig said, "If I'm ever down there when you're down there, Rock, will you introduce me to Marcy Miller?"

"Who's Marcy Miller?" Haig's father said.

"She's the girl we saw in the movie with Rock," Haig said.

"That's a very pretty girl, Rock," the man said in English.

"I'd like to meet her," Haig said.

"If we're ever down there at the same time," Rock said, "I'll introduce you to her."

"When are you going to be down there?" Haig said.

"Isn't it true," the woman said, "that the longer the war lasts, the higher the price of raisins will be? I'm sure you've heard."

"Yes," Rock said because he didn't want to disappoint her. "The longer the war lasts, the more the farmers will get for their raisins."

"Is it because the government is going to buy raisins for the soldiers?" the woman said.

"Yes, that's it precisely."

"Haig," the woman said, "do they feed you raisins in the Army?"

"I never eat in the mess," Haig said. "Will you be down there Saturday, Rock? I'll pay a pal five bucks to go on duty for me and I'll come down on my motorcycle."

"That's too far," Haig's father said.

"Have you heard how long the war is going to last?" the woman said.

"It looks as if it's going to be a long war," Rock said. "No, I won't be down there Saturday," he said to Haig.

"Was there not a twenty-year war?" the woman said. "It seems to me I read it in *The Asbarez*."

"There was also a hundred-year war," Rock said.

"Why not?" Haig said.

"That's too long," the woman said. "Twenty years is plenty. Life is short. Many of us will be dead in twenty years."

"I'd like to meet Marcy Miller before I get shipped," Haig said.

"Shipped where?" his father said.

"To the Pacific, or to Europe," Haig said. "That's where they're fighting, isn't it?"

"You stay at Hammer Field in Fresno," the father said.

"Is it true Roosevelt is a Jew, like the Germans say?" the woman said. "And that is why we are at war with them?"

"I don't know," Rock said.

"They say his name is Rosenfeld," she said.

"Plenty of time to meet Marcy Miller," Rock said. "Plenty of time to meet her husband and three kids, too."

"Husband and three kids?" Haig said. "Oh, frig her, then. I thought she was the way she is in the movies, a hot dame looking for a fine, healthy, red-blooded farmer's boy. You're kidding, aren't you? She isn't married, is she?"

"They say he changed his name," the woman said.

"She's been married six or seven years," Rock said.

"Well, I guess that's that," Haig said. "How about Clare Laney?"

"They say he changed his religion, too?" the woman said.

"Is it possible to do that? I mean, can one decide to become a Catholic, and become one?"

"Clare Laney's been married five years," Rock said. "I'll tell you what, Haig. I'd like you to take me for a little ride on your motorcycle."

He got up and went to Lula in the kitchen.

"I'm going for a ride on Haig's motorcycle," he said. "We'll be back in a little while. Is there anything I can bring you?"

"Go along," the old lady said.

She blinked both eyes, which was her way of winking, and Rock knew she was thinking of the water-level woman.

No man loves anyone but himself, but that is also a lie, as every man knows. Every man loves his own damned son, damned before he's born, damned to live a variation of his own damned father's life, damned to live a winking variation of the damned life every man lives. Every man loves his own damned winking daughter, winking in the eyes of her own damned mother. Every man loves his own damned winking daughter's mother. Every man loves his own damned mother and his daughter's mother and the damned nagging of them to get him to love them, notice them, remember them, and be their damned man.

SMALL boys and girls, cousins all, watched Haig and Rock drive off on the motorcycle, away from the house on Winery Street, but only around the corner, where they could not be seen, Haig brought the machine to a halt and got off. He began to jump with uncontrollable laughter.

"I hear Roosevelt's an Armenian," he said. "What do you hear?"

"I hear *you're* an Armenian," Rock said.

"*Me?*" the boy laughed. "You're crazy. Whoever told you that is a dirty liar. I'm just a little sunburned, that's all. I'm as white as the next man underneath. *Whiter.* Pale, you might say. Sickly. When did you ever see me peddling rugs? What makes Armenians so lovable?"

"Christianity," Rock said.

"That's it, that's it *exactly*," Haig said. "They're the first Christian thieves of the world, but I hear Armenians are not really Armenians. I hear they've been passing. I hear they're one of the lost tribes of Jenghis Khan, and I wish to Christ nobody found them."

"I hear they're not even Christians," Rock said. "I hear they're dervishes who got tired of whirling."

"Got tired because there was no money in it," Haig said. "Being a Christian's the softest spot in the world for a thief."

He watched the boy calm down, study his motorcycle, kick the tire, then bounce the machine violently.

"Well," Haig said, "there's your family."

"She's no Vagramian," Rock said.

"Her *kids* are," Haig said. "There's your Armenians for you."

"They're not so bad," Rock said.

"They make me sick to my stomach every time I see them," Haig said.

"Everybody's family does that," Rock said. "The Armenians have no more thieves among them than any other people."

"I'm sick of being an Armenian," Haig said.

"Why?" Rock said.

"I just think it's silly to be an Armenian," Haig said. "What nationality is *that*, anyway?"

"What's eating you?" Rock said.

"Nothing," Haig said. "We're all sick of being Armenians, aren't we? Aren't we getting tired of it? I'll be damned if I'll ever marry an Armenian girl. Inflict *that* on my kids? Not me."

"How long has this been going on?" Rock said.

"All my life," Haig said. "Who wants to be *any* nationality? Isn't it a lot of shit? A man's his own lousy self and nothing else, isn't he?"

"That's right," Rock said.

"No man belongs to any lousy nationality or religion or anything else," Haig said.

"He belongs to *something*," Rock said.

"To his own lousy self."

"Why lousy?" Rock said. "What's happened to you?"

"I want to lay Marcy Miller before I get killed," Haig said.

"You're not going to get killed."

"*Somebody* is."

"What's bothering you?" Rock said.

"I get shipped a week from Saturday," Haig said. "I haven't told Pop. I was just kidding about Marcy Miller. I just didn't want that woman to talk too much. She wants the war to last twenty years, so they can get more money for their raisins. They're loaded already but live like misers. A hundred-year war would be too long because she'll be dead. She was *born* dead, wasn't she?"

"No, she wasn't," Rock said. "And she's the mother and grandmother of quite a few people."

88

"Frig her and them, too," Haig said. He stopped suddenly. "I'm sorry," he said. "I take that back. She's your father's brother's wife. He seems like a nice guy. I guess I hate anybody who isn't in the Army."

"That leaves plenty to like," Rock said.

"And don't think I don't like them," Haig said. "I feel sorry for every sucker in every Army in the world. I like them all, just so they're in the Army, because in the Army you don't belong to any nationality, you don't even belong to your own lousy self any more, you belong to the twenty-year raisin war. Do they feed me raisins? she wants to know. When I can't get anything else to eat and I'm dying of hunger and there's raisins all over the place, I'll die of hunger."

"Grapes are pretty good," Rock said.

"So are raisins," Haig said, "but I'll die of hunger. I'm not going to help the price of raisins go up."

"How about the price of wheat and beef?" Rock said.

"O.K., I'll eat raisins," Haig said. "Let's go get a drink someplace. I apologize."

"For what?" Rock said.

"For everything I said," Haig said. "I love the Armenians so much it's stupid. It's just that loving anybody makes a fool of a man. If I wasn't in love, do you think I'd talk the way I've been talking?"

"Who are you in love with?" Rock said.

"Nobody," Haig said. "I'm just in love. I'm in love with any girl who happens to come along. You're not sore at anything I said, are you?"

"Come on," Rock said. "We'll go get a drink, but drive this contraption slow and easy, will you?"

89

They got on the contraption, and began to go, moving slower than a man walks.

"Sometimes I think I'll open the thing up and smash it against a brick wall," Haig said.

"Then what do you do?" Rock said.

"I slow down and get a root beer somewhere and bust out laughing," Haig said.

"Manic depressive," Rock said.

"Who? Me?"

"No. Human beings."

"What's a manic depressive do?"

"He gets depressed by the things that are depressing."

"Such as?"

"His own lousy self, as you put it."

"Is this slow enough?" Haig said.

"It's fine. It's just right."

"Three miles an hour."

"Fine."

"After the war, can you get me a job down there?" Haig said.

"I think so," Rock said.

"Acting?"

"I don't know why not."

"I can't act," Haig said. "What I want to do is loaf."

"It's a lot like loafing after you get the hang of it," Rock said.

"What *is* the hang of it?"

"The same as the hang of anything else."

"How do you get all those different expressions you get, like when you're mad but smile? How do you do that?"

"By being your own lousy self," Rock said.

"You want to get a drink at Fat Aram's?" Haig said.

"I'm half afraid to go into the place," Rock said.

"Why?"

"I may not want to leave it again," Rock said. "We laughed there years ago. We laughed three whole years. It wasn't so long ago. It *could* happen again."

"Quit kidding yourself," Haig said. "It's gone. Everything you had then is gone. You know it."

"I do," Rock said.

"How about it, then?"

"Sure. Let's go to Fat Aram's."

No man loves his own lousy self alone. Every man loves the men who were there then and laughed with him then because there was no telling then, and a man could wink and believe almost anything could happen.

Is every man a liar? Is there not one righteous man in the world? Is the small man a liar, and the great man, too? Is the lie in the man himself, winking? Is the man himself the lie? Is the lie the wink?

Is the kiss itself a lie, out of which he came?

Every man is a liar. He is a lie. The lie is in his eye all his life.

But what's a man to do, for all that? He is to wink and go about his business.

Is there not one righteous man in the world?

How could there be, since righteousness itself is a wink?

THE motorcycle moved slowly down Ventura Avenue and came to the old red-brick church.

"Let's go in," Rock said.

"What for?" Haig said.

"For the fun of it."

"Let's go in and pray for the price of raisins," Haig said.

"I want to see where I stood that Sunday my mother made me sing," Rock said.

"Did *your* mother make you sing, too?" Haig said.

"Just once, though."

"Mine did, too," Haig said. What did *you* sing?"

"The song of the alphabet," Rock said. "A for Art, most glorious. B for—— What was B for?"

"Bitlis?" Haig said.

"No," Rock said. "The Armenians from Bitlis aren't the *only* Armenians. They may be the most brilliant and arrogant, but they're not the only ones."

"And the crookedest," Haig said. "Aren't you going in?"

"Let's walk around the church first," Rock said. "B wasn't for Bitlis, it was for something else."

"Business?" Haig said.

"No. Wait a minute," Rock said. "A for Art. B for—was it Beauty?"

"Baseball?" Haig said.

"Or was it Birth?" Rock said. "Which one did you sing?"

"Morning Light," Haig said.

"How does it go?"

"You know how it goes."

"Sing it."

"I've forgotten the words."

"Hum it, then."

Haig began to hum. He was about to stop when Rock began to hum with him. They hummed the song as they wandered around the church, up the steps, and in.

"Shall we buy candles and light them for somebody?" Haig said.

"Yes," Rock said. "I want to light one for my father."

"O.K. I'll light one for my mother."

The candles were there to take. In the plate where the money for the candles was placed were two quarters and a half dollar. They took a candle each. Haig took the money out of the plate and put it in his pocket, and then they went down the center aisle. They lighted the candles and placed them in the place for them where three others were burning. Then they crossed themselves, and Rock went to one knee.

"I don't know what to say," he said. "I don't know if I've done anything right or not. I remember the poems. I'm sorry about the fight. I'm home and in the church, as you see. My cousin Haig is here, kneeling beside me, named after my brother, your son who died so long ago. I sometimes forget that this one is not the other one. I'm looking for a wife, for I cannot wait any longer to see my children. I shall soon see my mother. I shall speak to her, as I have already spoken to *her* mother. I thank you for the time and trouble you took for me, for the love you gave your wife, who lives in it still, and for the poems you spoke in our own tongue. I have lived poorly, but I regret none of it."

They got up together and left the church.

"Well," Haig said, "that's that. Let's get the hell to Fat Aram's if we're going."

Every man *is* a liar who in the end *cannot* lie.

Is a man many men, or vagrant parts of many men, each part desperate with failure? Is he something in shoes, which gets up and walks, all of the parts standing in his shoes?

93

THEY stood on the steps of the church and lighted cigarettes.

"Do you remember Easter here?" Rock said. "Five times as many people outside the church as in, everybody playing Eggs?"

"Do I *remember*?" Haig said. "I was *here* last Easter."

"I thought I'd fly here and get in the crowd with a dozen hard-boiled eggs in my pocket," Rock said, "but at the last minute I didn't do it."

"Why not?"

"I got scared," Rock said. "If I could have played Eggs and won a few or lost them all, it would have been great. It was what I wanted to do. I wanted to have a pocket full of eggs to play, tapping a stranger's egg, breaking it and taking it, or breaking my own and giving it. I hate eggs. To eat, I mean. But I like to *see* them, and any time I see them I remember Easter here, all of this area around the church full of them, playing Eggs."

"You should have come," Haig said. "You should have come out to the vineyard. I'd have got three or four of the boys together who look like you, and like me, and I'd have given you an old suit of mine to wear instead of your New York and Hollywood clothes. The five or six of us would have come here together and nobody would have known you from me or from any of them. I had two dozen eggs and lost all but six, which I ate. Pop came here with six eggs and brought home three dozen, but I think he either uses a phony egg or knows how to tap. He wins every Easter. I lose. You should have come."

"How did they look?" Rock said.

"They looked great," Haig said. "They had on their Sunday

clothes. No, their *Easter* clothes. It was a bright day. Everybody was talking and laughing and pushing and challenging and winning or losing, and every once in a while somebody would come out of the church and shout at the top of his voice, 'Quiet! Christ is risen, is He not?' Somebody would holler back, '*Who?*' They don't believe any of that stuff."

"They believe *something*," Rock said.

"They like sunshine," Haig said.

"They worshipped the sun in the first place," Rock said. "They probably still do, probably never managed to figure out anything as complicated as Christianity. How were the girls?"

"You know how the girls are," Haig said. "They're either Americanized, as they call it, or full of lustful looks accompanied by shameful blushing."

"Any of the Americanized ones any good?" Rock said.

"For what?" Haig said.

"For God's sake, for a smile, for instance," Rock said. "To say hello to. To talk to as if it didn't matter that they were Armenian."

"I thought you meant to lay," Haig said.

"Are they any good for that?" Rock said.

"Well, the answer is yes," Haig said. "The answer is they're just about the best in the world, and they'll do your laundry, too. Why? Don't you know?"

"Of course not."

"You're kidding."

"It's true."

"How come?"

"They were like sisters, every one of them," Rock said. "Do they still have the Water Day?"

"That's even better than Easter," Haig said. "Sure they have it. Everybody throws water all over everybody else. They really have a time that day. That's not a Christian day."

"No, it's not," Rock said. "They don't celebrate the Christian days the way other Christians do, anyway."

"Let's face it," Haig said. "They're not Christians."

"It's not important to be Christian," Rock said.

"It is if you want to be President," Haig said. "You can't even be a Catholic, you've got to be a Protestant."

"I never met anybody who wanted to be President," Rock said.

"Somebody seems to be getting elected every now and then, though," Haig said, "and he's never a Catholic, a Jew, or a Negro."

"Or a woman or a midget," Rock said.

"Or an Armenian."

"Have *you* ever run into an Armenian who wanted to be President?"

"No," Haig said. "The ones I ran into only wanted a vineyard and a family. I asked an old farmer why he wasn't President, and he said, 'The responsibility is great.' I'm not making this up. He couldn't speak more than twenty words of English, either. I told him he owed it to America. He said, 'I am bashful and peace-loving. If there was a war, we would lose.' I told him he might be provoked and angered. He said, 'In that case, we would win.' I go to the coffee house on Eye Street near Mono almost every day every summer and sit and talk with them, or I stop when I see them at work in the vineyards. I ask them all kinds of questions."

"That's *The Asbarez* across the street," Rock said.

"Yes," Haig said.

96

"Who's editor now?"

"How should I know? I don't read Armenian. You don't either, do you?"

"No, but I thought you might have heard from your father."

"No. He didn't say anything about it," Haig said. "Your father was editor for a while, wasn't he?"

"Everything," Rock said. "Typesetter, editor, writer, janitor. He was the whole paper for ten years or so when I was a kid. Want to go in and look around?"

"Sure."

They were walking across the street when Rock knew his cousin was going to ask him about his father's death.

"Can I ask you something, Rock?" Haig said.

"You want to ask me why he did it," Rock said, "or *if* he did it. Yes, he did it. I don't know why he did it. That's something nobody can ever know."

"Pop says he *didn't* do it," Haig said.

"He did it," Rock said. "He took his own life at the age of thirty-seven. He turned on the gas in the kitchen. He sat there writing, and died."

"What was he writing?"

"A poem."

"Who found him?"

"I found him," Rock said. "My mother had gone to your mother's. I'd just gotten back from driving Murphy to Bakersfield. I was sixteen. You know how the kitchen is in the house on Winery Street, door to dining room, door and two windows to screen porch. The two windows were always open, except in the winter. He'd shut them. I saw him from the screen porch and thought he'd fallen asleep, but when I opened the

97

door, I knew he wasn't. I shut off the gas, carried him to the couch on the back porch, and opened every door and window in the house because I didn't want my mother to know what he'd done. I put the poem in my pocket and I've still got it somewhere. I took off his coat and unbuttoned his collar and tried to make him start breathing again. I knew he was dead. You can tell the minute you look at a dead man that he's dead, but this was my father, and I kept believing he'd start breathing again. I tried to get him to walk, even. I didn't know what I I was doing. I was sick to my guts, because a dead man, even if he's your father, *is* sickening. I was scared to death my mother would come home and smell the gas and be even more brokenhearted than I knew she was going to be anyway. She loved him, as crazy as he was. She still does. She never got married again. We didn't have a phone, so I ran to Kazanjian's Grocery and called Doctor Burridge, the family doctor. I don't know what I told him, but I didn't tell him my father had killed himself. Burridge was in the house in ten or fifteen minutes. He asked me to tell him what had happened and I told him. He asked if anybody knew. I told him I had telephoned from Kazanjian's where the phone is on a shelf, and whoever was there heard whatever I said. He asked if I wanted my mother or my family to know. I said I didn't. He said he would stay in the house while I went to get my mother. He told her my father had died of a heart attack, and he wrote that down on the death certificate. My mother soon heard the gossip that her husband had taken his own life, but I've never told her. I think she knew, though. I think she knew from my face the minute she saw me at your mother's. If your father says he didn't, I'd rather you didn't tell him any of this."

"Of course not," Haig said.

THE MOTHER

They went into *The Asbarez* Building.

Rock looked at everything in the place, for a man *is* the vagrant parts of many men scattered and left desolate in many places, in rooms and in machinery, at tables and within walls.

A man is a traveler, a dreamer traveling the highways of sleep, a crusader on his way to the grave and the holy grail: around the clock, around the calendar, around the open eye of the wink, around the red-brick church, around the town, around the block, around the world.

THE typesetter of *The Asbarez* when he saw them got up from his work and went to them with his hand outstretched.

"Please," he said in Armenian. "Come in. I am Krikorian, Ahpet. Native of Van, in Ani, Ancient Armenia. Resident of Fresno thirty years, typesetter, editor, writer, janitor of *The Asbarez* six years."

He was a tall thin man who apparently smoked incessantly, his fingers and lips stained brown, a man perhaps sixty years old. His words meant that they were welcome, whoever they were, and they were a polite request for them to give their names.

"Arak Vagramian," Rock said softly, and the boy quickly after him, "Haig Vagramian."

The man looked from Rock to Haig, then back at Rock again.

"Arak Vagramian," he said.

"I am Vahan's son," Rock said.

"Yes," the man said. He did not speak for some time, and then he said, "Nothing's changed, as you see. Everything is

99

here. The machines, the type, the paper, the desks and chairs, and one of us is still here to get the paper out on schedule. Welcome, though I wish I could say we had come to a better time. Our story is the same. Fewer and fewer readers year by year. They are dying. Almost no writers at all, for a writer must have readers. We have even become resigned. That is a good thing, or a bad thing, depending on what your thinking is. Your father sat in this chair at this machine. He worked here, as I work. He got the paper out twice a week, as I do. I remember you as a boy coming here to watch him, coming with a small brother now and then. It *is* a wonderful place, a place of words, of print and paper. I was then only a contributor, unpaid."

"I remember you," Rock said, for as the man had spoken, slowly and with many sighs of despair and amusement, Rock had seen him again, tall, lean, hard, swift of eye and speech, his moustache then broad and black, a man with a shouting voice and a roaring laugh.

"You have come here to remember your father," the editor said. "Your coming gives me joy, for I am part of your father, all that is here is part of him. What is the paper we get out? What is it for? What is it supposed to do? What do we mean by going to so much trouble twice a week year in and year out? Well, we have our language, and it is a good one. Had we also half a dozen writers it could become a great one again. Having fewer and fewer readers, we have also fewer and fewer writers, but even these few writers have hearts that are no longer alive as they once were. Even so, twice a week the language must appear, and that is what we mean by going to the trouble. I am delighted to see you. Will you have a drink?"

As he had spoken he had walked, moving among the machines, and he had come to a bottle with a liquid in it that might have been water, which they knew was not water but rakhi. The editor removed the cork and handed the bottle to Rock, who lifted it to the man and said, "To you, sir." Rock took a swig and handed the bottle to Haig, who lifted it and said, "To you and the language, sir," and drank. Haig handed the bottle to the man, who lifted it to both of them and said, "To the Armenians, whoever they are, and to their language, whose majesty we all know, lost as it may be forever." He drank and handed the bottle back to Rock, saying, "Again, please."

"To my father," Rock said.

"To my mother," Haig said.

"To those," the man said. "And to those who are dear to *me*, and dead."

They went to the editor's study where the bound copies of the paper were. The editor removed one of the bound volumes from the shelf, placed it on the desk, and opened it.

"Here is a poem," he said, "written by your father, Vahan Vagramian. It is called *To My Haig*, the word meaning both a boy's name and our nation. May I read it? Would you mind if I read it?"

They did not speak, and the man read the poem. It was fourteen lines, Rock saw, and as the man read, Rock remembered his father reciting the poem in the house on Winery Street.

"That is a father speaking to a son," the man said. "*Any* father to *any* son, but it is also my friend speaking to his nation. It is also a great poem, never known to more than a handful of people, and now forgotten. These bound volumes contain many more poems that your father wrote, as well as stories, essays, and editorials. You do not read, I know. Even so, sit here at this desk where your father worked, and I will return to *my* work."

He embraced each of them and went off to the machine, and to his work. They heard the machine clinking out the letters of the alphabet, dropping them into the words of the language.

"Did you understand the poem?" Haig said.

"My father used to recite it at home," Rock said. "I had forgotten it, but when he read it I remembered it. I understand it. I always did."

"What does it say?"

"It says, Here is a world in which I am a stranger, given to me by a stranger, my own father. I give it to you, my own son Haig, and a stranger. It is a poor world. Give this world to another stranger, your own son, for that is all any of us can do with this world. But it says these things in a way that must be called Armenian, for it says them *in* Armenian."

"Didn't it say some other things, too?" Haig said.

"Yes, it did," Rock said. "It said, Would God this world were better and more, and you and I not strangers, for I love you, I love you so deeply that my love estranges you from me, me from myself, and love itself from love."

"Didn't you ever learn to read?" Haig said. "I mean, wouldn't it be a good idea to read *everything* he wrote?"

"I went to Armenian School across the street in the red-brick church for a while," Rock said. "I was just beginning to learn when I quit. I didn't *want* to learn. It's too late now."

"Do you want to say goodbye to the old man?" Haig said.

"He said goodbye," Rock said. "He knows we're not interested. He's back there doing his lonely work, as he always has. That work was supposed to be for *us*, but we're not interested. We never were. Let's go."

A man travels through a mournful dream seeking many things, but in the end they are all only one thing: the Word, and nothing in the lonely world is lonelier, for the name of the the word is Love.

What is it a man needs? Is it anything nameable? If it is named, does the name mean the need? Does it mean what it is supposed to mean? If what a man needs is named Love, does Love mean anything? If what a man needs is named Meaning, does Meaning mean anything? How long does Meaning mean whatever it means, and after that where is a man? What's a man supposed to do to be whatever he is supposed to be, to get whatever he is supposed to need?

A man is a wonderful and worthless thing. He is a rock but a swift one. Give him love, give rain love. Give him meaning, give fire meaning. Give him money, give birds money.

THE cousins walked across the street to the motorcycle in front of the red-brick church, but instead of getting on the contraption the older one walked to the top of the cement steps and sat there, while the younger one, foot resting on the curb, waited.

"How old was your sister Rose when she died?" the older said.

"She was three," the younger said.

"How old were you at the time?"

"Six."

"What did you think of her?" Rock said.

"I forget," Haig said. "I've forgotten. How old were you when your brother died?"

"Nine, and he was six," Rock said.

"What did you think of him?" Haig said.

"Before he died I thought he was the greatest man ever born," Rock said. "Next to myself, I mean. But differently, in his own way. He was a smiler. I never smiled. After he died I didn't know what to think. Finally, I decided that he did it on purpose, *let* himself die, because he *was* a smiler. I decided he was a smiling killer. He killed *me*. He killed me a long time. He helped kill his father forever. I killed my father for a while myself, but not forever. I didn't smile and die and kill my father forever. I fought with my father and killed him for a while. When he was angry at me, I was angry at him. When he wanted me to be better than him, I argued with him. When he didn't want me to be whoever it was I was going to be, I fought with him. I *had* to. I had to find out who I was going to be."

"Who did you turn out to be?" Haig said.

"The one you see sitting here on the steps of the red-brick church."

"Which one's *he?*"

"The father's son, after all," Rock said. "The Armenian, after all. The one he wanted me to be, after all. He broke my

104

nose. I broke everything he didn't break. It took thirty-three years."

"Could he fight?" Haig said.

"He was mad," Rock said. "He couldn't fight, but he was mad."

"If he couldn't fight, how did he break your nose?"

"You don't have to know how to fight to be able to break your son's nose, do you?"

"How mad was he?"

"Mad enough to kill me, I suppose."

"How mad were you?"

"About the same."

"Did you fight back?"

"I started to," Rock said, "but I changed my mind."

"Why?"

"I was afraid I *would* kill him," Rock said. "If it's not easy to be a son, don't think it's easy to be a father, either. He was right enough, but so was I."

"How did the fight start?" Haig said.

"He'd seen me standing on a corner talking to a couple of street girls," Rock said. "When I got home that night he told me that if he ever saw me doing that again he would give me a beating. He saw me the next night, and I saw him. The same girls. We were just standing there talking. He stood across the street, and then walked home. I didn't get home until around eleven. He was sitting in the parlor, waiting. My mother had gone to bed. He got up and went to the backyard. I knew he expected me to follow him, so I did. I knew he expected me to fight, too, since I had already disobeyed him, and was as big as he was, so when he began to fight I began to fight, too. He didn't say anything, and I didn't. We fought about a minute when I decided not to fight back any more. I didn't *stop* fighting, I just didn't fight back any more. My mother was standing on the steps of the back porch. She didn't say anything, either. He got me square on the nose and knocked me down. He walked to my mother and took her inside. My mother turned to me and said, 'Shame.' She said it softly. One word, in Armenian. The most painful word in our language. I walked to town, around town, all night. It was morning when I got home. I went inside to ask him to forgive me. He was asleep on his folded arms at the round table in the parlor. He sat up and looked at me and shook his head slowly several times. You know the way they do it.

"I said in Armenian, 'I ask you to forgive me.'

"He was dead tired and deeply angry. He stared at me a long time.

"'Go wash your face,' he said at last. 'Eat something, go to your bed.'

"I said, 'Do you forgive me?'

"'For the fight, yes,' he said. 'For the other, never. I will call Doctor Burridge in the afternoon to look at your nose. Is it broken?'

"'Yes.'

"'I'm sorry,' he said.

"After that, we were strangers. If we weren't a father and a son any more, we weren't enemies, either. We just didn't love or hate one another, that's all."

"Why didn't he want to see you standing on a corner?" Haig said.

"He wanted me to be a poet," Rock said. "A man who reads, who writes, who lives in a proud, lonely world."

"What did *you* want to be, a pimp?"

"Don't get funny," Rock said. "I wanted to be anything I felt like being. I didn't feel like being alone. A man's alone enough, anyway. I know I was, and I know I still am. I liked to read, I liked to write, and I still do, but I didn't want to read and write because he wanted me to. A man wants to do anything he does because he himself wants to do them. He wants to do them *as* himself, not as his father's son, not as a member of a family, a nation, a religion, a society, a class. All the same, it turns out that even if he does what he does *as* himself, he also does them as the other things."

"So you're a Christian," Haig said.

"I'm an Armenian," Rock said.

"What's your class?"

"The proud poor."

"What nation?"

"American."

"What race?"

"Human."

"What family?"

"Vagramian."

"Yes, you are," the younger cousin said. "All you are is a human being, and you know what phonies they are. You don't really want to go to Fat Aram's, do you?"

"I want Fat Aram's to be the way it was," Rock said. "I don't want it to be the way it is now."

"Well, it's going to be the way it is now, anyhow," Haig said. "Everything's going to be the way it is now, not the way you want it to be. You're getting tired."

"I know," Rock said. "That was the trouble with my father, too. Come on, we'll go to Fat Aram's and let it be any way it wants to be."

"And we'll like it, too," Haig said.

They sat on the motorcycle and went roaring down Ventura to Eye, up Eye to Tulare, and stopped in front of Fat Aram's.

What a man needs is unnameable, but he is forever naming it. Whisky—even the memory of whisky—helps him name it.

A man's mortality comes to him haphazardly in his mother's womb. His mortality is a disease. It is himself on schedule, in the beat of time. Whether it is pain a man knows or pleasure, his health is poor, for his illness is in him instantaneously and forever, and it is incurable, although every man is indestructible, as he himself knows.

OUTSIDE the Tulare Street door of Fat Aram's four young men stood. They watched the arrival of the cousins on the motorcycle, one in uniform, one in a pair of blue gabardine slacks and a blue-and-white plaid coat. The four young men were laughing and talking in Armenian. The cousins pushed open the corner swinging doors and stepped into the saloon. It was five in the afternoon and the place was jammed with drinkers, most of them women.

"What's happened to the place?" Rock said.

"It's doing well, that's all," Haig said. "It's not the old place any more, that's all."

"Where's Fat Aram?"

"He doesn't get around until after eleven," Haig said. "He closes the joint, counts the money, sits alone with a few friends, drinks and talks. The place is jammed. The tables and booths are all taken. Want to go?"

"No, let's get a drink, anyway," Rock said.

The bartender was an Italian boy.

"Be right with you," he said. He was busy, and at the other end of the bar so was the other boy.

"I like this," Rock said. "I wanted to see the place again. I'm seeing it. It's a money joint for sure now. What's Fat Aram doing with all the money?"

"He's investing it," Haig said. "He looks like a business man these days. He belongs to the Rotarians, the Chamber of Commerce, the Lions, and just about everything else there is to belong to, and I understand he gets up at the lunches every now and then and gives a success talk."

"That's great."

"The Indians clear out when it's busy this way. You saw some of them in the street."

"What's in the backroom now?" Rock said.

"Cards and the book when the town's open," Haig said. "It's closed now, on account of the soldiers. The Indians have games all the time at one or another of the hotels, though."

The bartender got to them at last, and Rock ordered double Scotches over ice.

The cousins touched glasses and Rock said, "Well, boy, I'm in Fresno, I've been to the house on Winery Street, I slept there last night, had breakfast there this morning, had a long talk with Lula, we've seen most of the family that's been near enough to come by, most of them are still in the house on Winery Street, we'll go back after a couple of drinks and have dinner with them, we've been to the red-brick church, we've lighted candles, we've prayed, we've been to *The Asbarez*, we've talked, and now we're at Fat Aram's. You're in the Army, and I'll soon be. Here's to us, boy. Take care of yourself."

"Here's to you, Rock," Haig said.

They finished their drinks, and as luck would have it the bartender was near and was pouring Scotch, so they extended their glasses and he poured for them again.

"I just wanted to see the place," Rock said. "I'm seeing it. It's not the way it was, but it's fine. It's another world now all right."

"It's the same world," the boy said. "It's just another time, that's all. We said we'd be back in a little while. We've been gone at least an hour, haven't we?"

"It's all right," Rock said. "We'll be back in time. Lula's rousting them all around, and they're having fun. I need these drinks badly, and *here* at Fat Aram's."

"Listen, Rock," the boy said suddenly. "Get out of it if you can. Don't fool with it. It's not for you. It's not for me, either. It's not for any of them who got drafted or any of them who enlisted because they knew they were going to get drafted, but it's especially not for you."

"No," Rock said. "I've turned myself over to the machine. Whatever it's got to do will be O.K. with me. I'll do what I'm told, go where I'm told, when I'm told. That's more than I ever did for my father, my mother, or anybody else I know."

"Well, get married, anyhow," Haig said.

"I'm thinking about it," Rock said.

"What's she like?"

"Beautiful, but a liar."

"How do you know?" Haig said.

"I know when a girl's beautiful," Rock said.

"How do you know she's a liar?"

"I know when she's a liar, too."

"Maybe the two go together," Haig said. "Is that possible?"

"It is."

"Marry her," Haig said. "Suppose she *is* a liar?"

"I like liars," Rock said, "but I don't know how it would be to be married to one, to have kids by."

"It would be fine," Haig said. "Marry her."

"I'm thinking about it," Rock said.

"Don't think about it," Haig said. "Just marry her. Where is she?"

"New York."

"Tell her to come out here," Haig said. "Tell her to fly out. What else has she got?"

"She's got seventeen years," Rock said, "but they're loaded. They're loaded with *something*. Damned if I know what, though."

"Marry her," Haig said. "Telephone her and tell her to fly out. What's her name?"

"Ann Ford."

"Marry her," Haig said. "You're too Armenian to marry an Armenian. Mix it up. For the sake of your kids mix it up. It wouldn't do to marry an Armenian, or anybody *like* an Armenian."

"I'm thinking about it," Rock said. "Let's go back to the house on Winery Street."

A man's mortality, his children's mortality, comes to him haphazardly in his mother's womb. It is a disease, and incurable.

If a man and his friends are liars to one another, is their lying worth the trouble? For is it not impossible to be a liar, after all? Is not the lie also the truth?

THEY were about to leave Fat Aram's when Rock saw the four young men who had been standing outside the saloon on Tulare Street come back in. They came over to where the cousins were standing and drinking, and one of them said in English, "Are you Rock?"

"Yes."

"A fellow was here about an hour ago asking for you."

"Have a drink," Rock said.

"We're not drinking," the speaker said. "We saw you come up on the motorcycle. We weren't sure it was you, but we decided to take a chance."

"Thanks," Rock said. "What sort of a fellow was he?"

"Fat."

"Schwartz?" Rock asked.

"Did he mention his name?" the speaker asked the other three.

"Did he?" they asked one another.

"No," the speaker said. "He just asked if we'd seen you. He said it was important."

"Did he say where he was stopping?"

"No," the speaker said. "If we see him again, shall we say we saw you?"

"You know the house on Winery Street?" Rock said.

"Yes."

"Tell him I'll be there."

"O.K.," the other said. "How are things going?"

"O.K. How about you?"

"We're going in, too. Maybe we'll run into you someplace."

"Sure," Rock said. "Come on out to the house later on if you feel like it."

"No," the other said. "We got a game coming up."

They went along, and Rock turned to his cousin.

"How about another?" he said.

"Sure," Haig said. "Who do you think it was?"

"It was Schwartz all right."

"Anything important?"

"No," Rock said. "Do you know these fellows?"

"Not by name," Haig said. "I've seen them around."

"They look alike, don't they?"

"They're not even from the same city," Haig said, "but they were all born in Fresno."

"I thought they might be brothers and cousins," Rock said.

"No," Haig said, "one's from Bitlis, one from Van, one from Moush, one from Harpoot."

"Which is our boy?"

"The one who spoke. He felt he had a right to, being from Bitlis."

"What do they do?"

"They work on the vineyards, in the wineries, in the packing houses, or they drive trucks."

"Weren't they a little reserved?" Rock said.

"They don't know you," Haig said. "They wanted to talk, but the one from Bitlis wouldn't let them. They wanted to come out to the house, too."

The bartender handed them fresh drinks. Drinking, Rock wished he didn't have to leave town. He wished he was back to stay. Even with Fat Aram's another kind of place altogether, he wanted to stay. He wanted to sit down in an all-night poker game, get up from the game at six in the morning, get in a truck loaded with muscats, drive to the winery in

Madera. He wanted to hang around the winery and smell the ferment of the grapes. He wanted to gamble all night and work all day and eat a bunch of muscats. He wanted to be back in Fresno, but it was too late. After the war, though, he'd come back, he'd buy a vineyard around Malaga, put up a house, have his wife and kids in it with him, and be home at last.

"I'm going to be drinking tonight," Rock said. "You going to be going along with me?"

"I'm supposed to go on duty at eight," Haig said, "but I'll get out of it. I'll telephone a pal and give him ten bucks instead of five."

"Can you find the game?" Rock said.

"Sure," Haig said.

"I'd like to get in it. How about you?"

"I could use a hundred or so. I need money in the Army."

"I hope you're lucky, then," Rock said.

"I like to gamble too much to be lucky," Haig said. "I love to gamble so much I always lose."

"Do they play high?"

"Not *too* high. You'll see a three-hundred-dollar pot every once in a while, though."

"Sounds like a good game," Rock said. "I hope you win yourself enough to pay a pal all through the war."

"Pals pay me, too," Haig said. "I run out of money, too."

They went out, got on the motorcycle, and slowly passed through the heart of the city, and then on to the house on Winery Street where the liars who were their family were telling lies to one another and little by little getting nearer and nearer to the truth, or something better, or something just as irrelevant.

THE MOTHER

The children of the family saw them coming, the motorcycle moving slowly, going from one side of Winery Street to the other. The children ran down the street to the motorcycle, and then ran after it. A man was on the lawn with a leather briefcase under his arm. It was not altogether unlikely that *he* was a member of the family, too.

Almost before the motorcycle had stopped this man went to Rock and Haig, both of whom were a little drunk by now, and said, "I am Craig J. Adams. My mother is the second cousin of the Vagramians which did not come to America but went to Beirut, in Syria. I practice in New York. Harvard. I am here on government business. It was by accident I heard you were passing through. I've spoken to your grandmother. Can I take you to dinner?"

"No," Rock said. "Have dinner with us. Have you met everybody?"

"Is he a dentist?" Haig said. "He looks like a dentist."

"Yes, I believe I've met everybody," Craig J. Adams said.

"Do you speak Armenian?" Rock said.

"No, I'm afraid I don't."

"He talks like a dentist," Haig said.

Rock opened his mouth.

"What's happened to this tooth?" he said in Armenian.

The lawyer, who wore a thin neatly trimmed moustache, looked into Rock's mouth.

"What is it?" he said in English.

"Can't you *understand*, either?" Rock said in English.

"Very little, I'm afraid," Craig J. Adams said.

"What's the matter with this tooth?" Rock said.

"Is something the matter with one of your teeth?"

"The nerve's been jumping in this one lately."

115

"I'm sorry."

"It's nothing," Rock said. "Do you enjoy dentistry?"

"I am not a dentist," Craig J. Adams said.

"Oh?" Rock said. "I don't know why I got the impression you were."

"No, I'm a lawyer," Craig J. Adams said. "Corporation and insurance, for the most part. A dentist would scarcely be out here on government business."

"Son of an Armenian," Rock said in Armenian to the lawyer. "Don't you understand? Aren't you an Armenian, a *little?*"

And then in English he said, "Listen, Abbott, I'm delighted to see you."

"Craig," the man said. "Craig J. Adams."

"Yes," Rock said. "You've lived in the East all your life, have you?"

"Yes," the lawyer said. "Our ties there with the older generation are not as close as yours are here."

"I want to ask a legal question," Rock said. "These children will witness it, and my cousin Haig Vagramian. Haig, this is Craig J. Adams." The cousin and the lawyer shook hands, Haig saying softly, "You should have been a dentist."

"This is the question," Rock went on. He turned to the children. "Witness this, please," he said in Armenian.

"He can't speak Armenian?" Haig said to Rock in Armenian. "What a phony."

"This is the question," Rock said again. "I love a girl who is not Armenian. If I marry this girl and we have children, who is going to teach them to speak Armenian?"

"That is hardly a legal question," the lawyer said.

"Who is going to teach them, however?" Rock said.

116

"I don't know," the lawyer said.

"Another question, then," Rock said. "The girl says she wishes to learn Armenian, so she can speak to me, to my mother, to my grandmother. If she learns to do so, will she *become* an Armenian?"

"Yes, that's right," a boy of eleven said.

"Who is this boy?" Rock said to Haig.

"That's your first cousin," Haig said. "Don't you recognize him? Avak Vagramian."

"Is that who you are?" Rock said to the boy.

"Yes," the boy said. "Avak Vagramian."

"Krikor's boy?"

"Yes," the boy said. "He's inside. We've been here about an hour. We came from Kerman. My father brought you two bottles of rakhi."

"That's my father's younger brother," Rock said to the lawyer. "He brought me two bottles. Will she become an Armenian?"

"Legally," the lawyer said, "a wife accepts or acquires the various identifying cultural or religious labels of her husband, insofar as he himself is aware of them or has employed or accepted them."

"Witnesses," Rock said. "You have heard for yourselves." He turned to Haig. "I'll telephone her as soon as I have a little of Krikor's rakhi. Let's go inside, cousin," he said to the lawyer, "and drink to your health." He turned to the children. "Any of you under twelve kindly drink strawberry pop." He put his arm around the lawyer and said to him warmly, "Please overlook my being so glad to be home. I'm delighted to see you."

They went inside, and Rock and his father's younger

brother Krikor embraced. Then Rock went into the kitchen to speak to Lula.

"Who's cooked all this food?" he said.

"I put them *all* to cooking," Lula said. "There is everything each of them knows best how to cook. I have done nothing but watch. There's an open bottle there on the table."

Rock poured a tumblerful of the transparent liquid and handed it to his grandmother. He then poured three more and handed one to the lawyer, one to Haig, and one to Krikor. He himself lifted the bottle.

"To Lula Vagramian," he said.

He lifted the bottle, as the others lifted their glasses, and everyone drank.

The old lady coughed and said, "It's good for my cough."

Rock found the water-level lady in the parlor and sat down beside her, drinking from the bottle.

"Please tell me about the water level," he said.

"It's falling," the woman said. "There's no telling when the whole place will become a desert again."

"Is there something we can do?" Rock said.

"I have been thinking that if we appointed a committee to write to Washington, it would perhaps help," the woman said.

Haig came to Rock and said, "Get on the telephone and talk to her. She'll be here tomorrow. Meet her at the airport. Take her up to San Francisco with you in the car. By the time you get there Lula will have her talking Armenian."

"I'm going to call her," Rock said. "Right after dinner."

"Call her now," Haig said. "I want to meet her."

"O.K.," Rock said.

He got up and started for the telephone in the hall, but on the way he ran into the lawyer and took him to the water-level lady.

"Here's the man to talk to," Rock said to the woman. "He has just come from Washington. He works for the government. He's a lawyer. Speak English. He doesn't speak Armenian."

He drank from the bottle again, and went to the telephone.

He was suddenly scared to death she wouldn't be home, that he wouldn't be able to reach her, that she was out with Junk, or with somebody like him. The operator went to work on the call, saying she would call him back. He stayed beside the telephone, hanging onto the bottle. When the bell rang he was so excited he had to take another swig.

"She's not in," the operator said. "Shall I try again in twenty minutes?"

"Where is she?" Rock said.

"Just a moment, please." The operator went off the line a moment, came back, and said, "Her mother's in, but she doesn't know where she is. Will you speak to her mother?"

"Yes," Rock said, "let me speak to her please."

And when the mother came on the line Rock said, "Where can I reach Ann?"

"She went out a few minutes ago," the mother said.

"I'd like you and Ann to fly to Fresno tonight."

"Fresno?"

"Yes. It's my home town. I'm visiting my grandmother, on my way to San Francisco, to visit my mother. I'd like you both to fly out and meet my family."

"I'm afraid I can't," the mother said.

"I'd like Ann to fly out, then."

"She couldn't," the mother said. "She's not eighteen yet."

"When *will* she be eighteen?" Rock said.

"Tomorrow night," the mother said.

"One day more or less doesn't make much difference," Rock said.

"Are you going into the Army?" the mother said.

"Yes. In a few days."

"Is there anything I can send you?"

"Ann," Rock said.

"What?"

"You can send me Ann."

"Ann couldn't come to California alone," the mother said.

"Send a friend with her," Rock said. "I'd like her to meet my family."

"Of course it's Ann's business where she goes," the mother said, "but I don't think she ought to go to California just now."

"Is she at the Stork?" Rock said.

"I'm not sure. Let me telephone a few places. If I find her, I'll have her call you."

Rock gave the mother the number, and then said, "Is she all right?"

"She's been unhappy because you said you wouldn't call her or see her again," the mother said. "She's been hanging around the house waiting for you to call."

"She thinks we ought to get married," Rock said. "Do *you* think we ought to?"

"I don't know," the mother said. "She's very young."

"That's what I told her," Rock said. "I'm thirty-three. She said she wouldn't think of marrying a man who wasn't thirty-three. She said she wants to learn Armenian. Do you think she could learn Armenian?"

"I don't know," the mother said. "It's a rather difficult language, isn't it?"

"Not after you get the hang of it," Rock said. "Do you think she could learn to be the wife of an Armenian?"

"I don't know," the mother said. "Is an Armenian very different?"

"Very," Rock said. "They order their women around and expect them to have a lot of children, keep house, cook, sew, sing, dance, and manage money. Do you think Ann ought to marry an Armenian?"

"I don't know," the mother said. "Are you drinking?"

"Yes," Rock said. "I'm home. I'm in the house I was born in. It's my grandmother's house now. I'd put her on to talk to you, but you don't speak Armenian."

"No," the mother said.

"She speaks Kurdish and Turkish, too," Rock said, "but all I'd want Ann to speak would be Armenian. Do you think Ann ought to get into something like this? Or do you think you and I ought to decide that she'd better not?"

"I know she'd be furious if I said anything one way or another," the mother said. "I know she'd like to *speak* to you. Let me call a few places and have her call you."

"I wish you would," Rock said, "but what do you think? If she decided she wanted to get into something like this, would you be unhappy?"

"I want Ann to be happy," the mother said.

"In that case," Rock said, "can you tell me what makes her happy?"

"Knowing someone loves her," the mother said. "Do you love Ann?"

"Yes," Rock said. "What else makes her happy?"

"She likes fine things," the mother said. "She likes to shop. She likes to spend money. She likes to dress and go out and eat at the best restaurants and meet nice people. Ann likes to be seen. You know what Ann likes. Of course you do."

"What else makes her happy?" Rock said.

"The things that make any girl happy," the mother said. "Have you gotten a commission?"

"What's that?" Rock said.

"A commission in the Army?" the mother said. "You must get a direct commission from the President. You must be at least a Captain."

"Must I?" Rock said.

"Of course," the mother said. "My husband can help you get a direct commission. He's done it for others. You mustn't waste yourself."

"I don't want a commission," Rock said.

"You've got a brilliant mind," the mother said. "My husband says your I.Q. must be very high. He says you're very intelligent. You mustn't waste yourself. Let him get you a commission."

"I'd have to be a General," Rock said. "He couldn't get me a direct commission as a General, could he?"

"No, I don't think they do that," the mother said.

"I wish you'd fly out with Ann," Rock said. "I'd like you to meet my family."

"I can't," the mother said. "I'm going away for a month with my husband. He's going on government business. We asked Ann to go with us, but she wouldn't. She's been irritable. I think she's in love. I'll find her and have her call you."

"I'll be waiting for Ann to call," Rock said. "If she asks for your advice, tell her the right thing."

"She won't ask for my advice," the mother said.

"Is that so?" Rock said. "She *should*. A girl should speak to her mother about everything that's important to her."

"Yes, I know," the mother said. "She's awfully independent. Always has been. And stubborn."

"And beautiful," Rock said. "Have a nice holiday, and thank your husband for saying I have a high I.Q. Goodbye."

"Goodbye," the mother said.

He hung up and took another swig from the bottle.

What does a man think? What does he ever think? All his life what does he think? What is his thought? What is his one thought which embraces all other thoughts? Is it the thought which is any animal's? This? This animal? Myself?

Or does a man regret and hope all his life? I am losing time, I am forgetting, I am lonely, I am frightened. My sleep has grown troubled. My nerves are on edge. My skin is dry. My hair is falling out. My eyes are dull. The nails of my hands and feet are brittle. I am growing old. I am beginning to find all things tasteless. I am beginning to be bored with the good things as well as with the tiresome things. I am dying. I am dying, and I have no children.

I must have children. I must see my children.

ROCK'S cousin took the telephone and dialed a number.

"Fox?" he said. "Haig. My cousin's in town. How about another deal?" He listened a moment. "I'll give you ten, then," he said. "Yes. Ten. I'll leave it in an envelope with the Company Clerk. No. It's worth it. Thanks. Take it easy." He turned to Rock. "Did you call her?"

"She wasn't home," Rock said.

"Who'd you talk to?"

"Her mother."

"What did she say?"

"She said she's unhappy."

"What's her mother unhappy about?" Haig said.

"Her mother's not unhappy," Rock said. "The mother said the daughter's unhappy because I told the daughter I wouldn't call or see her again."

"What did you tell her that for?" Haig said.

"I left New York for San Francisco," Rock said. "I'm going into the Army, and I wanted her to pick up where she left off when I diverted her attention. Has Catanzaro been around at all?"

"Who's Catanzaro?"

"Sam Catanzaro," Rock said. "Another grape shipper. He was from Pittsburgh. He used to divert more cars than anybody else in the grape shipping business. I used to take his diversions to the railroads for him. That was before I started driving for Murphy. What ever happened to Sam Catanzaro?"

"What happened to your girl?" Haig said.

"What are we talking about, anyway?" Rock said. "She's not my girl. She's Junk's girl. She's anybody's girl. Anybody famous, or anybody rich, or anybody who seems to be somebody. She's out somewhere in New York spreading it around."

"Who's Junk?" Haig said.

"Some New York punk," Rock said.

"What about him?"

"She's more his girl than she is mine."

"Why?"

"Because he's got more money."

"How much have *you* got?" Haig said.

"Listen to this," Rock said. "I'm flat. I haven't got anything but my car and some old clothes."

"You're kidding."

"I owe at least thirty thousand dollars besides."

"What did you do with all the money?" Haig said.

"Blew it," Rock said. "That's what comes of not getting married and having kids. It's gone."

"I've got two hundred bucks stashed away that you can have," Haig said.

"What are you talking about?" Rock said.

"You're going to need money in the Army," Haig said.

"I never gave you anything," Rock said. "Why should you give me two hundred? Are you crazy?"

"You can't go into the Army broke," Haig said. "It's bad enough when you're not broke. Have you got any money at all, for the game tonight, for instance, if we decide to get into it?"

"Forty bucks or so," Rock said.

"I've got about that much with me, too," Haig said. "If we go broke, we'll ride out to the house in Malaga and I'll get the money for you."

"You're crazy."

"No. You've got to have money. Has your mother got any?"

"Do you think I'd let my mother give me money? I'm going into the Army the way everybody else goes into it."

"What did you do with all the money, Rock?"

"I blew it, I said."

"Did you buy expensive presents for girls, or what?"

"I never bought a present for a girl in my life. I don't believe in it. What would I buy a girl a present for?"

"Well, what did you do with the money? Everybody in this house thinks you're the richest Vagramian in the world."

"I'm broke," Rock said. "I wish I had fifty thousand sitting somewhere, though."

"Did you gamble?" Haig said.

"Sure I gambled," Rock said. "I gambled all around. I always gambled. I just wasn't paying any attention at the time."

"How are you going to get married?"

"What's money got to do with it?"

"A marriage has got to have money to keep going on," Haig said. "What's it going to keep going on if there isn't any money? *Love?*"

"I'll get married on my Army pay," Rock said.

"Listen, Rock," Haig said. "This girl sounds like somebody to marry, but you can't do it on Army pay." He began to laugh suddenly. "You've been kidding me, Rock, God damn you," he said. "You're not broke."

"I'm *broke*," Rock said.

"It doesn't make any difference," Haig said. "You can borrow all you want any time you want to."

"No, I'm broke and I can't borrow," Rock said.

"Well, you could make a deal, then," Haig said. "You could get the studio to get you a deferment in order to make a patriotic picture, get a lot of money, pay your debts, and get married. You know you could do *that*."

"I could."

"Well, you'd better do it, then, if you haven't been kidding."

"I haven't been kidding," Rock said, "but I'm not going to be doing it, and the reason is this: I don't want to. I don't want to be bothered any more."

"You've really flipped your lid, haven't you?" Haig said.

"We're drinking, aren't we?" Rock said. "We're home, aren't we? What do we care about money?"

"*You* don't," Haig said, "because you've always had a lot. I care plenty, because I've never had a lot, and I can always use

126

a lot. We're drinking, aren't we! What's that got to do with anything? We'll be sober in the morning, won't we?"

"Don't worry about it," Rock said.

"Why not?" Haig said.

"It's not worth it," Rock said. "Let's go sit down and talk about the price of raisins. What kind of an Armenian is that lawyer?"

"Educated."

"I wasn't rude to him, was I?"

"Not *enough*. Where the hell did *he* come from?"

"He's a member of the family."

"What I want to know is what are you going to do about money?" Haig said.

"Don't worry about it," Rock said. "The car's paid for. Maybe I'll sell it."

"Sell *that* car?" Haig said. "The last of its kind? They won't make cars like that again for years. This is going to be a long war. That car's priceless."

"I'll sell some of my old clothes, then."

"They don't pay much for old clothes."

"I'll sell something else, then."

"What else have you got?" Haig said. "Any stocks or bonds or securities or any of that crap?"

"No, nothing like that."

"Jewelry?"

"What would I be doing with jewelry? I never wore a cuff button in my life."

"Well, what *have* you got?" Haig said.

"I haven't got anything," Rock said. "I've got a typewriter I've had since I was twenty."

"How much can you get for it?"

"I wouldn't sell it, though. I'll sell some of the overcoats I had made to order."

"How many did you have made? A dozen?" Haig said.

"I had two made," Rock said, "but I never wore them. They're like new."

"When did you have them made?" Haig said.

"Three or four years ago," Rock said. "But I wouldn't sell my overcoats, either. I had them made to order and I'll keep them. I won't sell anything. I don't need any money."

"Everybody thinks you're rich," Haig said.

Lula found them passing the bottle back and forth, standing in the hall. "Come to the table now, and eat," she said. "Plenty of time to drink after you eat."

She took the bottle from Rock and took a swig, pushing them before her as she coughed.

Why is a man nonsense all his life? Why is he the impractical joke of unknown enemies or beloved friends? Why the fellow a fraud? Why does he smile? Why is he forever smiling and looking to be smiled at? Why doesn't he invent a philosophy? Why isn't he the Ambassador to Spain? Why doesn't he compose a symphony so astonishing that midway in it the musicians die of joy? That is a good thing. Why doesn't he evolve a tree that grows a new kind of peach? That would be an honorable thing. Why is he a fool? Why doesn't he go to the capitals of the world and say, "One body, one soul, union, fraternity, friendship, accord, trust, and love"? That would be a noble thing, would it not? Why is he a joke? Why doesn't he apply himself to his religion and be the salvation of mankind? Why doesn't he go about in his bare feet, his beard full, his eyes shining with love, his mouth and teeth making kind words, his voice as soft as a dove's, his hand a healing hand? Why doesn't he go among the sick and mad, and restore them? Why doesn't he give the old the youth they wasted? That would be better than being a joke, wouldn't it? Why is he smiling all the time, several of his side teeth gone? Wouldn't it be better to help out? Wouldn't it be better to show everybody the foolishness of hatred and cruelty? Wouldn't it be nice to teach everybody to love everybody? Why isn't a man big? Wouldn't it be better to be big? Why doesn't he make a name for himself? Why doesn't he make his name stand for something? Why does he permit his name to stand for nothing?

Why doesn't a man crawl into a cave and scratch the outline of a lion, a bear, or an elephant on the wall? Wouldn't it be nice to be remembered a thousand years for having scratched on the wall of a cave? Why doesn't a man open his mouth and sing, making up a song so comforting as to impel beggars to transfer money from one pocket to another, or businessmen from one bank account to another? Wouldn't that be lyrical? Wouldn't it be practical and helpful? Why doesn't a man stop being nonsense and be something his mother can be proud of? Doesn't he love his mother? Why doesn't he say something his father can be happy about? Doesn't he love his father? Why does a man fall in with strangers whose sincerity is dubious? Doesn't he want to be something, make a name for himself in nuclear research, achieve the honor of a philanthropist, or the fame of an elder statesman? Why does he waste his precious time, annoy the hope everyone has put in him? Doesn't he know time lost can never be regained? Hasn't he heard? What's the matter with the boy? Will he never wake up? Will he never come to his

senses? Why doesn't he get into high finance and help out
that *way? Why doesn't he sit down and work out a plan, based*
on common sense, whereby all people will have steady work in
a factory? Why doesn't he think about the discrimination at
expensive hotels against minorities? Would it hurt him to have
strong feelings against intolerance and injustice? Couldn't he
teach manners? Why does he have to be chasing tail all the
time?

AS luck would have it, Craig J. Adams sat across the table
from Rock, so that it was necessary not only to have the
lawyer before his eyes, but to talk to him in English, which he
did, asking questions but getting no answers.

The children, at their own table, said to one another, "Hear
him? That's Rock. He's drunk. The one who's laughing,
that's Haig."

Everybody knew he was drunk, and ate heartily, as he ate.
There were twenty different kinds of things to eat. He ate
some of each, one after another. Then he went to his old
room, shut the door behind him, stretched out on his bed, and
fell asleep.

Haig woke him up to say, "There's a fellow at the front
door to see you."

"Bring him in," Rock said.

"Aren't you going to get up?"

"No. I just stretched out."

"You've been asleep two hours," Haig said.

"Two hours?" Rock said. "Did she telephone?"

"No."

"I'll marry somebody else," Rock said. "Bring in the man
at the door."

"One of the boys brought me out," Schwartz said when he saw Rock.

"What are you doing in Fresno?" Rock said.

"P.K. sent me."

"What for?"

"He had an idea you'd be here," Schwartz said. "He told me to look for you at Fat Aram's."

"What's he want?"

"He asked you to see him on your way to San Francisco, Rock."

"What's he want?" Rock said.

"He wants to see you, Rock."

"Well, sit down," Rock said. "This is Haig Vagramian. Haig, this is Sam Schwartz. Sit down, both of you."

"P.K. wanted me to phone him the minute I found you," Schwartz said. "Is there a phone here?"

"Sure there's a phone," Rock said, "but what do you want to phone him for? Why bother him? He's probably at Romanoff's with Vida. Why not let them have a quiet evening together?"

"They're not at Romanoff's," Schwartz said. "They're at home. I talked to him not more than an hour ago. He said to go back to Fat Aram's. That's what I did. At Fat Aram's they told me to go to room 606 at the Hotel Fresno. A fellow there got up and brought me here in a taxi."

"Where is he?" Rock said.

"He went back in the taxi."

"That's where the game is," Rock said to Haig. "Remember it."

"I've got it," Haig said.

"Can I use the phone?" Schwartz said.

"I'll talk to him, too," Rock said.

"I think he wants to fly up and see you," Schwartz said. "He doesn't want to talk on the telephone. He wants to see you."

"What's eating him?" Rock said.

"He's got a story for you," Schwartz said.

"I'm not interested in a story."

"I wasn't supposed to tell you about the story, Rock. I forgot. You won't tell him I told you, will you? He'll get mad at me. I can't stand P.K. getting mad at me all the time."

"If you'll tell me what else he asked you not to tell me," Rock said, "I won't tell him."

"That's all he asked me not to tell you," Schwartz said. "I swear on my mother that's all. I'm supposed to phone him the minute I find you. It's nine o'clock and there's a plane at ten, I think. He can just make it. You won't tell him, will you, Rock?"

"I won't tell him," Rock said. "I knew it, anyway."

"P.K. understands you like a book," Schwartz said, "and you understand him like a book. But he's your friend, Rock. Don't ever forget P.K.'s your friend."

"I won't," Rock said. "Take Schwartz to the phone," he said to Haig. "If the lawyer's out there, ask him to come in."

"He left a few minutes ago," Haig said.

"I was a little drunk at the table," Rock said. "I didn't mean to be rude."

"He didn't know the difference," Haig said.

"I'll be getting up in a little while and we'll go to room 606 and get in the game," Rock said.

"O.K.," Haig said. He went off with Schwartz.

"How do you feel?" he said when he came back.

"Not bad," Rock said. "How do you feel?"

"I'm sorry she didn't phone," Haig said.

"I said I feel O.K.," Rock said.

"Have you got it *that* bad?"

"I have."

"She'll phone."

"No," Rock said. "How do *you* feel?"

"I never felt worse in my life," Haig said.

"Why?"

"Because human beings are such dirty crooks," Haig said.

"Who?" Rock said.

"Everybody," Haig said. "Especially the bright ones, not the ones I see coming into the Army every day. *They* break your heart. I feel lousy because just staying alive calls for so much cleverness that it bores me to death. Just to stay alive you've *got* to be a crook."

"Maybe you do at that," Rock said, "but don't let it bother you too much."

"O.K.," Haig said. "If she doesn't phone, are you going to phone her?"

"I don't know," Rock said. "I'm thinking about it."

"Do you think her mother got in touch with her?"

"I'm thinking about that too."

"What do you mean?" Haig said.

"I mean Myra Clewes was probably right about her."

"Who's Myra Clewes?"

"She produces plays," Rock said. "I took her out a couple of times in New York. She told me to forget her. I'd planned to, but she phoned and I didn't want to make too much of a point of forgetting her. I thought not making a point of it would be the best way to get over it, but after a month I had it worse than ever. It was time to get back to San Francisco.

I wanted to drive across the country once more. I wanted to be alone. I told her it was over. I said I wouldn't call her. That was eight or nine days ago, or six or seven. I've forgotten."

"What's the matter with her?" Haig said. "What's bothering you about her?"

"I don't want to marry a girl who's been around," Rock said. "I told her so. She swears she's had nothing to do with anybody except me."

"Maybe she's telling the truth," Haig said.

"No," Rock said. "She's lying. She lies all the time. If she told the truth, clean, I think I'd marry her anyway. I've been all over the place, so if she has too, maybe we could make a good marriage. I don't think she can tell the truth. I mean I think it's unnatural for her to tell the truth. I think it's deeply painful. I think she hates the truth. I can't imagine why, though."

"Are you sure you've got her right?" Haig said.

"You don't spend two months with a girl and get her wrong, do you?" Rock said. "The trouble is I've got it so bad, I don't mind any more that she *is* a liar. At the same time, I'm angry at her because her mother hasn't been able to reach her. I'm burning because maybe she *is* in bed with somebody. I don't want anybody to get near her any more. I want her to tell me the truth about herself, forget it, and be my wife."

"You want a girl to be your wife who's been with other men?" Haig said.

"*This* girl," Rock said. "I told you I've got it bad."

"What's she got?"

"I don't know."

"Is she *that* good?"

"No," Rock said. "She doesn't know enough to be good. She

fools around at being real, for *me*. That's because she's a baby. I told her long ago I liked her the way I felt she *really* was."

"What way is that?" Haig said.

"The way of a *truly* beautiful girl," Rock said. "It's all there. It just needs somebody—*me*, of course—to notice and cherish it. There wouldn't be much to notice and cherish, though, if she had to go on being a liar, or if she *preferred* being a liar, or if she just didn't want me to have anything special to notice and cherish. She says she's not lying. She says she wants to be what I think she really is. She says she loves me and wants to marry me and have children, and doesn't want anything else—ever. And here I am in Fresno, wanting to believe her."

"Maybe you'd better find a girl who *can't* lie," Haig said, "instead of a girl who can't tell the truth."

"I'm thinking about that too," Rock said. "Between the two of them, the one I'm involved with, and the one I haven't found, it looks pretty hopeless, though."

Schwartz came back into the room.

"He'll be here sometime tonight," Schwartz said. "He wasn't sure he could get to the airport in time to get the next plane, but he'll be here sometime tonight, Rock."

Rock got up.

"We'll be in the game at the hotel," he said.

"All right," Schwartz said. "Can I come up there until it's time to go out to the airport to meet P.K.?"

"Do you want to play?" Rock said.

"If it's all right," Schwartz said.

"It's all right," Rock said.

He went into the parlor, to his grandmother, and said, "I may not get in until morning. We'll drive to San Francisco soon after I get in. When they go home, go to sleep. I won't say goodbye."

"Who is the English-speaking lawyer?" Lula said.

"He's a member of the family," Rock said. "Never saw him before in my life."

"He's no member of the family," Lula said.

"He's an Armenian, anyway."

"He's no Armenian. He neither speaks nor understands the language."

"Well, he's a lawyer, then."

"Beware of lawyers," Lula said. "Keep away from them."

"It was a wonderful dinner," Rock said. "I'll see you when I get home."

He went out and found his cousin and Schwartz standing beside his car, waiting. They got in and he drove off, thinking, "A man is no joke. No man is a joke. Having life is no joke, but wouldn't it be nice if he went to the capitals of the world and said, 'One body, one soul, union, fraternity, love,' and all the other nice things?"

Every man is afraid of something, but most of all he is afraid of death and disgrace. There are few moments in the life of any man in which there is no disgrace, and none in which there is no death. The nobler the man is the more aware he is of the disgrace in himself, the nagging absence of grace. The more alive the man is the more aware he is of the death in himself. Everything he is afraid of is himself, as he himself knows, going about his business, which is a business of deathly struggle all his life. But every man is fearless, too. He is afraid of nothing. Having fearlessly emerged from the womb, he is forever after fearless. Having fearlessly accepted his head, he

can never again be afraid of anything. Having fearlessly got-
ten onto his feet and walked, he can go anywhere fearlessly.
Having fearlessly looked into the eyes and face of his mother
and father, he can forever after look into the eyes and face
of any man or animal. A man is a bold fellow. He is a game
fellow. He is a fearless fellow.

THE only thing Sam Schwartz was afraid of was his uncle
Paul Key. He was afraid of everybody else, too, but as he
didn't have time to notice, he didn't know or care that he was.
He noticed that he was afraid of Paul Key all the time. As a
child his mother had spoken of no one but Paul Key, her
younger brother. He was the man Sam should try to be like.
This was unfair, because Sam was big and soft and heavy-
laden, whereas Paul, twenty-five years his senior, was small,
hard, and all nervous gristle. Still Schwartz wanted to be like
Paul Key. At last, working without a contract, they reached
an agreement. It happened when Schwartz was twenty-two.
The agreement was as follows: Samuel Schwartz would attend
Paul Keesler.

Sam would be available at all times to do anything Paul
asked him to do. The young man was thrilled. He said nothing
about money or hours, and nothing was ever made specific in
these matters. Still, it was part of Sam's work to take two
hundred dollars and go out and have himself a new suit of
clothes made to fit his new body—larger than it had been a year
ago. It was also part of Sam's work to get on an airplane and
fly to New York, go to a certain address, speak to somebody
there, and telephone Paul Key.

Once it was a girl who worked in a retail baker's. Somebody
had told Paul Key that the girl was Joan of Arc herself.

Sam telephoned Paul and said, "She's crazy, P.K. She said I'm Death. She said it in Yiddish."

"Yiddish?" Paul said. "Isn't her name Marie Gallimard?"

"I don't care what her name is," Schwartz said. "She's crazy. What do you want me to do now?"

"Did she say anything else in Yiddish?"

"Everything she said was in Yiddish."

"Does she look like Joan of Arc?"

"What's Joan of Arc look like?" Schwartz said.

"Well, does she look strong and fearless and like an angel?" Paul said.

"No," Schwartz said. "She looks like a girl who works in a bakery. I'm next door to the bakery now. What do you want me to do?"

"Buy a dozen bagels and take the next plane back."

"They don't sell bagels."

"Buy a dozen sugar doughnuts and take the next plane back."

Another time it was a cellar room in the tenements, in which Sam was supposed to find a new writer. Sam found a man who lived with eight alley cats. He was sixty-five years old and had been writing all his life.

"What do you write?" Sam said. "Books?"

"No," the man said. "Just inspirational things I get out of the air."

"Like what, for instance?" Sam said.

"Well, here's one I got this morning out of the air," the man said. "I come right home and wrote it down. Here it is on this paper bag. 'Be good to your mother. Your mother was good to you.' How true that is. These things come to me out of the air as I walk."

Sam listened to eight or nine of the things that had come to the old man out of the air, and then he telephoned Paul Key.

Paul had his secretary take down everything Sam remembered. A year later one of Paul Key's biggest successes was called *Be Good, Baby*, and Sam believed his work had been well done.

He often told his mother about the old man with the cats.

"He was a saint," Sam said. "A saint. It was no good hauling him to Hollywood. It would have spoiled him. We changed his idea around a little."

Sam was in fact good to his mother, and she wasn't in fact good to him. He was a disappointment to her.

Her brother Paul Key was the man: swift, brilliant, intelligent, dynamic.

Now, sitting alone in the back seat of the new car, Schwartz said, "What's that nice new smell in this car, Rock?"

"That's the leather of the seats, Sam."

"Makes you feel good to smell something new like that," Schwartz said.

"It goes away after about a year," Rock said.

"Why does it do that, Rock?"

"Time," Rock said, thinking of other things. "The same thing happens to everything else. At first it's new and has a new smell. Time goes by and it's no longer new and hasn't got a new smell. How much money you got on you, Sam?"

"Three or four hundred," Schwartz said. "You need some money, Rock? You can have all I've got."

"No, but I may want to borrow some later on."

"Any time, Rock."

"How much money have you put away?" Rock said.

"I don't know," Schwartz said. "P.K. gives the money to my mother, to keep for me."

"He does?"

"My mother keeps it for me," Schwartz said. "My mother and I, we've got a fine house, nice furniture, good clothes, money in the bank. P.K.'s like a father to me. He gets mad at me sometimes, but he's like a father. You won't tell him I told you about the story, will you?"

"No," Rock said. "He may not decide to mention it himself."

There were five in the game in room 606. The room was quiet. The game was quiet. The men were at work, and it was serious work. Schwartz moved around on tiptoe. Places were made, and the three new players sat down to play. After an hour Schwartz got up to go to the airport, the game stopped a moment while everybody got a fresh drink. Everybody met and talked.

Two hours later Paul Key came into the room with his nephew Sam Schwartz.

He saw that Rock Wagram was drunk and busy, so he sat down to wait.

Half an hour later Rock counted his chips and pushed them across the table to Haig.

"I've got to go for a while," he said. "Play these while I'm gone."

"I may lose them," Haig said.

"Lose them."

"Cash in a hundred, anyway," Haig said.

"No," Rock said. "Cash in when everybody else cashes in."

"You want to get back in the game, Schwartz?" one of the players said.

Sam looked at his uncle, who didn't look very pleased about what he'd heard.

"You lost about a hundred," the player went on. "You've got a place in the game any time you want it."

Sam looked at his uncle again.

"Go ahead," Paul Key said. "Sit down and play."

Sam was sure P.K. was being sarcastic. He was sure this was nothing better than a trick. He waited patiently for the knife. Would it be the biggest knife yet? Would he be knifed to death this time?

His uncle got up, smiled, and took him by the arm. There was laughter in his voice, and it wasn't mean laughter.

"Go ahead, Sam," Paul said. "Sit down with the boys and play. Play until the game stops. If you run out of money—— Well, here. Here's a blank check with my signature on it. Fill it out and remember how much it was, so I can keep my records straight."

The nephew sat down. He was stunned. He looked up at his uncle. He didn't have far to look. There were tears in his eyes, and he wished to God he knew what had suddenly come over Paul Key, or people, or the world.

Was P.K. planning to do a picture about a poker game? Was this just another assignment that Sam didn't understand? Or did his uncle actually want him to do something Sam himself wanted to do? Sit down in a quiet poker game and play all night and not have to be scared to death every minute that his uncle would hear about it? And knife him half to death about it? His uncle *seemed* truly earnest and truly kind. Was it possible that, even so, he was being sarcastic, more deeply so than ever? Was he going to knife him later on? Or was it the real thing at last? Did his uncle really feel at last that it was all right for Sam not to be exactly the same kind of man that he was? That it was all right for Sam to be Sam? For Sam not

141

to be swift and clever and far-thinking? For Sam to be fat, to sit comfortably in a chair in a quiet poker game and look at the cards and play?

Rock saw what was going on between the nephew and the uncle. He poured three straight shots, handed one to Sam, another to Paul, and lifted his own.

"Here's to my pal, Sam Schwartz," Rock said.

"To my pal, too," Paul Key said.

"Good luck," several of the players said quietly. They drank, Sam gulping his down eagerly, and smiling.

Rock and Paul Key went out and walked down the long hall to the elevator.

"He worships you," Rock said. "I'm glad you'd rather he *didn't*, though, at last."

"Where can we go to talk?" Paul said. "What's Fat Aram's like these days?"

"We can go there," Rock said.

In the street Rock said, "I'm getting scared to death I'm seeing a lot of people I like to see for the last time."

"Nothing's going to happen to you," Paul said.

"I'm getting to feel something's going to happen to *them*," Rock said. "I don't mean they're going to die. I hope Vida and the kids are well. I hope you're O.K. Everything's got to die, but that doesn't mean I've got to like it when it happens *inside* people I like."

"I want to have a long talk with you, Rock," Paul said. "It's very important.

They walked in silence to Fat Aram's, everything everywhere scaring both of the fearless men half to death.

Every man needs his family, but is his family his mother and father and their mothers and fathers? Or is his family his sons and daughters and their sons and daughters? Or is his family anybody's mother and father and son and daughter? Is a man's father his father, or anybody's father, or is his father anybody's son?

"YOU'RE like a son to me," Paul Key said.

"I wasn't much of a son to my father," Rock said. "Take it easy."

"I know you've been drinking," Paul Key said. "I mean, for a couple of months, but don't you think I have, too?"

"Don't want me to be like a son to you," Rock said.

"I had a talk with Myra Clewes night before last," Paul said. "Did you read Patrick Kerry's play?"

"I read it," Rock said.

"I'm sure you think it's a good play."

"Have *you?*" Rock said.

"Have I *what*, Rock?"

"Have you been drinking a lot for a couple of months?"

"Yes, I have," Paul said.

"I thought so," Rock said, "because you think you're my father, and you're sure I think the play's a good play, and so on and so forth. You *must* be drunk."

"I'm not a *mean* drunk, at any rate," Paul said.

"I didn't mean to be mean," Rock said. "I ate too much for supper. I met most of my family again for the first time in years. The supper's made me sleepy, the family's made me ashamed. It's made me want to get married and have a family of my own, the last resort of the failure. Being sleepy and ashamed, I probably *seem* mean, but I don't mean to be mean. Tell me your story and I'll tell you mine."

"What story, Rock?"

"You didn't fly here to tell me you think you're my father," Rock said. "You didn't fly here to tell Schwartz he could sit down with the new Armenian hoodlums of the town and play poker, either. That was nice of you, but you didn't fly here to be nice to your sister's fat son. Her *fine* son, I might add. As fine a son as I ever heard about. A finer son than I've ever been. A real son, a true son. So what's your story, Paul?"

"I'm glad we're here in your home town, in the saloon I found you in, Rock," Paul Key said. "This is my story. I can tell it to *you. Here* at Fat Aram's. I couldn't tell it to anybody else anywhere else. I wrote the play Myra Clewes asked you to read, *The Indestructibles.* I've been writing since I was a kid. Everything I ever wrote seemed to be sicker than anything in this world has a right to be. Except this play. Over there at that bar seven or eight years ago I stood waiting for you to stop talking to your pals and give me a drink. I wrote the play the way you talked that day. I wrote it swiftly and easily, as if it wasn't myself writing it. It was no trouble at all. I felt glad every minute I was writing it. I sent it to New York and had it typed. When it came back I read it, and couldn't believe I had written it. I looked at other things I had written to see if they were at all like it. They weren't. They were sick, and the play wasn't. What are you smiling about, Rock?"

"Am I smiling?" Rock said.

"Yes," Paul said. "What's it about? Is something the matter with the play?"

"Go ahead with the story," Rock said.

"What's the matter with the play?" Paul said. "There isn't any more to the story if something's the matter with the play. *Is* something the matter with it?"

"No. Go ahead."

"Is it a good play?"

"Yes. Go ahead."

"Would you have liked to have written it?" Paul said.

"It didn't occur to me to wonder," Rock said, "but yes, I would."

"Do you see yourself in it?"

"I see myself in everything I read."

"Rock," Paul said, "only Myra Clewes knows I wrote that play. Myra Clewes, and yourself. Vida doesn't know. A man can do things like that. I had expected to hear from Myra that you were crazy about the play. When she said you had read it but didn't want to appear in it, I didn't know what to think. I thought you thought it was no good, and if you did, that was too bad for me."

"Why?" Rock said.

"Why?" Paul said. "A man's only got so long. I haven't got forever. That play is my life. Why shouldn't you know I'm dying? I'm dying, Rock. I'm scared to death. I'm sixty, Rock, but that isn't why I'm dying. I've had three heart attacks in seven years, but that isn't why I'm dying, either. I'm dying because until I wrote this play I knew in my heart that I was a lie. A *whole* lie. A man can be a lie only so long. If the play is what I think it is, I know I've stopped being a lie. I know I've stopped dying, and so it won't matter any more that I am actually dying. It won't scare me any more. You saw what happened between my nephew and myself a few minutes ago. That was because I'd written that play. That was because I believed I had stopped dying and could therefore stop killing."

"It's a remarkable play, there's no doubt about that," Rock said.

145

"Nobody's ever written anything like it, have they?" Paul said. "The English never did, the Russians never did, the Germans, the Italians, the French, the Scandinavians, the Americans. None of their best playwrights ever wrote one like that one, did they, Rock?"

"No," Rock said. "It's a new thing, the first of its kind, maybe the last."

"Is it great?" Paul said.

"In a new way, it is," Rock said. "In a *truer* way, it is."

"Then, how does it happen you didn't get excited about it?" Paul said.

"I don't get excited," Rock said.

"Didn't you tell Myra anything?"

"I told her I thought it would be a good play to see on the boards. I told her I thought it would fail."

"Why? Why do you think it'll fail?"

"It's new," Rock said. "It's true, and most people in the theatre are neither, and don't know how to become either. They'll only make it *seem* bad. It will only make people uncomfortable."

"Did you tell her these things?" Paul said.

"No."

"Why didn't you, Rock?"

"I didn't think I needed to," Rock said. "I didn't know you had written it. I thought Patrick Kerry had. I didn't know you were out here dying of anxiety. I just thought it was a play that seemed great that I couldn't do anything about."

"Aren't you astonished that I wrote it?"

"It never occurred to me that you could find time to write."

"Do you remember when I was asking you questions that

first time at Romanoff's and you said you liked to read and write?" Paul said. "It never occurred to *me*, either, that you could find time to do anything except hang around, the way I had seen you hanging around this saloon, standing behind that bar, telling stories to the boys. I was astonished. Now that you know I wrote it, aren't you astonished that it's the kind of play it is?"

"I'm not astonished," Rock said. "I'm glad, because it's the kind of play that *should* have gotten itself written at last. I'm glad *you* wrote it, because I happen to know you. Any more to the story?"

"That's it," Paul said, "except for the details. I've told you my story. You tell me yours."

"I'd like the war to be over," Rock said, "so I won't have to go into the Army."

"Anything else?" Paul said.

"No."

"Can we talk about this?"

"I'm comfortable," Rock said. "The girl is bringing us drinks whenever we want them. Schwartz and my cousin are in the poker game. I'll be going back to get in after a while. We can talk."

"The war isn't going to be a short war," Paul said.

"I know," Rock said.

"Being a Private in *any* Army is no fun for *any* man."

"I know," Rock said.

"One day is a long time for the kind of man I am, and the kind you are," Paul said.

"Yes, it is."

"A year is a very long time."

"Very."

"Two or three years are long enough to change a man, or finish him."

"Most likely."

"What do you want to do, Rock?"

"I want the war to be over."

"It won't be over for two or three or four or five years, Rock."

"I suppose not."

"What do you want to do?"

"I want it to be over."

"A lot of people who think they're in good physical shape actually aren't," Paul said. "I don't know why you don't let a first-rate physician give you a complete check-up."

"I've had my physical and I'm O.K.," Rock said. "I saw the others who had their physicals at the same time and were classified O.K., and I know I'm certainly as O.K. as they are. If a first-rate physician gave me a complete check-up and discovered that I *wasn't* O.K., I know he would also be able to discover that every man in the Army isn't O.K., if they or he or friends of theirs or his wanted him to go to the trouble. I've heard what the boys are doing. I don't blame them. Besides, they are going to help sell War Bonds, and entertain, and things like that. I wouldn't do any of those things."

"Do you want to kill yourself?" Paul said.

"I don't believe in killing," Rock said, "but I will not do anything to keep myself from being as *apt* to be killed as any of the others who are unable to do anything to keep themselves from being apt to be killed by the war. Don't be unhappy. It's a good play, and you're not dying any more. Myra may find somebody to direct it who will make it come across the stage as simply and effectively as it came across the page when I read it. I want to get back to the poker game now."

"I'd like to get in the game, too," Paul said.

They got up and began to walk back to the hotel, neither father nor son, nor brother, nor friend, but accidents which had happened to meet by accident, and by accident had continued to meet, to tell one another the unfolding of the accidental story, something winking in each of them, knowing the story was enormously meaningless, unfortunate, depressing, and something to be instantly forgotten.

Is it a world that dies in a man when a man dies, a world he never knew, never understood, never improved, never inhabited? Is a man, inside his small sack of skin, a whole world once he has fearlessly come out of the womb, fearlessly accepted his head, fearlessly accepted his schedule, winking fearlessly as he goes? Is a man a whirling dervish in his own whirling world and desert? Is he a man or a world? Is he good or is he bad? Is he true or is he false? After he has fearlessly stepped forward among the multitudes of his kind, is he fearlessly among friends and unalone, or is he fearlessly among enemies, incurably alone, but forever innocent, and forever indestructible? After he has fearlessly seized his woman and fearlessly loved her, loving mother and father, daughter and son, has he come to meaning? Or is this also nothing? After he has fearlessly loved life, world, beauty, and truth, is a man any closer to anything good than he ever was, than he was in the winking womb?

"ROCK," Paul Key said as they walked fearlessly back to the hotel, each of them fearlessly drunk, fearlessly friendless, a world fearlessly dying in each of them. "Rock," he said, "I don't like what's happening."

"You don't like what's happening to the play?" Rock said. "Is that it?"

"Not to the play," Paul said. "To everything. To everybody. Something's the matter. I thought you'd do the play, first in New York, then in films, for the whole world to see. Something's the matter that I don't like that's so nearly not the matter that I believe it could be quickly stopped if something could be quickly done that had nothing the matter with it."

"You're drunk," Rock said. "A big man in a small body drunk, stumbling around trying to stop dying. The dying's not to be stopped. It's not to be stopped by not liking what's happening to *anything*. I had my shoes shined in this Shoe Shine Parlor. I sat in that second chair there."

"What's that mean, Rock?"

"It means the Parlor's still there," Rock said. "The chair's still there. My feet have grown. I'm wearing another pair of shoes. The man who shined my shoes is dead. I was eleven or twelve. It doesn't mean anything. Why do you want it to mean something?"

"Everything means something," Paul said. "You had your shoes shined. What about it?"

"He shined them for me," Rock said. "I sat there and he shined them. Shines were a dime then. A dime was a dime then. I gave him a quarter."

"What about it, Rock?"

"He's dead," Rock said. "The Parlor's still there, the chair's still there. I'd just had a haircut, too, and my ears were cool. The way I felt, anything could happen."

"What happened?" Paul said.

"Anything," Rock said.

"How about now?" Paul said. "Can anything still happen now?"

"No," Rock said, "because he's dead. *Something* can happen, but not anything. Anything's happened already."

"What can happen, Rock?"

"The play can be produced," Rock said. "You can sit there on the opening night, all alone in your seat, all alone in your clothes, all alone in your head and hide, and hang your head and try to hide because the play is there, it *is* the play for them, but they don't want it. So they're *not* there, only *you* are there, and you had your shoes shined long ago. Everything in this miserable town is mine. Everything I see here now I saw here long ago. Look over there. Look across the street there. At the corner there. My father stood there watching me talk to the two street girls the night we fought and he busted my nose. I know that corner. I remember him standing there, burning with Armenian anger, burning with his own Vagramian anger, because his son, whom he'd believed was himself again, did not love him, did not respect him enough to obey him, to obey his anger, to stay away from street corners and street girls. I see him standing there still. He wasn't much older than I am now. But he was mistaken about himself, about his son, and about the girls. We were talking about better things than I have ever found people anywhere to talk to about."

"What things, Rock?"

"We were talking about the accidents that had happened to each of us," Rock said, "each accident small and unimportant, sometimes amusing and pleasant, and how out of these accidents each of us had come to that corner, that evening, in this town. We were talking about the fun we'd had having our accidents and about the fun we were going to have having more of them, because they were on their way to the S.P. Depot, to go to San Francisco, and we had stood on the corner and talked a couple of times before and laughed and knew we'd never do that again, never have another chance to stand there and talk to one another about nothing in particular again, and I never saw them again. He was wrong about them. He was wrong. He was wrong about himself and myself. My father's all over this town. He couldn't stand it, but he couldn't go anywhere else, either, for he had to be where his family was, his people, where he could write what he had to write and know his people would read it. He wrote and they read. The play will be performed, and you will see it. One of your sons will stop someplace in Beverly Hills some night, outside Romanoff's maybe, or outside the William Morris Agency, and remember that you and he had been there once together, that you'd worked hard all your life at work you hated but did because you were mistaken about yourself and about him, and that you wrote all the time but didn't like what you wrote and didn't let your wife, his own mother, know that you wrote, and then after a whole lifetime of being mistaken about everything, you wrote a play in which you weren't mistaken at last, and it was performed and nothing happened, and there he is, your son, a man of thirty or thirty-five himself now, himself mistaken about himself and about his wife and his son and his daughter, and there's Romanoff's, or there's the William Morris Agency, and that's all it came to. Why couldn't you have been a tailor?"

"A tailor, Rock?" Paul said. "Why should I be a tailor? My father was a tailor."

"Didn't he want you to be a tailor, too?"

"Yes, but *he* was mistaken, too," Paul said. "He didn't understand that he should never have been a tailor."

"What should he have been?" Rock said.

"He should have been a clown," Paul said. "He was even smaller and uglier than I am, but I never saw him when he wasn't laughing in his eyes or moving his arms and legs in a way to amuse God. It was an accident that he was a tailor, just as it was an accident that you stood on the corner and talked to the girls about accidents, but it was no accident that I got into the world of ideas. I did that, Rock. I decided to do it, Rock, and I *did* it."

"You shit," Rock said. "You decided to do it, and you did it! That was an accident, too. It was an accident you wrote the play, too. It was an accident you met Vida, an accident she saw you weren't ugly, an accident you saw that she *saw*, an accident you loved one another and had kids. If you'd been a tailor, you wouldn't have come into Fat Aram's, and by now I would have had a vineyard and three or four kids. Accidentally the vineyard and accidentally the kids, and accidentally I'd be the same man I am, bored the same as I am, and unwilling to trade places with anybody in the world, the same as I am. I'll tell what Jews and Armenians have in common."

"What, Rock?"

"Fathers," Rock said. "They have mothers in common, too, but the way they have fathers in common is the way that comes to something accidentally. Of course he was a clown, and there was never a series of accidents by which you could ever forget it, and none by which your son shall ever forget what you were accidentally."

153

"I was a man who worked hard, and loved his wife and kids," Paul said.

"That's not what he'll remember," Rock said. "He'll remember that you were small and ugly and knew it, but the handsomest and swiftest man he ever saw. My father was mad. I suppose his father was, too. My mother's father was, at any rate. We have fathers in common. We're fathers ourselves the minute we're born. We get over being sons quicker than any other people in the world. Our sons do, too. We fix our fathers, and our sons fix us. That's the reason we're intelligent. That's the reason we know so much more about everything than other people do without needing to go to the trouble of studying anything. We have fathers in common, and we're fathers at birth because we want enough of us to be around to receive the accidents, just in case an assortment or series of them is going to happen to somebody some day that is going to make a difference. You'll see the play, but your son, or both of them, won't know, even if they see it, any more about what it is—a new thing, a true thing—than the sons of strangers. It may even turn out to be a joke they will be able to laugh at. Shall we go up and get in the game?"

"I thought you'd do the play, Rock," Paul said. "I thought you'd do anything to do it."

"I wouldn't do anything to do it," Rock said. "Accidents happen to me. I don't do anything to stop them from happening. I never have. I never have, because I'm curious to know what the accidents are going to be, and what they are going to do and how they are going to do it, and because I'm not sure the accidents aren't at last going to come to what I want and have always wanted anyway."

"What's that?"

154

"To be, to have been, a good witness," Rock said. "Did your father kill himself, or did somebody else kill him?"

"He killed himself," Paul said. "He irritated himself to death threading needles and sewing buttonholes. How did your father die?"

"He died of old age," Rock said. "Let's go on in and get in the game."

"How about one drink in the hotel bar?" Paul said.

"Make it two," Rock said. "The game's there. It'll keep."

They went into the hotel bar and had two, then three, then four. Rock asked the bartender to hand him the telephone. He called Ann Ford and talked to her mother again.

"It's four o'clock in New York," Ann's mother said.

"Is there any madness in the family?" Rock said.

"Any *what?*"

"Any madness. I haven't met Ann's father. Was he mad?"

"Mad?"

"Yes."

"There is no insanity in my family, or in Ann's father's family. They are all property owners."

"I didn't say insanity," Rock said. "I said madness."

"They are all practical," the mother said. "Scotch-Irish on her father's side. Russian-French on her mother's. All well-to-do and well-mannered."

"She didn't telephone me," Rock said.

"I wasn't able to reach her," the mother said.

"Where is she?" Rock said.

"In bed, I suppose," the mother said.

"In bed with who?" Rock said.

"Alone, of course," the mother said. "My daughter enjoys going out and having fun, but all her people behave like ladies and gentlemen. Alone, of course."

"You mean she's in her own bed in her own room?" Rock said.

"Yes, of course," the mother said. "It's four o'clock."

"I'd like to talk to her," Rock said.

"I didn't think you wanted to talk to *me*," the mother said. "She's got a phone beside her bed. I guess she's unplugged it. I'll go wake her up and have her plug it in. Hold on. You must be drunk to call at four in the morning and ask if we're mad."

"I've got a high I.Q., though," Rock said.

"I'll go wake her up," the mother said.

"That's her mother," Rock said to Paul Key. "She's gone to wake her up."

"Where's her father?" Paul said.

"I don't know," Rock said. "They're divorced. Her mother's married again. The first husband was her own age. This one's older. I haven't met her father. I hear he's a gentleman drunk. A Scotch-Irish gentleman drunk. The daughter of that ought to go all right with the son of an Armenian manic depressive poet. The son and daughter of fathers like that ought to have pretty good sons and daughters."

"You want to marry this girl?" Paul said.

"I want to find out if I do," Rock said. "I expect to find out now."

"Now?"

"More or less."

"What do you know about her?"

"Wait a minute," Rock said. "I think she's plugged the phone in."

"You dirty dog you!" Ann said. "You said you weren't going to phone, then you phone at four in the morning! What

156

do you want, you dirty stinking dog? My mother's standing over my bed. Go away, Mother! She says I ought to be ashamed to talk the way I'm talking. Oh, go away, Mother, and don't you dare listen on the other phone! You hang up the minute you get back to your bed! And don't you dare life the receiver later on, either! She's gone now. Listen, you dirty dog! You've made me sick as a dog. I can't stand being made sick as a dog. What do you want?"

"I'm driving to San Francisco in a few hours," Rock said. "Take down this number and this address."

He gave her the telephone number and the address, then said, "Fly to San Francisco. Phone me before you leave. I'll pick you up at the airport and take you to the St. Francis Hotel."

"Do you want to marry me?" Ann said.

"I want you to meet my mother, and *her* mother."

"I want to meet your *grandmother's* mother," Ann said. "Where's *she*, you dirty dog? You want me to meet your mother and her mother! Don't you love me? Don't you want to marry me? I can't wait to meet them. I hope they'll like me. Do you think they will?"

"Yes, I do."

"If they like me, I'll love them madly," Ann said.

"I hear you're eighteen now," Rock said. "I hear it's your birthday."

"Yes. What are you going to give me?"

"Eighteen."

"Eighteen *what?* Oh, you dirty dog! I love you, Rock. Do you love me?"

"Yes."

"I'll phone you," Ann said. "Don't you dare make a pass

157

at any of those California girls, do you hear? Wait for me."

"I'll wait," Rock said. "Happy birthday."

He hung up and turned to his friend.

"I'm going to marry her," he said.

"Why?" Paul said. "Who is she? You don't know her. Myra Clewes said something about her. Myra knows her. You don't know her. Myra doesn't think she's the girl for you at all. Why are you going to marry her?"

"For my kids," Rock said. "I was a father the minute I was born. No sense being a father without kids. I want to see them now. I'd like to see them looking at least half like her. Let's go get into the game. Schwartz and my cousin are probably broke by now. Let's go sit down and look at the cards."

Is a man his father and his son fighting in him for a chance to share in the common indestructibility?

Every man's life means more than any other man may ever guess or suspect, more than any man himself may ever guess or suspect, as he himself knows. The mystery of every man is a full-grown thing while he is still in his mother's womb. To live, to go on living, is to have this full-grown thing worn away by time until nothing is left. As the wearing away proceeds the meaning of a man's life grows farther and farther past knowing or guessing, until meaning and no-meaning are one and the same.

What does a man mean, for instance, sitting in a poker game at two in the morning? What does he mean, carrying this full-grown but vanishing thing to the cards and their values? Does he mean it is he who is lucky? Does his sitting there mean he is drawing nearer with each hand dealt to fatherhood

*and proud unimportance, to love and fun, to health and glad-
ness? Does it mean that if he makes a heart-flush the war will
end by morning? Does it mean that if he draws to two pair
and makes a full house his children will be handsome and have
fine hearts and minds? Does it mean that if he is dealt a pat
queen high straight the girl he marries will be the one woman
in the world to send him by accident to the best end he could
ever reach?*

THE boy whose parents were from Bitlis, who spoke to
Rock at Fat Aram's, who took Schwartz in a taxi to the house
on Winery Street, was Bakrat Bonapartian, called Buck Bonapart. He was one of the last box-makers of Fresno, a once
proud calling, in recent years all but made extinct by the
machine. He took his bench, nail rack, and hatchet from one
small grape shipper to another, nailing three or four days for
one, five or six for another. The owners of the box-making
machines asked a dollar sixty-five for a hundred lugs, Buck
Bonapart asked a dollar fifty. Thus by underselling the machine he practiced his proud trade, nailing at top speed a
hundred lugs in two hours. In twelve hours he earned nine
dollars. Sometimes, however, he worked on and earned twelve
dollars. Still, he gambled as if he had gotten his money from
his father.

Rock Wagram was glad to see that after losing two hundred
dollars on an eight full to a ten full, Buck Bonapart was able
to win four hundred from Paul Key on a pair of sixes against
a bluff.

"How did you know I was bluffing?" Paul Key said.

"I didn't," Buck said. "I just had a *hunch* you were."

"Old Buck," one of Buck's friends said, a man of twenty-one called Pitcher because he had pitched for Fresno High the only year they beat Bakersfield and won the Valley Championship. "The heart of a lion, the brain of a boob."

"Boob," Buck said quietly. "Brain of a boob. I suppose I played that wrong?"

"Call a three-hundred-dollar bet with a pair of sixes, and right or wrong you'll soon be sleeping in the streets," Pitcher said.

"You're talking about pitching," Buck said. "This is poker. I got the same idea Paul did. I was going to bet three hundred to try to get the hundred in the pot. When he beat me to it, I asked myself if he was bluffing and the answer I got was yes."

"Where'd you get it, Buck?" Paul Key said. "Where'd you get the answer?"

"I don't know," Buck said. "I got it. I got it clear. You drew two to something, a flush most likely. I drew three to a pair of sixes. You got nothing and I got nothing. But I got the answer when I asked the question. Isn't that what poker is? Isn't it asking them and answering them? I never try to trick another player into telling me what he's got. I never look at him, I never ask him anything, I never tell him anything. I play poker with God." He laughed softly. "I guess that's where I get the answers, and the questions, too."

"You're entitled to *that* money," Paul Key said. He shuffled and dealt. "This time it'll be a different story."

"My grandmother," Buck said, "always used to say, 'God is big.' A different story, a different God. There's enough to go around, I guess. Anybody here can take my money if he's got a better in with God than I've got."

The cards were dealt, the talk stopped. It had been so quiet in the first place as to have been not much more than the game's continuous quietude. No one had paid much attention to the actual words said, or the actual meaning of them, except Paul Key.

Rock was thinking of Ann Ford, of having her meet his grandmother and his mother.

Next to Rock, on his left, Buck Bonapart was thinking of the vineyard he would buy after the war.

Next to Buck, Schwartz was thinking the world must be coming to an end for his uncle to be sitting in a poker game with an assortment of Armenians, a most happy end, for there was his uncle losing and winning, but mainly losing, and happier (or something) than he had ever before seen him.

Next to Schwartz, Haig Vagramian was thinking that if he could get through this game without losing he was a cinch to get through the war without getting killed, for he had gambled the only way he knew how, innocently and wildly, with astonishment at his mistakes, with gladness at his successes.

Next to Haig, Pitcher was thinking that if he was lucky he might still have a pretty good arm after the war and might be signed by one of the teams in the Coast League, the San Francisco Seals, he hoped.

Next to Pitcher, a man of twenty-seven with black bushy eyebrows called Aslan was thinking it must be a small world, after all, for a man who was supposed to be as famous as Rock Wagram to come back to Fresno and sit down with him and the other boys and play poker, for he had never believed Fresno would ever again see Rock Wagram, or that he himself would ever speak to him in Armenian, and hear Rock speak to him in Armenian.

Next to Aslan, Paul Key was thinking that if Rock could

come through the war all right, Paul Key could write a play even better than *The Indestructibles*, and Rock would appear in it and it *would* make a difference, a great difference, but at the same time he was thinking he might never see Rock again, might never know how Rock made out in the war, might be dead before the war was over.

Next to Paul Key was a man called Manuel. This man was thinking that if it was the Turks they were fighting he would feel better about it, for they were the only people he hated, since they had killed most of his family when he had been five years old, a man of thirty-five now who sometimes had difficulty about his hatred of the Turks. This happened when he remembered the Turks who had been kind to him, who had taken care of him, given him food and shelter, and even tried to give him love.

At half past six the game stopped. It stopped by itself. Buck Bonapart got up to yawn. While he was doing so, Haig Vagramian got up to get himself a fresh drink. Sam Schwartz got up to see about getting a little more comfortable inside his tight pants. The others pushed back their chairs, but did not get up.

Haig had won a hundred and seventy-five dollars. Schwartz had won exactly one dollar. Buck Bonapart had won three hundred and thirty dollars. Pitcher had won fifty-five dollars. Aslan had lost eleven dollars. Manuel had lost eighty-five dollars. Rock had won nine hundred and ninety dollars. Paul Key had lost a little over two thousand dollars, less than half a week's wages.

Rock spoke to Manuel, the orphan, the loser of eighty-five dollars, in Armenian.

"What is your city?" he said.

"Moush," Manuel said.

Then in English Rock said, "Cut high card for a hundred."

Rock took the deck and quickly cut to an eight.

"I haven't got any more money," Manuel said softly in Armenian because he was ashamed.

"Cut," Rock said in English.

Manuel cut to a nine, and Rock handed him two of Paul Key's fifties.

They moved around the room now, talking and laughing, and then it happened. Sam Schwartz heard his uncle Paul Key laugh. Paul Key had told Buck Bonapart a joke. Buck had liked the joke so much he had leaped and whirled with laughter. Sam Schwartz had seen his uncle come alive in a way that he had never before seen, and for the first time in his life he had heard Paul Key laugh as if Paul Key had the equipment for it.

"What will they do next?" Sam asked himself, deeply puzzled by what was happening to the world.

Everybody stretched and joked and laughed. The game was now a thing of the past.

What good is it for a man to lose his soul if he does not gain the world? What does it profit him? What is the joy or comfort of it? What good is it for a man to gain his soul, only to discover that it was not worth gaining?

PAUL KEY had long ago gained the world, and lately he had also gained his soul, but what good was it? The world he had long ago gained was a poor one, the soul he'd gained was poorer still.

He stood in front of Fat Aram's with Rock and Rock's

cousin, and with his nephew Sam Schwartz, and he said, "Good luck, Rock."

"The same to you, Paul."

He turned to Rock's cousin. "Good luck, boy."

"Thanks, Mr. Key," Haig said.

"Mr. Key my foot," Paul said. "My name is Paul, boy. Paul. That's all." He turned to his nephew. "Good luck, Sam."

"Thanks, P.K.," Sam said.

"P.K.'s chewing gum," Paul said. "Don't ever call me that again, Sam. Paul."

The small man, who was drunker and tireder than ever before in his life, said, "Give my love to your family, Rock. I love them all. I love them deeply. Take care of yourself for them. Come on, Sam, back to Hollywood, back to U.S. Pictures, back to lies, Rock. Take care of yourself."

"I'll drop you off at the airport," Rock said.

"No, you won't," Paul said. "This is our corner, Rock. Fat Aram's. This is where we met. This is where we say so long. The joint's closed, but this is the place. I loved them all. I loved them all deeply."

"We'll meet here again," Rock said.

"Will we, Rock?"

"Sure we will," Rock said. "Take it easy. Take it easy, Sam. So long."

Rock and Haig turned and walked across the street, to get back to the car parked in front of the hotel, Haig saying, "You worked something out, didn't you, Rock?" Haig was speaking in Armenian when Rock heard Sam shout, "Rock!" He turned and saw the nephew holding the uncle in his arms.

He went back, not hurrying, and looked at the man's face.

"He's all right, Sam."

"I think he's dead, Rock."

"No," Rock said. "He's passed out. He's drunk, that's all. Come on. I'll help you get him back to the hotel. Let him sleep it off, then fly back."

"Isn't he dead, Rock?"

"No."

"The way he looked at me, Rock, I thought he was dying."

"No."

They got him to the hotel, onto the couch in the room they had just left. His face was white and sticky. Haig was downstairs trying to get a doctor. At last Haig came up with somebody old and dirty from the Emergency Hospital in the Police Department across the street.

"He's had a little to drink," Rock said. "He's all right, but take a look at him."

The man worked over the body a few minutes and then said, "I think he's had a heart attack. He's not dead, though. I'll give him a shot, sit around a minute and see what happens."

"Shall I call Vida?" Schwartz said. "Shall I call U.S. Pictures, Rock?"

"No."

"What shall I do, Rock? He's going to die. I saw him when it happened."

"He's not going to die," Rock said.

"You never know about these small fellows," the doctor said. "They take a lot of punishment and then something happens that would kill anybody else, but it doesn't kill them." He examined the tube and needle, jammed the needle in gently and slowly pressed the handle, forcing the fluid out. "We'll know in a minute. In the meantime I'll fill out this report. Who is he?"

Schwartz was about to tell the man who his uncle was when Rock said, "Patrick Kerry." Rock glanced at Schwartz. He gave the man the other information he needed, and then they talked about highway accidents because that was what the man worked at for the most part. The man was ready, though, when Paul Key opened his eyes.

"How do you feel?" the man said.

Paul Key tried to sit up.

"Not for a moment, please," the man said, holding him down.

"I want to get to the airport," Paul Key said. "Rock, I'm all right. Tell him."

"He's all right," Rock said.

"I know," the man said. "Let's just give it five minutes, though."

Paul Key laughed softly, closing his eyes a moment, then opening them again.

"Go ahead, Rock," he said. "You've got to drive to San Francisco. I'd rather you didn't wait. Take care of yourself."

"O.K., Paul."

Rock and his cousin left the hotel. Rock drove to the red-brick church, and went in. He crossed himself, then knelt and prayed for Paul Key. When he went back to the car the boy said, "What happened, Rock?"

"He's dying," Rock said. "He's been dying for years."

"Patrick Kerry? Who's that?"

"Paul Key. Shut up a minute."

They drove in silence to the house on Winery Street. It was eight o'clock in the morning now. The old lady was sitting on the sofa in the parlor, a small satchel at her feet.

"Are we driving now to San Francisco to see my daughter?" she said.

"Yes," Rock said. "Have you been waiting long?"

"I wanted to be ready."

"Let me use the bathroom," Rock said, "then we'll go. You'll like the car. It's new. Leather seats."

"Has it got a radio?" the old lady said.

"Oh yes."

"If you get tired talking to me, you can listen to the radio."

"No," Rock said. "I want to talk to you. I want to talk to you all the way to San Francisco."

Haig stood in the bedroom and talked to Rock in the bathroom, vomiting in there, trying to vomit silently.

"You worked something out, didn't you, Rock?" he said.

"A lot of things," Rock said.

"Is he going to get you a deferment, so you can make a patriotic picture?"

"No."

"Did you borrow a lot of money from him?"

"No."

At last Rock came out of the bathroom.

"Telephone the hotel and ask the desk about Paul Key, will you?"

"Sure," Haig said.

"Now?" the old lady said. "Are we leaving now?"

"Right this minute," Rock said.

She got up and went to the door with her satchel. Then she went out onto the front porch. Rock went to the kitchen for one more look at the table where he'd found him. Haig came from the telephone.

"He's dead, Rock."

"Fuck him."

"Aren't you going back to the hotel to help Schwartz?"

"No."

"Shall I go back?" Haig said.

"Get on your bike and go home and go to sleep," Rock said. "Send me your number and everything else I ought to know."

They left the house, locking the door behind them. From the street he looked back at it. He helped the old lady into the car, then drove off, the boy on the motorcycle racing past the car to wave solemnly and disappear. Rock never saw him again.

"Are your affairs in good order?" the old lady said. "Are they going well?"

"Now, in the morning, when you were a girl," Rock said, "was it like this?"

"*This?*" Lula said. "This is no morning."

"Tell me about a morning, then," Rock said.

"When I was a girl—ten or eleven, the year before I got married—my man was a young man," Lula said. "He was twenty-two or twenty-three. I used to get up at dawn because it was then I knew I would see him walking to the city. I used to climb to the roof and from there watch him. He knew I was there every morning. I waited for him to notice that I was there, but he only walked by. One morning, though—and that is the morning I am talking about—he looked up and noticed me. He stopped and smiled. 'Good morning, Lula Khanoum,' he said. *That* was a morning."

"Yes," Rock said. "Tell me all about it."

They were on Highway 99 now, just past Roeding Park, headed for the river at Skaggs Bridge where he'd gone swimming, where Dick Cracker, ten years old, almost twenty-five years ago, had drowned at sunset one night, trying to swim across the river with the rest of them, turning to them to say, "I can't make it, boys. So long, Vahan. So long, Shag. So long, Rock."

It doesn't do a man any good or any harm to lose his soul or lose the world or gain his soul or gain the world. If he's swimming the San Joaquin River, all he's got to do is get across. All he's got to do at any time is not drop dead.

Driving across the bridge, Rock glanced at the place where Dick Cracker had drowned. He'd been a game boy, a red-headed boy, Dikran Kirakjian. They'd all been half-drowning. Dikran Kirakjian didn't ask any of them for help. He just turned and said so long. It doesn't do him any harm or any good. All he's got to do is not stop.

Chapter III

:

THE SON AND THE DAUGHTER

What is it that happens? What is it that comes to pass?
A man who was thirty-three is now forty-one, the
year is no longer 1942, it is 1950. The month is no longer
September, it is February. He is not driving his new Cadillac
through the desert, on his way from Amarillo to San Francisco.
He is lying, half-drunk, on a bed in a hotel room in New
York.

What is it that happens that a man can understand?

A man lives to be older than his father.

A man has a son of six, named Haig after his brother who
died when the man was nine.

A man has a daughter of three named Lula after his mother's mother.

A man has a divorced wife, now twenty-five, named Ann Ford, called Ann Wagram. A man has a nine-year hang-over on a February afternoon in New York, a black day of snow.

For nine years the man has been winked, but still he winks back. In nine months of separation, three months of divorce, the weight of the man has fallen from 190 to 160 pounds.

What is it that happens?

This is what happens. A man's weight increases, or decreases, but one way or another a man is winked, as he himself knows. Money comes and goes, or doesn't come and go, or neither comes nor goes, and he is still the same man. He is still the same man, but can never again be the same, for the time is another time, several of his children have come, several more of his family have died, several more of his friends have died.

The world is still the same world, but it has been so wickedly winked that it is blurred, and it is not easy for the man to get up and see his way to the table to pour another drink.

There is a gray blur in the world. It is in the faces of the strangers the man has lately seen. The way they walk is strange now, too. They walk nervously and swiftly, seeming to look about as they go, seeming to turn to look back, seeming to expect the return of something lost, or the catching up of something evil, seeming to expect something unspeakable.

Or if they do not walk nervously and swiftly, they go as in a trance, as if to execution.

It is in the young, too. They are not young. The telling of jokes is not in them. The living of jokes is not in them. They think, and think bitterly. They get married before they're twenty-two, hating one another and one another's parents, hating art, hating religion, hating places, hating biology, hating chemistry, hating anthropology, hating history, hating children, hating science, hating shoes, hating machinery, hating trees and grass, hating rabbits and flies.

What is it that happens?

The telephone bill rings, and a man reaches over to the receiver, puts it to his ear, and says, "Yes."

"ROCK?" a voice said. "Sam Schwartz. I just flew in. I'm at the St. Regis bar. Come and have a drink."

"No," Rock said. "Come up here and have one."

"David's with me."

"Who's David?"

"P.K.'s son."

"Who's P.K.?"

"Is that Rock Wagram?"

"Yes, yes," Rock said. "I know. *You're* Sam Schwartz, Vice-President in Charge of Production at U.S. Pictures. *I'm* Rock Wagram. P.K.'s Paul Key. I forgot. You're the only man in the world who ever called him P.K., and I haven't talked to you in years, Sam. What's David doing?"

"He's working with me," Schwartz said. "He's twenty-four now, you know."

"How old are you now?" Rock said.

"Forty-nine," Schwartz said, "but never felt better in my life."

"Come on up and have a drink," Rock said. "I'd like to see you both."

"You come here, Rock."

"Come on up and have a drink."

"I'll call you back in a few minutes," Schwartz said. "I don't know if I can make it."

"*What?*" Rock said.

"What's the matter with you, Rock?" Schwartz said. "I thought you'd be glad to hear from me."

"I asked you to come up and have a drink," Rock said.

"Can we meet somewhere for dinner, then?" Sam said.

"No."

Rock laughed to himself as he put the receiver back in its cradle.

At the table at the other end of the line Sam Schwartz said to his cousin David Key, "Well, I guess they're right all right. He's gone crazy all right. He hung up on me. He's cockeyed drunk. He's up there drinking. Why should we get up and go there? Who does he think he is, anyway? He hasn't worked in years."

"Why hasn't he?" David said.

"He's crazy," Schwartz said. "He's too tough to get along with. Nobody can talk to him. Pretty soon there won't be anybody left who will *want* to talk to him. He was good all right, but that was a long time ago."

"My father liked him very much," David said. "I believe my father admired him."

"Your father was a brilliant man," Schwartz said. "He liked to give difficult people the *impression* that he admired them. The people he really admired were the ones he treated like dirt. The people he loved he treated like dirt. He was the most brilliant man the industry's ever known. Everything I know I learned from P.K. He had a way with difficult people who happened to have temporary value. He knew how to get full value for his money out of them. What's the best way to get something out of somebody? Give him the impression you admire him."

"Yes, I suppose so," David Key said, "but my father gave *me* the impression that he admired Rock. He didn't give me that impression about very many others who visited us, and a lot of people visited us."

"Rock's all right," Schwartz said, "but let's face it, he never stopped being an Armenian."

"He *is* an Armenian," David Key said.

"So what?" Schwartz said. "So who cares?"

"I've never stopped being Paul Key's son," David said. "I've never stopped being a Jew, either. I like being my father's son and I like being a Jew, Sam."

"You're a baby," Schwartz said. "You're a baby, David. It's not what you are, it's what you *make* of yourself. What *you yourself* make of yourself."

"You're not ashamed of being a Jew, are you, Sam?" David said.

"I haven't got time to be ashamed," Schwartz said. "I'm too busy achieving things that *must* be admired. He had his nerve hanging up on me."

The boy got up.

"I think I'll go for a walk," he said.

Schwartz watched him go.

"I've been like a father to him nine years," Schwartz said. "I've been like a father to him since P.K. died, so what does he do to show his appreciation? He insults me. Am I ashamed of being a Jew? he wants to know. When I did the dirty work for his father, I never asked insulting questions. I did my work and helped his father get to the top of the industry. I worked hard. I didn't travel around with his father like an equal, the way his son travels around with me, and then insults me. That's what I get for being kind. I helped make his father. Who does he think he is to ask me insulting questions?"

What else happens? What else is it that comes to pass?

The children are born one after another, named, and noticed. They are heard speaking. They are heard living, making the noises of living. They are seen watching, examining, opening and looking into. They are loved, they love.

What else happens, winking?

The telephone bell rings again.

"Yes."

"Rock? Myra Clewes. Did you read the play?"

"No," Rock said.

"Rock, please read it," Myra said.

"I can't read it. It's dull."

"He's one of the most famous playwrights in America," Myra said. "How can you say it's dull?"

"He may be one of the most famous," Rock said, "but the play is dull just the same. I can't read it. I read the first nine pages."

"Rock," Myra said. "You can't just say *everything's* dull."

"Everything *isn't*. Just this play."

"Rock, it's too bad *The Indestructibles* failed the way it did," Myra said, "but that was three years ago. Please read the play. I know you're going to like it. It gets much better as it goes along."

"I read the last six pages, too," Rock said.

"It's awfully powerful in the middle," Myra said.

"I read three pages in the middle, too," Rock said. "Everybody screams, but it's not powerful. It's noisy."

"How do I get you mad, Rock?"

"You don't have to get me mad," Rock said. "The theatre stinks. We know it does. What do we want to kid ourselves for?"

"It *is* a lousy play, isn't it?" Myra said.

"Yes, it is," Rock said. "But that's not the point. We could do the play, but what would be the point of that? It would go, most likely, but that wouldn't mean anything, either. The play doesn't say anything. It doesn't say anything in the words, and it doesn't say anything in the stuff that's not in the words."

"Well, anyway," Myra said, "I'm giving him a birthday party tonight. Everybody's going to be there. I want you to be there, too."

"How old is he?" Rock said.

"Fifty."

"That old?"

"Yes," Myra said. "I told him you'd be there. You won't let me down. It's upstairs at 21. Any time after eight."

"I don't feel like going to anybody's birthday party, Myra."

"It'll do you good."

"I don't feel like bothering with a lot of people."

"I'm expecting you, Rock. There'll be a lot of beautiful girls."

"Don't make me laugh."

"There *will*, Rock."

"I married the most beautiful one there is," Rock said.

"Yes, I know," Myra said. "Well, just come to the party. I want to talk to you."

"O.K., Myra, I'll try to make it," he said. "Thanks for asking me."

That's what happens.

It isn't much, item by item, but it mounts up, it mounts up, it winks and mounts up, and a man smiles as he shuts his eyes to see if he can sleep a moment in the afternoon, since he can't at night. He shuts his eyes and falls into something that is almost but not quite sleep, he falls into remembering what *was*, what *might have been*, and what *is*. It means something, perhaps something fine, only a man can't make out what it means, he can't make it out for the winking and the mounting up of it.

Whatever the time of him, a man is his own poor friend, his own proud stranger, his own cunning enemy, watching with sharp eyes his mother's own son. It is himself who is the luckiest man, as he himself knows. It is his own half-words and half-acts left in half-places at half-times that grow whole in all men, winking in them and in their children, for a man is the race, every one of him is the race, and each is good, each is innocent, each is winked into his own innocence, as he himself knows. A man lives out his time in secret, leaving behind no word of what he was or did or knew, or leaving only half a word, mixed with coughing or laughter, or half an act of dancing on the floor of his own mother's kitchen when he was five and loved the promise of time and the world.

HE had almost fallen asleep when he heard the knock at the door.

"Come in, David," he said.

Paul Key's son found him lying on his bed, the room dark, the dark snow falling softly outside the window.

"Did you say, 'Come in, *David*'?" David said.

"Yes," Rock said. "Pour yourself a drink. Pour me one, too, please."

"Did you mean *me?*" David said.

"Yes."

"How did you know it was me?"

"Sam told me you were with him."

"Do you remember me?"

"Very well," Rock said. "And your brother. And your sister. And your mother. And your father."

"How do you like yours?" David said.

"Over ice, please."

Rock received the glass from the hand of the son of his dead friend, tasted the liquor, tasted it again, and then lighted a cigarette.

"Will Sam be coming along?" he said.

"I don't think so," David said.

"Too bad. I wanted to see him."

"Is there something you'd like me to tell him?"

"No," Rock said. "I'd just like to see him again. How does he look these days?"

"Well, he's bigger than ever," David said. "Still, he's got a lot of stamina for a heavy man."

"Yes, he gets things done, I hear."

"What do you think of his pictures?" David said. "I mean, I don't mean to—I mean, I've been working with him a year and I've gotten a little confused. I'm beginning to believe they're *good.*"

"Does it make any difference?"

"I don't know. I'm not sure. It must make some sort of difference."

"Does it make any difference to *you?*" Rock said.

"No, I guess it doesn't," David said. "I'm supposed to be learning production. The trouble is there isn't anything to learn. I mean, the most I can learn is to make more of these pictures that I know have got something the matter with them. I don't know what it is, but I know something *is* the matter with them."

"Are you trying to guess what to do about it?" Rock said.

"Yes, I am," David said. "I admired my father very much."

"I liked your father," Rock said.

"I've always felt I'd like to do what he did," David said. "Did he do what Sam's doing?"

"Yes, he did," Rock said, "but Sam isn't the man your father was."

"Did my father make bad pictures that he himself *knew* were bad?"

"Yes."

"Did *you* make bad pictures that *you* knew were bad?"

"Yes," Rock said.

"Why?" David said. "Why did my father do it? Why did you do it? I thought it was because of Sam."

"No," Rock said. "It's not because of Sam the pictures Sam makes are bad."

"Why are they bad, then?" David said. "Why did my father make them bad? Why did you?"

"We don't know what we're doing," Rock said. "We do our best. It isn't good enough. We do our best when we're *not* working, too. We do it all the time. It isn't good enough. It always seems as if it *may* turn out all right at last, and then it turns out bad again."

"I can't decide what to do," David said.

"About what?"

"About having always felt that I'd like to do what my father did," David said. "If he made pictures he knew were bad, what shall I do? I mean, I like fun and money and all the rest of it, the same as all the others do, but I *thought* my father *tried* to make good pictures. I *believed* the ones he did make *were* good. Sam tries to make bad pictures and he makes bad pictures."

"They make more money than pictures that are less bad," Rock said.

"Yes, they do," David said.

"Your father *tried* to make good pictures," Rock said. "He did *try*."

"Didn't he try hard enough?" David said.

"It's not as simple as that," Rock said. "The way it was was this, and that's the way it is now, too. You had to try to make a picture that would make money and at the same time be a good picture. You never believe this *can't* be done. You never *want* to believe it can't be done."

"Can it be done?" David said.

"It never has," Rock said.

"What about Chaplin?"

"They're very bad. All of them."

"Why?"

"They put sleeping, weeping people into deeper, weeping sleep."

"The last ones, too?"

"No," Rock said. "The last ones *try*, they try for *something*, but they don't make it. It's not simple at all. It involves everything."

"What about the English ones lately?" David said. "The Shakespeare pictures?"

"They're bad."

"Everybody seems to like them."

"That happens. I don't like them. Do you like them?"

"I *thought* I did," David said.

"Then you did," Rock said. "I was *sure* I didn't. I'll tell you why. Kings and their wives and brothers and sons and daughters bore me. Most other people do, too. After they've bathed and put on clean clothes and are comfortable and feel fine, they bore me. Before they do these things they fascinate me, and I think I love them. While they're working, while they're struggling to get to the bath, to the table, to comfort and well-being, they delight me, but once they get to where they believe they will finally be all right, they bore me, for they are nothing then. Kings are always supposed to be all right, and it is a shock to discover that they are nothing. You had to try to make a picture that would make money and at the same time be good. Your father tried. He tried every time."

"What should I do?" David said.

"At the same time," Rock said, "there's another way of looking at it. It's this. You decide they're *all* good, and you observe that this one is better than that one. You let it go at that. It doesn't make for the worst life in the world. You should do what you like, or what you must, or what's most convenient at the time."

"I thought my father was—well, a great man."

"He was greater than most," Rock said. "There are no men who are not great. You happen to like some men enough to believe they're the ones who are great. You happen to dislike others enough to believe they're the ones who aren't, but actually any man who lives, any man who stays alive, *is* great. Having stayed alive *demonstrates* that he is. As to the ones who die, it's hard to say. Most likely they were great as long as they lasted. Would you pour me another, please?"

"I thought my father was *truly* great," David said.

"You knew him better than you knew the neighbor boy's father," Rock said. "A man's father is always great. A man's family is always great. How could there be any question about that? How many children has Sam Schwartz?"

"He isn't married."

"Well, as soon as he gets married and has children, his children will know *he* is great."

"Maybe we don't mean the same thing by great," David said. "My father was a *kind* man."

"He was as kind as he could be under the circumstances," Rock said. "There's no limit to greatness or kindness."

"What's *anything* mean, then?" David said.

"Not very much," Rock said. "Your own animal health, mainly. Your own animal fun. Your own animal cleanliness."

"Animal?" David said. "All animal?"

"Yes," Rock said. "I'll tell you what, David. I don't sleep nights. I think I'd like to sleep now. Call me any time tomorrow and we'll go sit down somewhere and talk. Thanks for coming by. Is Vida well?"

"She misses my father," David said. "She *still* misses him. I'll call between two and three if it's all right."

"That'll be fine," Rock said.

He stretched back on the bed and began to go over everything again, the half-words and half-acts left in half-places at half-times, for whatever the time of him, a man is his own proud stranger, and the luckiest one that ever was born.

A man lives his life in ignorance. He lives his entire life alone, out of touch with a secret, an instantaneous thing forever longing to be in touch with the secret, which he believes

183

is in his woman. But his woman is not his woman, and the secret is not in her. His son is not his son, and the secret is not in him. His daughter is not his daughter, and the secret is not in her. Each of these is also alone, and out of touch. Each is a man's own sad achievement, his own sad failure, his own instantaneous self, but they are not his own, as he himself knows.

During the February afternoon sleep Rock Wagram drew close to the secret. When he awoke his soul wept. His sleep had been without action, without thought, but in it he had gone closer to the secret than ever before in his life.

What is it? What is the secret?

HER lawyer telephoned and said, "I just had a talk with Ann. If you want to see the children, she wants you to know you're welcome."

"I'll go right over," Rock said. "I haven't seen them in a month."

"It's the nurse's day off," the lawyer said. "Ann's taking care of them."

"Then I'll go tomorrow," Rock said. "Are they well?"

"Ann said they're fine," the lawyer said. "She asked me to call you. You can go tonight or any other time."

"I'll go tomorrow," Rock said. "Thanks for calling."

What is it? What is the secret?

He began to move swiftly, for deep inside something had stopped, and he knew something would have to be done about it.

What had stopped he did not know. What he was to do about it he did now know.

He shaved, showered, put on fresh clothes, and went out

into the snow. It was night now, but not yet five o'clock. He got into a taxi and went to his lawyer's.

"I saw Ann's lawyer last night," Rock said. "There's to be no legal fight for the children. She is to do what she pleases. I am to see them whenever I like, but for reasons of my own only when she's not there. She's there now and asked her lawyer to phone me to say that I could see them tonight. I'll see them tomorrow."

"What made you change your mind?" Rock's lawyer said. "We were to file the papers tomorrow."

"Night before last my mother telephoned," Rock said. "We talked an hour. There's to be no fight for the children. She loves Ann. She understands Ann."

"Are you all right?"

"Yes," Rock said. "I'm going to a party Myra Clewes is giving John Flannery at 21 tonight. Tomorrow I'm going to work. I'll take anything. I've got to have money."

"Something seems to be the matter," the lawyer said. "What is it?"

"I don't know," Rock said. "I took a nap a little while ago. I guess I'm still half-asleep, that's all."

"Do you want to come to early dinner?"

"No. I want to read the play, so I can talk to Myra and the playwright about it."

"Everything's off, then?" the lawyer said.

"Yes."

"If it's what you want, Rock, I'm glad."

"I want the kids," Rock said, "but that's silly. My mother told me so in Armenian. I want Ann, too, but that's sillier still. There is no marriage, she said. There is no divorce. There is Ann, there is Rock, there is Haig, there is Lula. There is change. Each is each. Each is alive. Let each live, she said. Let Ann live as she pleases. My grandmother used to say the same thing. She loved Ann more than she loved anybody else in the world, except her dead husband. Ann went to my grandmother's funeral in Fresno. Women understand and love one another. Women married to Vagramians do, I mean. Have I got time to read this play outside in the waiting room?"

"Of course," the lawyer said. "Stay as long as you like. I'm leaving in a moment, but you stay. Stay where you are."

He was an hour reading the play. It was bad, but it didn't matter. It didn't matter any more. He would do it.

What had happened? What was it that had stopped?

He dropped the play on the leather sofa and left the office. It was one of those plays he could read once and remember forever, for there was nothing in it he needed to make a point of remembering. He walked up Fifth Avenue, turned left at 52nd, and went to 21, to the bar, to drink alone until he saw somebody he knew.

He hadn't finished his first drink when he saw Myra herself. They sat down and Rock said, "I just read it. Do you want to do it?"

"Do you, Rock?" Myra said.

"Yes."

"Is it good?"

"No," Rock said. "I want to work. I want to go to work the way any working-man goes to work, to get his pay. I need money. Do *you* want to do it?"

"Of course," Myra said. "It's better than we think. Besides, he'll be on hand to work on it as we go along. I'm delighted. What happened?"

"I took a nap this afternoon," Rock said.

"So what?" Myra said.

"When I woke up my whole life inside me wept."

"Why? Do you know?"

"No," Rock said. "Something stopped. I don't know what it is."

"This party tonight will do you good," Myra said. "Do you know a girl called Eve Ellis?"

"No. Why?"

"She's going to be at the party," Myra said. "I think you'll like her. I mean, why not *look* at another girl? You've been separated a year. It isn't the end of the world, Rock. There *are* other girls. This one's a beauty. I'm having her sit at your table. Will you meet with me and Flannery at lunch here tomorrow to talk about the play?"

"Yes."

"One o'clock?"

"I'd like to get away around two," Rock said.

"What's the hurry?"

"Make it twelve to two, then," Rock said. "Paul Key's son David came by this afternoon. He seemed troubled and wanted to talk, but I got sleepy. This sleep wanted to happen, I guess. This isn't silly. I don't understand it, but I know it isn't silly. I told David to call tomorrow and we'd meet somewhere and talk. He said he'd call between two and three."

"What sort of a boy is he?" Myra said.

"He doesn't look like Paul, but he's in trouble about Paul," Rock said. "He's beginning to suspect his father wasn't the man he thought he was. Does he know about Paul's writing?"

"Paul had only one play produced," Myra said. "I produced it, you appeared in it. It played two weeks to empty houses. I don't know whether he knows or not. I don't even know if

Vida knows. Surely they *must* by now. They must have come across the manuscripts."

"They came across the manuscripts of hundreds of writers," Rock said. "How would they know Patrick Kerry was Paul Key?"

"You think you ought to tell David Key about his father. Is that it?" Myra said.

"I don't know what the other things he wrote are like," Rock said, "but I know he wrote a great play."

"*Was* it great, Rock?"

"Yes."

"Then why did the critics attack it? Why did the audiences resent it?"

"It broke a habit," Rock said, "and habits are cherished. It broke the habit of thinking the particular is great. It achieved a new greatness. It said something never before said."

"What did it say?"

"It said *all* is art, all is great, because all is indestructible."

"This party'll do you good," Myra said. "I'm sure you're going to like Eve Ellis."

"I'll tell him," Rock said. "I think he ought to know. He can go through the manuscripts if they haven't been thrown away and pick out the plays by Patrick Kerry and examine them for himself. I don't think I ought to let it go."

"Do you like Richard in the play?" Myra said.

"Not at all," Rock said, "but I'll do it. He'll be all right."

"You'll help me with Flannery, won't you?"

"Of course."

"Shall we go upstairs?"

They went upstairs. The party was already in progress, with eight or nine men and as many women having cocktails.

"There'll be about a hundred," Myra said. "That's Eve over there."

"She looks a little like Ann."

"Oh, Rock!"

He stood at the bar with Eve Ellis and talked. More and more people arrived, all of them people he knew. The girl was light, as Ann was, smaller, and finally not at all like Ann. She said she would like him to hear something by Mozart that she believed was the most exciting music ever composed. He said he would like to hear the music.

He knew her feet wouldn't be Ann's, nor anything else of hers anything at all like Ann's. Still, it would do. He talked swiftly with almost everybody at the party, wandering around with a glass in his hand, and he knew this would do, too. He told a half dozen people two jokes he hadn't told since he had tended bar at Fat Aram's, and he heard them laugh. He knew this would do, too, for he was trying to forget the thing that had stopped.

The main course was being served when a waiter came to whisper in his ear, and the forgotten thing was instantly remembered.

"Telephone, Mr. Wagram," the waiter whispered.

It was his lawyer.

"San Francisco's trying to reach you," the lawyer said. "It's operator 76."

"Thanks."

It was his sister in San Francisco.

"What is it?" Rock said.

"It's Mama, Rock," his sister said. "She's at the St. Francis Hospital."

"What's the matter?"

189

"I went over early this morning," his sister said. "She was still in bed. All of a sudden Mama said, 'Vava, please get a doctor, I'm dying.' You know how Mama hates doctors."

"What's happened to Mama?"

"She's had a cerebral hemorrhage."

"I'll take the next plane."

"I've been with Mama every minute," his sister said. "This morning the doctor told me not to call you. A few minutes ago he told me to call you."

"I'll take the next plane," Rock said.

He hung up and asked a waiter to tell Myra that he had had to go. He hurried down the steps, out of the place, and to his room, where he telephoned and learned that the next plane would leave in ten minutes. He reserved a place on the one following, which left at eight in the morning.

He packed, went back to the party, sat down beside Eve Ellis, and began to drink again. He took the girl home at two, got back to his room at six, showered, dressed, checked out, and went to the Waldorf for his ticket. He wired his sister and asked her to have her son Joe drive his car to the airport and meet him. He wired Myra. He wired David Key.

When the plane took off he went to sleep and slept all the way to Chicago.

There was twenty minutes in Chicago, so he telephoned the Armenian doctor he had met in London when they had both been in the Army.

"What do they do for cerebral hemorrhage?" Rock said.

"Nothing, Rock," the doctor said.

"What do the best men do, the ones who know what they're doing?"

"Nothing, Rock."

THE SON AND THE DAUGHTER

"Who's the best man in San Francisco?"

"They're all the same, Rock."

His friend spoke in English at first, then in Armenian, explaining how it was.

He got back on the plane and slept or half-slept most of the way to San Francisco.

No man loves anyone but himself, not even his own mother, not even his own wife, not even his own daughter, for love is a lie.

No man loves anyone but himself, but this, too, is a lie, and no man loves even himself.

Every man is damned, as he himself knows, and the damned hate one another, each in his own damned way. They hate one another, pity one another, regret the failure of one another.

A man's own mother happened to meet his own father at a time of hunger and need in each of them, and every wedding is a wedding of male and female needs and failings, and a lie.

Every wedding is a wedding of failure to failure, one boy and one girl in love with the terrible hope of one another, the girl in love with herself and boys, the boy in love with himself and girls, the wedding itself in love with weddings and the world. But the love is damned, the wedding is damned, and so is the world. The unborn children they are in love with are damned. The longing of each of them, the boy and the girl wedded, the son arrived, the daughter arrived, is damned. The love is a lie, the wedding is a lie, the politeness is furious and brave, the tenderness is fierce and bitter, the doing of time together is fearful and beautiful.

The doing of time together, winking at the posture of time, at one another, each of them flying, and time doing noth-

ing, loving nothing, hating nothing, wanting nothing, receiving nothing, giving nothing, is holy, and hell.

HE was asleep on an airplane, flying through the posture of time to death, to the end of his mother, to the departure of another of his girls. The old Lula was gone three years to her husband Manuk. Ann was gone a year to safety and silliness, hats and hotel rooms. Little Lula mistook the men of the hotel rooms for her father.

And now his mother was lying in a bed in a hospital in San Francisco, lying and dying, asleep in the violent sleep of dirty death, lying in a strange and hateful building, her helpless body cared for by gentle and hateful strangers, her sleep clamoring with the lies she had always believed, lying there and knowing at last how all of it had been lies.

Yesterday he had slept in snow, in a storm of black snow, in a bed of cold, and he'd drawn close to the secret, which is death.

Another of his girls had been struck down. Her being in him had fallen at the feet of standing time, to the bottom of time's posture. Hadn't he danced in the kitchen of the house on Winery Street, danced for joy at the smell of his girl and the bread she had baked? That girl now fallen? Araxi Vagramian, the daughter of Lula Karagozian who married Manuk Vagramian? Araxi Vagramian who married Vahan Vagramian, bringing together two unlike families bearing the same name, the female side laughing at the male side for being unworldly, the male side looking down on the female side as scoundrels with good-looking daughters? That girl fallen?

Ann was gone to safety because marriage to a Vagramian was too much trouble: a Vagramian who had contempt for everybody she knew, for everything she believed was important—clothes, hats, cosmetics, shoes, parties, nice people, famous people, exciting people, happy people, plans for parties, plans for eating and drinking and talking the rest of their lives with nice people. Ann was a year gone to the resignation of their failure, to the social smartness of their divorce, of being seven years married, the mother of two kids, still only twenty-five, still a beautiful girl, a girl with many old friends and many new ones. She was gone to safety.

Lula was gone to Manuk in Bitlis by way of a weed-covered grave in the Armenian Cemetery in Fresno, Ararat.

Little Lula was gone with Ann.

Each had fallen, and now it was his girl Araxi, too.

One by one the girls had fallen and gone.

He had been at a party, sitting at a table, talking to a girl named Eve Ellis. A waiter had taken him to the telephone and in a moment he was listening to his sister.

"Mama's dying," his sister was saying. "What shall we do to keep Mama from dying, Rock? Mama's in the St. Francis Hospital, dying, Rock. They pierced her spine and took out fluid. It was full of blood. It was black, Rock. Mama's not Mama any more. She's asleep, but it's not the way Mama slept. When she wakes up it's not the way Mama wakes up. We talked this afternoon, but it wasn't Mama the way Mama talks. She talked about the bread she was supposed to bake when she got up this morning, but didn't bake because of her head. She told me to be sure to bake the bread. She told me not to call you, Rock. She said you've got troubles enough of your own, but the doctor told me to call. Mama's dying, Rock."

He left the party angry at his mother. He'd just run into a girl he wanted to know. He'd just decided to go to work.

He'd just gotten hungry for the first time in months, and wanted to eat. He'd just decided that he had lost Ann and the children forever, and he'd just begun to love them all the more for being lost. He'd just begun to go back to being a son again until he could find another girl to marry and by whom to have children, and through whom to become a father again. He'd just decided it was time to begin again. To eat, to drink, to tell jokes, to look at girls again out of the eyes of a son, to talk to them with the voice of a son, to begin again. To begin everything again, to put aside the father's wisdom and take up again the son's confidence that he can achieve anything.

He was pleased when there was no plane until morning.

"She's dead," he said. "She's dead now. The rest is foolishness. Araxi's dead, too. Back to Eve Ellis, then. Back to food and drink, then. Back to the jokes, the looking and the laughing. Back to the fun of the son."

He went back and told no one, not even Myra Clewes, who said, "Is anything the matter, Rock?"

"No, Myra."

"Was it Ann?"

"No. Everything's all right."

He would fly out and see her, talk to her, and she would be home again baking bread in a few days. When he returned to New York he would go to work. He would visit the kids when Ann was out. He would find an apartment. He would have them visit him, stay overnight, hear him talk and sing in Armenian.

Lula had been almost ninety when she had died. Araxi was only sixty-six. She wasn't going to die. He'd fly out and talk to her. He'd let her know how much more he loved Ann and the kids now, now that he knew they were lost, now that they were less Vagramians than New Yorkers, now that learning to speak Armenian was out of the question for them, now that he had stopped being infuriated about what was happening to them, what was going to happen to them, now that he knew that anything that happened to them would have to be considered good enough, and from this knowing, which would come from beginning again as a son, his old girl, Araxi Vagramian, would begin again, too, getting up and going home to bake the bread Vahan had loved so much, and her son Arak and her daughter Vava, and as long as he had lived her son Haig.

He *had* to begin again. This time he had to begin in New York, for that was where he *was*, where he would be no matter where he happened to go. He was there in Ann, in Haig, in Lula. He would fly to San Francisco to get his mother home for twenty years more of it, and then he would fly back to forty years more of it for himself, beginning in New York.

"What happened?" Eve Ellis said. "Where did you go? I've had three propositions since you left. I didn't even know if you were coming back, but I turned them down. Are you really fond of Mozart?"

His mother wasn't going to die because he was going to begin again with this girl.

A man's truth is instantaneous and everlasting, marvelous and miserable. There is nothing in him which is not true, wonderful, pathetic, delightful. He is drenched in innocence. He is anything he decides he is at any moment he chooses to decide, his hat on his head.

A man is an actor, as he himself knows. He acts all men, and each is a lie, as he himself knows, but he himself is not a lie, he himself is the truth, for it is himself which is himself, which cannot be acted, which is, which is truth itself, bellowing and bloody, or bright and bland. A man is a liar who cannot lie, a crook who cannot be crooked, an imitation who is an original, for a man is an actor, he is all men, all things, the original lie, the final truth.

A man invents truth as he goes, he invents mankind as he goes.

There is no end to a man's acting. The bounce of his acting is everlasting. The measuring of it is instantaneous and impossible. A man cannot lie, cannot know the truth. He can only be innocent, as he himself knows. He is a true thing come from nothing. He is a false thing come from everything, high-rolling for home.

LET her be awake when I get there, he said. Let me see her. Let her see me. Let her seeing of me tell her there is time. The dough is in the tub, ready to cut and shape. The bread will be made. Her son's daughter lives, a woman like herself, and there is time for them to go to one another, see and smell one another, speak to one another, know themselves in one another. Let her see her son and know his son lives, a man like her father Manuk, like her husband Vahan, like her son Arak, and there is time for her to see these men in Haig, and take him in her arms. There is still time for them to be alive together. Let her hear him when he tells her in words which deal in other things that there is time, time for bread, time to hear the voice of his daughter, the laughter and shouting of his son, the chanting, embracing speech of Ann, even. Let me get her up and home for twenty years more, he said. Let me get her into my old car and drive her along the ocean, high above the ocean, beside the sand cliffs and the rock cliffs. Let her see the sunset upon the water, and let me speak to her in Armenian.

"Would you like a blanket over your feet?" the girl on the airplane said.

"No thanks," Rock said. "How long do we stop in Chicago?"

"Twenty minutes," the girl said.

I'll do this, he thought. I'll telephone Doc Kirmoyan and ask him to tell me what to do. Only, I know it's the end. I know it's death. What can the Doc tell me about *that?* Araxi's dead. She had almost thirty years more than Vahan, but twenty years less than Lula. What's Vava going to do now? She has her husband, her three sons, her two daughters, but what about her pal Araxi? She used to go to Araxi's house every morning and call out, "Araxi, are you up? It's Vava." And her pal used to laugh and call back, "I know it's Vava. Do you think I forget overnight?"

He would telephone Doc Kirmoyan, anyhow. There might be something new now, a mystic powder. You take this powder and instantly it heals the broken vein. It makes *all* of the veins young and resilient. It was figured out by a druggist's clerk in Cincinnati, a remarkable thing called Nu-Vein, thirty-five cents a packet.

Already he was on the phone.

"Doc, what about this Nu-Vein?"

"It works, but only on people past sixty-five."

"Wonderful, Doc. She's sixty-six. Is there anything else she ought to have? Air? Water? Light?"

"Yes, those are the things. She'll be fine."

"Now, Doc, about later. Her mother died several years ago,

almost ninety. There wasn't anything they could do. Have they got something for that?"

"Yes, they've got something called Nearing-Ninety, it's a powder, white, teaspoonful in a little water. Half a dollar a throw. Most people that age have got great-grandchildren who can afford it. It only came out this year. Too bad."

"Yes. I knew there ought to have been *something*."

"Yes, Rock, they finally figured it out."

"Now, Doc, after ninety, what?"

"They're working on it, Rock. Another couple of months, another year. A lot of them when they get that old don't want to spend the money. They want the funeral. But they're working on it. There's a fellow's got a powder almost worked out, not quite white, a little gray, that seems to be effective where they want the funeral. A teaspoonful to every member of the family and they don't want the funeral."

"Oh, it's for the family, not for the old lady? Is that it?"

"That's right, Rock. That one—he hasn't given it a name yet—it has to be something polite—is for the family."

"Now, Doc, tell me. What have they got for Death?"

"Oh, the usual. Everything. The mind boys are in on some new things. Anybody can get his Death in no time at all just by concentrating on it."

"No, Doc, I mean what have they got—what kind of mystic powder have they got that *prevents* it?"

"Well, they haven't got that, Rock. But what you want is Nu-Vein. It's fine."

He turned in his seat, as if to get away from the mystic powders, saying, What's the poor sick girl dreaming? Do they know anything about that? Can they guess what a dying girl dreams?

198

Poor Mama, he said. Poor Araxi. Well, let her see me. Let me see my old girl before she goes. Let her see her own body's stranger once more before she goes.

A man's truth is instantaneous and preposterous, as he himself knows, as he is carried by a piece of junk that flies through the posture of time to Death, to the end of his mother, to the death of the bread-maker, a man's own girl, a man's own mother.

A man is many men. He is each of his friends and enemies, each of them going, taking him with them, as he takes them. He is the men who made him, each of them in despair about his own failure.

Day-dreaming on the airplane, morning-dreaming, after-noon-dreaming, night-dreaming, sleep-dreaming, life-dreaming, death-dreaming, he wandered among the girls.

HE hugged the one Myra Clewes was sure he would like, as sorrow hugs and heals sorrow, healing itself upon it, with tender arrogance and violent pity, each sorrow watching the body of the other sorrow.

"This is my name," she said. "This is my address. This is my telephone number here. This is the number where they'll know where I can be reached when I'm not here. I'm writing it down because I want you to hear the Mozart."

"O.K."

"I mean the music itself I told you about," she said. "I think *you* especially will like that music."

"I like it."

"I mean, when you actually hear it."

"I hear it."

"I understand," she said. "Yes, you do."

"Everybody hasn't got the taste for Mozart you have," he said.

"You *will* keep the numbers and call, so we can hear the music itself, won't you?" she said.

He fished into his pocket, brought out the card, looked at the writing, and put the card in his wallet, a man flying through the posture of time, hanging onto the girls, trying not to let any more of them get away, to get lost in the crowds, or in safety, or in the grave.

A man is forever asking questions.

WHY did she lie? he said. Why is she a liar? Why did I fail to win her away from lies? Why did I fail?

For the sake of my children why didn't I marry the girl in Dublin? She may not have been a liar.

Why did I drive for Murphy instead of going the way my father wanted me to go? Why didn't I learn to read and write the language and go with my father to the paper and work there? Why didn't I work there, and buy a small vineyard around Kerman, Clovis, or Malaga? Why did I turn away from my father? Why did I stand on the corner of Eye and Tulare and break his heart? What good did it do me to stand there and talk to a couple of street girls when I knew it meant to him the failure of the language itself, the failure of the word as he knew it, the failure of the people, the failure of the family, the failure of his own fatherhood?

Why did I turn away from my father? What harm would it have done to put on the red shirt Sunday mornings and sing the song of the alphabet or the one of morning light in the red-brick church? Why couldn't I have made a gift to my mother of the voice singing the songs she had known from childhood, who is now dying, who is now coming to the end? Why couldn't I have made a gift to my father of knowing his language?

He drove for Murphy because he liked Murphy.

The year before he had gone to an employment agency to get a job during summer vacation. He had filled out the application.

"Here under nationality," the woman said, "you have written American."

"Of course."

"Aren't you——? Isn't that name, Vagramian——?"

"Armenian?" he said. "Of course. I was born in Fresno. I was born on Winery Street."

"Hadn't I better put down Armenian?" the woman said.

"No," he said. "I'll tell you what you do. Change the name from Vagramian to Basoglu, change the religion from Christian to Mohammedan, change the nationality from American to Turk. My father and his father filled out forms for the Turks long ago. They filled them out accurately, too. They were Armenians, not Turks. They were Christians, not Mohammedans. They lived in Armenia, not Turkey. If you're going to change my nationality, let's have some fun. I don't want the job anyway."

Murphy said, "What are you, another Armenian?"

"That's right," Rock said.

"Can you drive?"

"Yes."

"Fast?"

"As fast as you like."

"A dollar every day you drive," Murphy said.

"A dollar and a half," Rock said.

"A dollar and a quarter."

"O.K."

"Get in the car and drive," Murphy said. "I want to go to Reedley, then to Sanger, then to Clovis. Bring me back to the Hotel Fresno. Put the car in the garage down the street. Go home. See me at the hotel five o'clock tomorrow morning. We've got to drive to Bakersfield and back."

Rock got into the bright yellow-green Cadillac, and drove. Murphy sat in the back.

"Food is your own problem," he said. "Girls, too. Your pay is a dollar and a quarter a day. I pay for gasoline, oil, garage, tires, repairs."

In Reedley, though, Murphy asked Rock to have lunch with him. After the drive to Bakersfield and back the next day, Murphy paid Rock two dollars instead of a dollar and a quarter. A couple of days later he paid Rock three dollars. After that he paid three dollars every day whether Rock drove or not, and when he went back to Brooklyn at the end of the season Murphy gave Rock a hundred dollars.

"You drive good, Rock," he said, "but you tell the best jokes I've ever heard. This is for the jokes."

Driving for Murphy meant a lot to Rock. He liked Murphy. He liked a man who didn't keep his petty word but kept his unspoken word, lived in laughter, loneliness, and swift action, said nothing unkind to those who were false, but looked at them with contempt, amusement, and charity.

The airplane flew through clouds over mountains. The traveler slept and asked questions, awoke and remembered answers.

THE SON AND THE DAUGHTER

Why did she lie? he asked.

She was *driven* to lying, he answered. She thought there was something better for her to be than the wonderful thing she was because snobbery had looked upon that wonderful thing as an inferior thing. She lied to reach the truth, only she got tricked along the way, and instead of reaching the truth reached other lies, the lies that kill.

A man needs few material things, but he ought to have his portion of them: to eat, to see, to smell, to kiss, to sport with, to be astonished by, to keep him going. The things of matter that a man needs are few, but they are magnificent things, and without them the achieving of things of non-matter is either impossible, undesirable, or irrelevant. A man must have his portion, for a man is flesh, he comes from flesh, he inhabits it. He is not a soul, though he may have one, or several. He is swift-dying stuff, not slow-living stuff, he must have his portion, for it is little enough, as he himself knows.

A man needs girls. He needs civil liberties, too, but not the way he needs the daughters of strangers.

He needs humor, and he can't have humor if he can't have his portion. He needs girls, and money. He needs them in order to have the humor he needs.

A man needs to take himself seriously. A man is a serious matter. He is worthless, but seriously so. His head and hide aren't worth a dime in the open market. He is an unmarketable commodity. Only his soul is worth something, something in the neighborhood of fifteen cents. It is never off the market. If the body goes with the deal, as it does in certain contracts, in marriage, in personal appearances, in acceptances of in-

*vitations to dinner, in day labor, and so on, the whole soul
does not go with the deal, inasmuch as no man in the world
knows a soul from a hole in the ground. A good deal of a man
is always out in the green, scouting around for a deal, as he
himself knows, looking for the connection between the soul
and the hole in the ground.*

ONE day when they were riding up Highway 99 to Madera
Murphy said, "Do Armenians hate Armenians?"

"Some do and some don't," Rock said. "Some hate some
and don't hate others. Some hate most and don't hate a few.
Some hate all, and some don't hate any."

"Jews hate Jews," Murphy said.

"No, they don't," Rock said.

"I do," Murphy said, "and I'm a Jew."

"One," Rock said. "Only one."

"One's enough," Murphy said. "I hate all Jews."

"Nah," Rock said.

"Nah?" Murphy said. "Jews say that. Where'd *you* learn
that?"

"Right here in this car," Rock said, "from you."

"I hate people who say nah," Murphy said. "Do you hate
Armenians?"

"Nah."

"Why not?"

"Like them."

"Don't you get sick and tired seeing their faces, hearing
their voices, watching them eat? They're always eating, aren't
they? Don't you get sick and tired of them?"

"Nah."

"Nah," Murphy said. "Don't you think they're silly when they go to church?"

"Nah. Like them at church."

"Don't you think they're stupid, the way they're always trying to make grapes grow on the vines?"

"Nah. Like grapes. Like vines. Like them always trying."

"Don't you think they're ugly, with their ugly faces?"

"Nah. Like their faces. Like their ugly faces. Like their handsome faces."

"Don't you think they're mean, the way they push their old people around when their old people die?"

"What do they do to their old people when they die?" Rock said.

"Don't you think it's pretty Goddamn mean to bury them?" Murphy said.

"What else can they do with them?" Rock said.

"I'm talking about the cemeteries where they put them," Murphy said.

"We've got a good cemetery," Rock said. "Ararat. All our dead are in there."

"That's not nice," Murphy said.

"*What's* not?" Rock said.

"Putting them in the cemetery," Murphy said. "Putting them in Ararat. Is that the mountain?"

"Yes. It's in the Armenian flag."

"You got a *flag*, too."

"Yes, we have."

"What do you do with the flag?" Murphy said.

"Wave it," Rock said.

"You got a Navy?"

"No. Inland."

"You got an Army?"

"Six or seven."

"Who do they fight?" Murphy said. "Each other?"

"Only in times of peace," Rock said. "The rest of the time they fight the Turks."

"They're no different," Murphy said.

"The Turks?" Rock said.

"Yes, the dirty Turks," Murphy said. "They're just as dirty as the dirty Armenians and the dirty Jews. I met a Turk once. The son of a bitch was a liar, but I fixed him. I lied better than he did. Don't you think it's mean to put them in a dirty hole in the ground?"

"Nah," Rock said.

"Why not?"

"It's the rule."

"Who made the rule?"

"It's natural. Ashes to ashes."

"Is a man ashes?"

"Dust."

"Is a man dust?"

"Earth."

"Earth," Murphy said. "Who made the rule?"

"I did," Rock said.

"All right," Murphy said. "Stop the car and get out."

Rock stopped the car and got out. It was a fine vineyard of Red Emperors, and they were ripe and ready. He went into the vineyard and took a bunch off a vine, a bunch that had three or four dozen fine large berries, each of them held firmly to its stem, the skin of each grape hard and tight, with a fine bloom. He began to eat the grapes. Murphy was stretching himself beside the car, feeling good. He liked to get out of the car every now and then and stretch and look around.

"What you got there?" he said.

"Fine Red Emperors," Rock said.

"Bring me a bunch," Murphy said.

Rock found a fine bunch for Murphy and took it to him.

"What makes them fine?" Murphy said. "They all look alike to me."

"Large berries," Rock said. "Good color. Good bloom. Clean stems. Skin hard and tight. These'll keep a long time."

"Where'd you learn all that stuff?" Murphy said.

"Driving for you," Rock said. "Talking to the government inspectors."

"How long will they keep?" Murphy said.

"Most of the winter," Rock said. "It's a fine grape to put on the table at Thanksgiving."

"Remember this place," Murphy said. "We'll go in sometime and talk to the farmer, the son of a bitch."

"He may not *be* an Armenian," Rock said.

"Whatever he is," Murphy said, "he'll be a farmer, and I've never met people like farmers. They think this stuff's gold." He was eating the grapes swiftly, making a lot of noise chomping down on them and swallowing them entire, seeds and all. "It's *grapes*, not gold."

"You can *eat* grapes," Rock said. "What can you do with gold?"

"Don't be a smart aleck," Murphy said. "You can buy *anything* to eat with gold."

"You can't if there's nothing to buy," Rock said.

"Smart aleck," Murphy said. "Get in the car. There's

207

always farmers to grow stuff. There's always stuff to buy. The thing to get is gold."

Rock got back into the car, behind the wheel. Murphy got back in his place in the back, still chomping down on the Red Emperors, his thick lips and big mouth making a lot of noise.

"There you are," Murphy said. He spit a grape out of his mouth into his hand. "What about *this* grape? This one's bad."

"Mildew?" Rock said.

"Rotten."

"That happens," Rock said. "That's what the girls in the packing house are for. To clip off the mildewed, smashed, or rotten berries."

"Do you remember the place?" Murphy said.

"I remember it," Rock said.

"On the way back let's stop there," Murphy said.

"You want to talk to the farmer?" Rock said.

"Farmer?" Murphy said. "Who wants to talk to a dirty farmer? I'm talking about the cemetery. Do you remember the cemetery?"

"I know where it is," Rock said.

"You got anybody in there?"

"Yes."

"Who?"

"My brother Haig," Rock said. "He died when he was six. He would have been twelve years old now."

"You want to visit his grave?"

"Nah."

"Nah," Murphy said. "Why nah?"

"What good does it do?" Rock said. "Don't you want to talk to the farmer? Get those fine Red Emperors?"

208

"Talk to him tomorrow," Murphy said. "Talk to him the next day. What *good* does it do? Visit your brother."

"He's been dead six years," Rock said.

"Visit him," Murphy said. "Show a little courtesy. Don't be mean about *everything*. Was he a good boy?"

"I'm sore at him," Rock said. "He didn't need to die."

"He didn't need to die," Murphy said. "He died, didn't he? Why do you say he didn't need to die?"

"He didn't need to," Rock said. "I'll never forgive him."

"You're crazy," Murphy said. "Everybody in your family crazy?"

"No," Rock said. "My brother was crazy."

"Why?" Murphy said. "Because he died?"

"Yes, because he died," Rock said. "He didn't *need* to. Everybody got the flu. Everybody got better."

"I read in the papers where a lot of people died," Murphy said.

"You didn't read in the papers where a lot of people in my family died," Rock said. "Just *him*. I'll never forgive him. When he was sick I said to him, 'Haig, I'm going to let you go around with me, everywhere I go. I'm going to take you catfishing as soon as the ditches get full of water again. I'm going to take you stealing watermelons as soon as they're ripe again. I'm going to take you sneaking into the Hippodrome Theatre. I'm going to take you to the Public Library.'"

"What's the Public Library got to do with it?" Murphy said.

"That's where the books are," Rock said.

"What books?"

"All the books."

"What about them?"

209

"Nothing," Rock said. "I just told him I'd take him to the Public Library and let him see the books."

"What for?" Murphy said.

"Books," Rock said. "Got to see books. Got to open them up. Got to read them. Got to know them."

"Why?" Murphy said.

"Don't you know about books?" Rock said.

"Book*keeping*," Murphy said. "I know about keeping the books that'll tell you if you're getting rich or going broke. I know about books you put numbers in. What's in the other books?"

"Everything's in them," Rock said.

"You read books?" Murphy said.

"Sure I read them."

"You don't *have* to read them," Murphy said, "but you read them just the same?"

"Sure."

"Why?"

"I like to read them," Rock said.

"When do you do it?" Murphy said. "When do you read them?"

"Any time," Rock said. "Any time I feel like it."

"You want to be a professor?" Murphy said.

"No."

"Then why do you read? You want to be a preacher?"

"No."

"What do you want to be?"

"I want to be a lot of things," Rock said.

"You want to be a lot of things," Murphy said. "What do you want to be? A thief?"

"Does reading books make you a thief?" Rock said.

"You get smart reading books," Murphy said, "and smart people are always thieves."

"I don't want to be a thief," Rock said.

"You want to take him stealing watermelons, but you don't want to be a thief?"

"That's not being a thief," Rock said. "I'll never forgive my brother."

"He had the flu," Murphy said. "He died. Why will you never forgive him?"

"He didn't *need* to die," Rock said. "I know what I'm talking about."

"What's a small boy know, six years old?" Murphy said. "Does he know something?"

"He knows," Rock said. "He knows plenty. He knows what he did to my mother. He knows what he did to my father. All of a sudden he was dead. He was lying there dead. Haig, you son of a bitch," Rock said suddenly. "You don't do things like that, you don't stop that way, Haig, you don't stop things inside your own people that way."

"We'll go visit him," Murphy said.

"Do you really want to see his grave?" Rock said.

"Do *you*?" Murphy said.

"Yes, I'd like to," Rock said. "It'll be the first time. I've never gone there. My mother and father go a couple of times a year, come home and can't talk. They look at each other, but they can't say anything. They try to smile. My sister watches them, and then she runs out of the house. They've got a stone there. They've got his name on it. We'll find it. I'd like to go all right. I won't let them know I went, though. What do you want to go for?"

"I like to walk in cemeteries," Murphy said. "I like to

walk in a *real* city. Any chance I get I like to go where I'm going. It reminds me not to get too smart."

"How smart are you?" Rock said.

"Too smart," Murphy said. "So smart I'm the kind of man everybody hates. The kind *you* hate, too."

"Nah," Rock said, "I like the kind of man you are."

"You're a liar," Murphy said.

"It's the truth," Rock said.

"Why do you like a man like that?" Murphy said.

Rock knew the time had come to give Murphy an inside laugh.

"Because he's got a Cadillac," Rock said.

"I thought you were going to say something good about me," Murphy said.

"Nah," Rock said.

A man needs few material things all right, but he ought to have his portion. He ought to have things of flesh *in* the flesh. His brother should live in the flesh, not die in it. His mother should abide in the flesh, not forsake it.

The minute the airplane came down in San Francisco he would drive to the St. Francis Hospital and see her. He would get her to abide. He would take her home for twenty years more of it.

A man's mortality comes to him in his mother's womb, and it comes as a sickness. He is the only animal which knows enough to get sick and die. All animals die, but no other animal dies as a man dies, as he himself knows. A man is sick every minute he lives, for he is his sickness, he is the one who lives his life. When he dies it is not another who dies. Now and then a dog may die like a man, but all men die like dogs.

THE SON AND THE DAUGHTER

THE name of the Erie Railroad man was Elton Fickett. He was a vice-president. He wore a gray business suit, conservatively cut. He was probably a Mason, a Sciot, an Elk, a Woodman, and a secret riot. He was either a Methodist, a Baptist, or an Episcopalian. He was a big man, very nearly as big as Murphy himself, who was six feet tall, and 250 pounds in weight. Fickett had a clean face with clean features. His hair was gray and parted on the side. He was not bald, or beginning to be bald, as Murphy was. Murphy wasn't beginning. The top of Murphy's head, the entire crown, was clean bald, and what was left seemed tired, dry, and absurd. It would have been better if he had been all bald, clean finished with hair on his head. Murphy's face was swarthy, and he always looked as if he needed a shave. Fickett's face had a color that is associated with health. A man of sixty, he seemed both boyish and adult. He spoke in a calm, deep, and warm voice. He had married well, had two sons and three daughters, each of whom had gone to good schools and colleges, places with names. Only one daughter, a girl of nineteen, remained unmarried. The others were married, successful in business and in society, with children of their own.

The railroad man *was* impressive, and Rock Wagram, almost fifteen years old, *was* impressed by him. He seemed to Rock a real American, the first he had run into, and he was glad the man had had to do with railroads all his life, for Rock loved railroads.

Fickett had come to Fresno to see some of the bigger carload shippers of grapes. Murphy had shipped almost a thousand carloads the previous year. The cars that had not stopped at Chicago had gone to the Eastern cities over the Erie line.

Murphy had sent them over the Erie because one line was as good as another as far as he was concerned, and it was simple to say Erie. Fickett, however, wanted to show his appreciation for the enormous business Murphy had given his line, and his way of doing it was to permit Murphy to look at him, to be in his presence, one of the most successful railroad men in the country, one of the most famous in railroad circles, as well as a man with social background, and offhand membership in the best clubs.

Murphy, sitting beside the elegant but very manly man, was ill at ease.

Murphy talked automatically, without thinking, with excitement, loudly, and with all the dirty words he needed in order to more accurately convey his meaning.

Fickett talked thoughtfully, slowly, carefully.

When Fickett had left his card the previous night in Murphy's hotel box and Murphy had read it, and the message on the back of it, Murphy thought it would be a good thing to have a word with Fickett about last year's claims. Murphy had filed them at the end of the season, claiming damages due to negligence on the part of the railroad, but nothing had come of it. About forty out of almost a thousand cars had been involved. The damages came to around nine thousand dollars. He telephoned Fickett, who suggested a meeting in the morning. Murphy explained that he had to go to Bakersfield in the morning.

"When do you plan to leave, Mr. Murphy?" Fickett said.

"Five," Murphy said.

"In the morning?"

"Yes. It's a hundred miles. I go and look things over and come back the same day. Why? Do you want to go?"

"I'd like to very much," Fickett said. "At five, then. In the lobby?"

"Takes about two hours," Murphy said. "We can have coffee before we leave, breakfast in Bakersfield."

"Very good," Fickett said. "I look forward to meeting you."

Now, at half past five, Fickett had met Murphy, Murphy had met Fickett, and Rock Wagram was watching both of them in the rear-view mirrow of Murphy's Cadillac, crossing the railroad tracks on the way to Highway 99.

"I leave early," Murphy said, "because it's cool early in the morning. Also, I can't sleep."

"Is that so?" Fickett said. "Have you tried a warm bath before bed?"

"No. Is that good?"

"I find it relaxing," Fickett said. "I made the discovery thirty years ago. A bath before bed, a shower on rising."

It seemed to Rock that Murphy was trying to remember if he had taken a shower on rising, or if perhaps he smelled a little anyway.

"That's a lot of bathing," Murphy said.

"I find it well worth the time it takes," Fickett said. "Ten minutes at night, ten minutes in the morning."

"What do you do?" Murphy said. "You take the bath and go to bed, and then you go to sleep? Is that it?"

"*Warm* water," Fickett said. "A tubful. Relax in it ten minutes."

"Warm water," Murphy said.

"Yes. Not hot. Not cold."

"Puts you to sleep?"

"Relaxes you, so you can *fall* asleep."

"You sleep well?"

"Quite well."

"*Every* night?"

"Yes. I assure you it's an excellent treatment for insomnia, Mr. Murphy."

"Maybe you haven't got any worries," Murphy said.

"Oh, I have my responsibilities," Fickett said. "I don't take them to bed with me, though, because I've found that I can't do justice to my work the next day if I lie awake all night. Work when it's time to work. Play when it's time to play. Sleep when it's time to sleep."

"I work all the time," Murphy said. "I work when it's time to work, when it's time to play, and when it's time to sleep."

Murphy felt sure that Fickett had left his card in his box because he had a settlement of the damages to report, and he believed the amount of the settlement would be made known after a few minutes of small talk, but even after they had reached and passed Tulare the talk was still small, although it was no longer about bathing, sleep, work-time, and play-time.

It was about the kinds of people in the world, as Fickett understood the matter, his voice calm and deep, his face clean and relaxed.

Rock Wagram watched and listened.

He watched the road carefully, too, because he was driving around seventy, but there was little traffic, except trucks loaded with grapes on their way to packing houses, so he was also able to watch the faces of the men as he saw them reflected in the rear-view mirror. They could scarcely notice that he was watching them. He listened very carefully.

He still admired Fickett, but he found that as time went on he admired Murphy much more, a man it hadn't until

216

now occurred to him to admire, a man whose very nature seemed to insist on no admiration, seemed in fact to demand that there be none, a man for whom it was easy to work, whose presence it was inevitable to enjoy, whose swiftness and richness of mind it was refreshing to notice.

Twenty or twenty-five miles past Tulare, Rock still admired Fickett, but it was nothing to the affection he felt for Murphy.

"It takes all kinds to make a world," Fickett said. "I have associates who have lost patience with this people or that, generalizing about all of them solely on the basis of experience with a handful of them—a hundred or so. The Italians, for instance. Hot-headed, excitable, emotional, overwrought, occasionally hysterical, but for all that, as far as my own experience has been, lovable, child-like, and deeply honest, however confusing some of their behavior may sometimes be. I have given this matter thought, and my conclusion is that this behavior is the result of high spirits, a love of fun and mischief, and nothing else. They don't expect their demands to be met, and they only pretend to be astonished when their demands are not met."

"That's the Italians?" Murphy said.

"As far as my own experience has been," Fickett said. "They are a people who *sing*. Hearty. Spontaneous."

It was here that the admiration Rock Wagram felt for Elton Fickett began to go.

Who asked you? Rock thought. If you're going to talk about people, talk about your own, whoever they are, because you *know* them, and *don't* know other people.

"The Scotch, on the other hand," Elton Fickett said. "The popular misconception about the Scotch is that they are tight-fisted, stingy, miserly, dour, severe, excessively money-loving, thrifty to the point of impracticality. My own experience with the Scotch, however, leads me to believe they are sober, serious-minded, dignified, and honorable."

"They're nice people," Murphy said rather pathetically, for it seemed to Rock that what Murphy really wanted to say was something dirty and accurate about Elton Fickett himself.

"The French," the man went on. "The absurd misconception here is that the Frenchman thinks of nothing but coarse pleasure, food, drink, and so on and so forth. My own experience with the French, however, tells me that they are cultivated, refined, and devoted to the highest ideals of western civilization."

Rock noticed that Murphy was becoming uneasy, waiting with apprehension for this authority's verdict on the Jews.

"I make it my business to find out the truth about people for myself," Fickett said. "I'm not interested in what the majority of people think of one people or another. That's *their* business. I will *acquaint* myself with what they think, solely as a guide, but that is all. The Jewish people, for instance. The vast majority of the public is convinced that the Jewish people are materialistic, clever, aggressive, overbearing, demanding, and so on and so forth. What nonsense!"

Fickett smiled, then said, "My own experience tells me that the Jewish people are intelligent, quick to adapt themselves to a new environment, a new tradition, a new order, a new trade or profession. They have speed, plus patience, a rare combination. They love good things, the things money can buy. Good homes, good clothes, good cars, good investments. I have always admired the Jewish people. I marvel at their cunning in the achievement of good. I take off my hat to them."

He removed his hat, apparently by accident, and began to fan himself with it.

Murphy, uncomfortable and bewildered, removed his hat, too, and also began to fan himself.

What a crook! Rock thought. What a clean-cut crook!

In the rear-view mirror he noticed that Murphy was dying like a dog, and in the airplane, more than a quarter of a century later, Elton Fickett long since dead, Murphy himself long since gone to the real city, Rock could not forget how, sooner or later, every man dies like a dog, moaning and wagging his tail.

A man is a born liar who cannot tell a lie. A man can be a decent animal. His friends are meaningless unless they are decent animals. But a man's friends are polite and lying animals, as a man himself knows. There is never a lie in the life of any animal that is worth being told, or any truth that is worth being concealed.

Thus, in the end, a man's best friend is his money, his tobacco, his whisky. A man's best friend is his feet, his hide, and his head. A man's best friend is his own time. His best friend is the sun, the very same which made light and heat for his father, and for his mother: the same that shined on him when he was no older than his son, on whom it shines now. A man is a born liar, born of liars, the father of them, and his best friend is his own animal which cannot lie, but may lie down in the heat of the afternoon, in the shade of a tree, and be there, be a friend there, be alive a moment there, half-asleep and half as if he had been there all the time. A man's

*own brother cannot be his friend, but a man can be the friend
of his poor world and time. There is no truth for a man, there
is no friendship for him except the truth of the sun, the friendship of time, his own personal sun and his own personal time.
There is nothing to say of these things. They are there and a
man is there, and there's his truth and there's his friendship.*

ON the airplane, he woke up with a start and looked for
somebody in uniform, for they were the ones who had the
needed information. They were the ones who started elevators
with castinets, who kept fools behind ropes outside moving
picture theatres, who were members of the academy, who
opened the doors of taxis at hotels, restaurants and fashionable
saloons, who knew the answers. He saw one in uniform, and
called to her.

She came to him, beside him, upon him, as if to be embraced, her eyes and lips smiling a little, which is the way of
them on airplanes, and she said, "Yes, Mr. Wagram." She
spoke softly, as if they were somewhere where this might be
explored, worked upon, given any life it might be entitled to.

"Will you tell me when we will reach San Francisco?" he
said.

"We're on time," she said.

"Even so," he said. "When will we reach there?"

"At half past five," she said. "It's almost half past four now.
You've had no lunch. You were asleep, and I thought it best
not to disturb you."

"I had coffee and doughnuts in Chicago."

"Would you like something now?"

"No thanks."

"Magazine?"

"What magazine?"

"*National Geographic, Esquire, Secret Stories.*"

"They still publishing *Secret Stories?*" he said.

"Somebody who got off at Chicago left an old one on his seat," the girl said. "February, 1930. I've been looking through it. Would you like to look through it, too?"

"No, I think I'd better not," Rock said. "What sort of secrets were they?"

"You know," she said. "Love, marriage, lies, adultery."

"You like this work?" Rock said.

"Love it."

"You like travel?"

"People," she said. "I'll sit down a minute if you don't mind."

"Please do," Rock said. "What do you like about them?"

"Oh, I don't know," she said. "I just like them. Don't you?"

"I don't *dislike* them," Rock said, "but mainly they break my heart."

"Why?" she said.

"They're always lying, or dying," Rock said. "They tell lies all their lives, and then they die. As long as they're alive, I don't mind the lies, but when they die, the lies break my heart."

"What do you mean by lies?" she said. "Like a girl tells her boy friend she loves him, then two-times him?"

"That example's all right," Rock said, "but it's not what I mean. Have you had any experience at all with cerebral hemorrhage?"

"What do you mean?" the girl said. "Have I had one?"

"No," Rock said. "Have you known anyone who's had one?

A grandfather, or somebody your father knew. How *is* your father?"

"He's fine," the girl said. "No. We've had some experience with heart. Attacks, you know. On the plane, I mean. Had a man die on us one time between San Francisco and Chicago. We came down of course to get him to a doctor, but he was dead."

"Does he worry about you?" Rock said. "I mean, you're not much more than twenty-one or twenty-two."

"I'm twenty-four," the girl said. "Of course he worries about me. He thinks being a hostess on an airplane is a foolish career for a girl, but I don't expect to be a hostess *all* my life."

"What do you expect?" Rock said.

"You know."

"You mean to get married?"

"Of course."

"To somebody you meet on an airplane?"

"Just the first time on the airplane," she said.

"Oh yes," Rock said. "Meet later on, *off* the airplane."

"Of course," the girl said. "Although we did have a girl who got married on an airplane. Publicity, of course. Miriam."

"What's *your* name?"

"Miriam. *Hers* was, too."

"Well, I guess if she could do it, you can do it, too. What's your last name?"

"Schwarzschild. Isn't it awful?"

"Not at all. You *are* a dark child."

"I'd love to change it, though. Miriam Merlin."

"You know somebody named Merlin?"

"No, but I like to put Miriam with other names. You know."

"How about Miriam Morgenthau?"

"All that money?" the girl said.

"What money?" Rock said.

"Wasn't he Secretary of the Treasury?"

"I guess he was at that," Rock said, "but the money wasn't his, was it?"

"Well, he was *near* it," the girl said. "Anyway, I don't like Morgenthau with Miriam."

"Is your mother well?"

"Oh, swell."

"Haven't you ever heard anybody speaking about some-body who had had a cerebral hemorrhage and got over it all right?"

"A cyst," she said. "I heard about a cyst once."

"No, that's something else," Rock said. "The veins get brittle, or a vein is weak someplace, and if the blood pressure has been high, and then gets higher, well, wherever the vein is weakest it breaks."

"Do you want some gum?"

"No. Why?"

"It helps when you can't hear," the girl said. "I just said a cyst isn't serious."

"Oh, I'm sorry," Rock said. "I guess I'll have some gum, after all. I didn't hear you."

He received the packet containing two Chiclets from the girl, removed the cellophane and began to chew, making a saliva he hadn't tasted in years, a hot, sick saliva, and he knew instantly when it had been. He had come home from school to find his father consoling his mother because his brother Haig was dead. He went into the room in which they both slept, and looked at his brother, and saw that Haig was dead. His father was walking in and out of the rooms of the house with his mother, and his sister was following them. He sat on his own bed and looked at his brother in the other bed. He never did know how or why he took the wrapping away from the two sticks of gum and got them into his mouth and began to chew, making the hot, sick saliva, the same saliva that was in his mouth now.

"Haig," he said.

He didn't cry. His father didn't, either. It was just his mother and his sister Vava crying. His father was saying her name to his mother again and again. Rock sat on his bed, looking at his brother's face, chewing the gum, as he was chewing it now, swallowing enormous mouthfuls of hot saliva.

"God damn you, Haig!" he said.

"Araxi," his father said.

"What did you say, Mr. Wagram?" the girl said.

"Oh," he said. "I wonder if I might look at that copy of *Secret Stories*, after all?"

"I'll get it for you," the girl said. "It's a scream. All lust, adultery, and murder, you know."

She brought him the magazine and said, "It's been awful nice talking to you, Mr. Wagram."

He took the magazine and opened it somewhere near the middle, looking at the print, but not reading. "Araxi," he said, the hot saliva pouring down his gullet. He stepped out into the aisle to the open area just behind his seat, to the water tap. He filled a paper cup full of water and tried to drink away the taste of death in his mouth. He drank many cups of water, eight or nine at least, but when he sat down again the taste was still there, for a man's own brother cannot be his friend, and a man cannot be a friend to his own mother when she has reached the quarrel with her own time, a man is helpless and he can do nothing but chew gum, look at the blurred

print of *Secret Stories,* and swallow as hot saliva the lie that
was her life, the truth that is her death.

*The only thing a man does all his life is breathe. The in-
stant he inhales he is alive, the instant he exhales but does not
inhale again he is dead. A man is very nearly everything the
first time he inhales, he is very nearly nothing the last time
he exhales, but between the first inhale and the last exhale a
man is many things, and the things he does are many and
strange. A man is a breathing thing. He breathes all the time.
No matter what else a man does he also breathes. Breathing's
what a man is. He is born to breathe. His life is a life of breathing. A man's appetite for air is everlasting. He stops breathing
with violence. A man wants air to breathe, he wants the
ability to breathe to stay with him, but in the end, in the time
of his own end, every man is denied, he is denied the air
he wishes to breathe, he is denied the ability to breathe, he
stops breathing, he can laugh no more. Never again can he
look at something and see it: at a face and see a face: at a tree
and see a tree: at a sky and see a sky: at the sun and see the
sun. Never again can he reach out to the things which are
and touch them. Never again can he listen and hear: the crying of his infant son, the laughter of his infant daughter, the
speech and song of both of them, the whispering at night of
his woman. Let him be denied air to breathe and it is never
again for him. Let the miracle of breathing be denied him, and
though the earth be filled with the scent of water, grass,
leaf, blossom, bee, and butterfly, it is never again for him.
There will be no more dandruff from his head, no more junk
for him to accumulate, no more gadgets to operate. He will
make no more debris, he will be debris, he will be the original*

debris, silver and gold in his dead teeth. Never again will he be a man who could stand on a street corner, look around, and speak to somebody. Never again will he be a king, a commander in chief, a millionaire, a vice-president in charge of production, a philanthropist, a labor leader, a locomotive engineer, a poet, an actor, a convict, a warden, a preacher, a doctor, a dentist, a lawyer, a schoolboy, a son, a brother, a father, a good man, a bad man, a man of truth, a man of honor, a man of dignity, a crook, a deceiver, a sneak, a liar. If he can't breathe, he can't be anything but debris. If he can't breathe, he can't love anyone or hurt anyone. He can't get into a car and drive, he can't take a train, he can't get into an airplane, he can't get aboard a ship, he can't ride a bicycle, he can't walk. He can't stand to walk. He can't sit. He can't lie down. He can't sleep, he can't sleep worth a damn any more. His memory fails him. He doesn't seem to remember anything any more. He has no taste for meat or bread or wine or water any more. He doesn't care which pair of shoes he puts on his feet. He doesn't even remember if he had feet. Didn't he go another way than by foot? Worst of all he can't laugh any more. He can't joke any more. He can't tell stories any more. He can't talk any more. He can't understand the alphabet any more. He can't say cat. *He can't talk with words and be saying at the same time other things than what the words are saying, funnier things, better things, more loving things, kinder, gentler, more gently wicked than the violent wickedness of literalness. Something's happened. He's exhaled and he can't inhale any more. It is the end. It is the end of the world he was. It is the end of being out of touch. That which he knew would happen has happened. A man is dead, he is dirt, he is given a funeral, he is buried, he is no more, and never again will he go there.*

THE SON AND THE DAUGHTER

THE airplane came down in San Francisco. He was the first to step out onto the steps, down, and across the asphalt pavement to where they stood: his sister Vava, her husband Sark, their son Joe. He walked slowly to the gate where they stood, not letting them know that long ago he had noticed their faces. He looked at each, said their names, walked with them to the waiting room, and out to where the baggage would be distributed. He handed Joe his baggage checks. They walked again and came to the car, his old Cadillac. After everybody had been seated he got in, taking his place behind the wheel.

"Rock," his sister said. "It was yesterday morning. The night before we'd gone to an engagement party and Mama felt fine and had a wonderful time."

"Wait," he said.

When they were on the highway he said, "Vava, how's Mama?"

"She's better," Sark said. "She's much better."

"How is she, Vava?" Rock said.

"I don't know," his sister said.

"She's going to be all right," Sark said. "Mama's a strong woman. She's much better, Rock."

"Who spent the night with her?" Rock said.

"I did of course," his sister said. "They put a cot in the room for me, but I didn't sleep."

"How is she, Vava?"

"I don't know," his sister said. "Sark came to the hospital a couple of hours ago to get me. She was sleeping then and Sark thinks she's better. Dovey's with her now. She sleeps most of the time, wakes up for a few minutes, says a few things, goes back to sleep."

"She's much better," Sark said.

"Who's the doctor?" Rock said.

"Lowell, Mama's regular doctor."

"What's *he* say?"

"Well, he doesn't have much to say, Rock."

"Has he tapped her spine again?"

"Yes. This afternoon."

"How was it this time?"

"Not as black maybe."

"What's the shortest way to the St. Francis, Sark?"

"Come to our house first," Sark said. "Relax, take a shave and a shower, have a bite to eat, then we'll go visit Mama."

He turned to the boy beside him.

"What's the shortest way, Joe?"

"Straight ahead to West Portal," Joe said. "I'll tell you after that."

"Do you want me to drop you at your house, Sark?"

"No, but Mama's much better," Sark said. "Mama's going to be home in eight or nine days."

"Sure she is," Rock said. "I want to see her. I want to talk to Doctor Lowell. Is he around now?"

"Well, it's almost six," his sister said. "He goes home at six. His office is across the street from the hospital. He visits Mama every hour or so. You know how he loves Mama. He had tears in his eyes this afternoon."

"What's Mama say?" Rock said.

"Well, Rock, I don't think she knows what's happened," his sister said. "She's got a tubful of dough that's ready for baking, and every time we've talked she's talked about it. Sometimes just a few words, sometimes all the time. She's told

228

me exactly what to do. Half the dough is for flat bread, half for small loaves. A bread-man for Haig, a bread-woman for Lula, a flower loaf for Ann, and a star loaf for you, Rock. Every time she makes bread she makes those, too. How are they?"

"They're all well," Rock said.

"You need a shave, Rock," Sark said.

"I know."

"You ought to stop and shave."

Rock turned around, even though the car was traveling swiftly. He looked at his brother-in-law. There were tears in his sister's eyes. It was his brother-in-law's nature to hold fast to anything that he believed in, and he wanted to hold fast to the theory now that Rock should stop at his house before going to the hospital. This happened every time Rock and his brother-in-law met.

"Give me a cigarette, will you, Sark?" he said.

The man held out a package which Rock took. They were Camels, which he didn't like, and he had Chesterfields, which he did like, in his coat pocket. He removed a cigarette, lighted it, and began to smoke. The boy beside him took one, too. They drove on in silence a minute or so.

"Mama's only sixty-six," Vava said. "Sixty-six is nothing any more, Rock."

"What's the nurse like?" Rock said.

"All three of them are very good," Vava said, "but you know what nurses are. It's a job for them. They talk about it that way."

"Three of them?"

"One comes on, another goes off. Doctor Lowell did it. They keep the chart, and every time he visits Mama he examines it. One's Irish, one's Italian, one's German. She's the one who comes on at midnight. She's deaf."

"Does Mama like them?"

"They're strangers, Rock, but they're very nice, too, and they know what they're doing. They move her in bed, and work with pans, and massage her forehead and her wrists, and they sit there and read."

"What do they read?" Rock said.

"Movie magazines."

"Every one of them?"

"Every one of them brings her own movie magazine and reads it," his sister said. "There was a story about the break-up of your marriage in one of them, with pictures of you in some of your movies, and pictures of Ann in different places in New York before you got married, with different men, and pictures of the four of you together, and the nurse showed it to Mama."

"Which one?" Rock said.

"The Italian one," Vava said. "The one who comes on at eight in the morning."

"Will she be there when we get there?"

"No, the Irish one will be there. She's the best."

"There wasn't anything like that in *her* movie magazine, was there?"

"She didn't mention it. Don't you think, Rock, you ought to go back with Ann and the kids? Live in California where you belong?"

"No," Rock said. "I've lost them."

"You haven't lost the kids," Sark said. "Those kids are your kids, Rock. They'll always be your kids."

"I've lost them," Rock said.

230

"Just Ann," Sark said.

"How is she?" his sister said. "Is she all right?"

"We haven't spoken in a month," Rock said. "She's all right, I guess."

"Don't you think it's because she's young and wants to be seen all the time by a lot of people, Rock?" his sister said. "Don't you think it's something that doesn't mean very much, and you ought to go back?"

"No," Rock said, "but if you want me to tell Mama we're going back, if you think I *ought* to tell her that, if you think it'll mean something to Mama——"

"She loves Ann, Rock," his sister said. "Old Lula loved her, too. To tell you the truth, Rock, I love Ann, too. She's a very difficult girl, I know, because she and I had a lot of long talks, but even so, I love her."

"I love her, too, Vava."

"Then why did you have to divorce her?" his sister said quickly, with a speed of speech that tells the person spoken to that he has been a fool.

"She lied to me, Vava," he said. "I can't live with a liar. I can love her, but I can't live with her."

"Ah," his sister said. "What's lying? Who cares?"

"I care," Rock said. "I didn't divorce her. I gave her the divorce because she wanted it—she wouldn't have lied if she hadn't wanted it. I gave it to her because I always gave her whatever she wanted. I spent six weeks in Nevada, so she could stay home with the kids. It was her divorce. If you think I ought to tell Mama Ann and I are going back, I'll tell her, though."

"I don't know, Rock," his sister said. "Mama loves Ann. She loves Ann because Ann told her so many times how much

231

she loved you. Mama wants to know what's happened to you. You haven't done anything for so long."

"I was about to go to work in New York," Rock said.

"In a movie?"

"In a play," Rock said. "I'll be going back to work just as soon as Mama's on her feet again."

"You *should*, Rock," his sister said. "Work is life, Rock. If I didn't work every day in my house, in my garden, I'd die. Work is life. I don't think Mama should have spent so much time these past ten years reading *The Asbarez* and all the other Armenian papers and magazines and books that come to her."

"No," Rock said. "Reading *The Asbarez* is all right. Mama works all the time, too."

"Not the way she used to," his sister said. "Her house is the easiest in the world to keep. Nobody but herself to take care of and cook for. Triola fools around in the garden every Saturday for three hours. Once a month Mama has a big baking, and once a week a little one. The dough that's ready now is for a big one. I'm coming over sometime tomorrow to bake the bread and take some of it to her. Just to *see*, of course. She can't eat. If she eats, she vomits. Your apartment downstairs is in order. All your junk is there, and I gave the place a thorough cleaning. There's logs in the garage, and I've got everything set in the fireplace for a fire. Have you got your keys to the house?"

"I've got them," Rock said.

They came to the hospital. Rock parked the car, got out, and looked around.

"Is that the building where Doctor Lowell's office is?" he said.

"Yes," his sister said.

THE SON AND THE DAUGHTER

"Joe," he said, "will you please go up and see if he's in. If he is, will you ask him to please wait a moment, as I want to talk to him. Then come to Mama's room."

"O.K.," the boy said, and bolted across the street.

They went into the place, rang for the elevator, got in, went up to the third floor, and walked softly down the long corridor to the last room.

"I'll peek in first," his sister said. She pushed the door open, looked in, then nodded to Rock that it was all right.

The room was no place to be of course, but there wasn't anything anybody could do about that. The nurse was sitting beside the bed, reading a magazine that probably was a movie one. His mother had turned away from the nurse, but perhaps not intentionally, just to be comfortable. She hadn't heard him. He moved along the bed and saw her an instant before she saw him, the woman in whose kitchen he had danced thirty-five years ago when she had been baking bread. Her hair was gray now, and very dry, hair that he had never thought of as having been anything but black. There was still a good deal of black in it, but not the black that he remembered. Her face seemed larger, hot and swollen. When she saw who it was she was astonished. She sat up, and instantly the nurse was out of her chair, to help hold her up. Her eyes were still the same, but everything else was changed. He took her in his arms very slowly, kissed one cheek and then the other. He took her hands and kissed them, then held them tightly, looking into her eyes, for she was his girl, she was the first of his girls, and he didn't like to see them go.

"Where you come from so quick, Rock?" she said in English, for she tried not to speak Armenian when there were those nearby who could not understand the language.

233

"I came from New York, Mama."

"Why you come all the way from New York, Rock?"

"I came to see my girl," he said.

His mother laughed as a girl laughs, then turned to the nurse.

"Miss Gillen," she said, "you know who this is? This is my son. Rock Wagram."

"Yes," the nurse said softly. "I recognized him, Mrs. Vagramian."

"Is it all right for her to sit up a moment?" he asked the nurse.

"Yes," she said.

The nurse placed two pillows behind his mother, so that she needn't make an effort to stay up.

"How is your wife, Rock?" his mother said.

"She's fine, Mama."

"How is your son, Rock?"

"He's fine, Mama."

"How is your daughter, Rock?"

"She's fine, Mama."

He saw her eyes fill with concern, as they searched through his eyes and along the lines and outline of his face and head.

"You excuse me, Miss Gillen," she said, "I going to talk in Armenian."

"Oh, Mrs. Vagramian," the nurse said. "Please."

"Arak," his mother said in Armenian, "how are *you?* You, yourself."

"Araxi," he said, "do not worry about me. I am well."

"You are tired, Arak?"

"No."

"You are finished with the lawyers?"

"Yes."

"In family affairs it is no good to have lawyers, Arak."

"I know," he said. "I got angry."

"It is no good to get angry," his mother said.

"I know."

"I've got a tubful of dough at home for bread," she said. "Vava will make you some fresh bread tomorrow. You sit down quietly at your table, and you eat fresh bread with butter and honey and tea."

"Yes, Mama."

"You be a good boy and send your beautiful wife money." She looked at him severely and then said, "Let Ann do anything she wants to do. What do you care? You be a good boy, let your children love their mother, let their mother enjoy herself, let her be beautiful, let her put on the clothes she loves so much and go out and have fun and laugh and talk and be happy. Ann is that kind of girl, Arak. You just be a good boy. You do your work and send her money. Is there something else honorable a man can do? You do not do this because you *must* do it, you do it because you *want* to do it. You do it with love, not with anger and hatred. You love Ann, no matter what she does. Ann is the mother of Haig and Lula, Arak. She is always the mother of your children. You love her."

"All right, Mama."

He laughed inwardly because he believed she must be all right if she could give him instructions.

He had something important to tell her when Sark came in and stood behind him. His mother and Sark greeted one another and then the nurse said, "I think she'd better lie back and rest now, Mr. Wagram."

235

"Yes," he said.

The nurse took away the two pillows and eased his mother down. Rock kissed her hands again and then said in Armenian, "Just rest, Mama. Don't think about anything. I'll be here tonight with Vava."

He left the room feeling deeply glad, for he did not know that he would never speak to her again. His sister and her husband and their son and daughter were in the hall.

"She seems all right," Rock said. "But I want to have a talk with Doctor Lowell. Let's none of us go back in there for a while. Let her rest."

"He's waiting in his office," Joe said.

They walked down the hall, took the elevator, and left the building. He visited the doctor alone.

"How about it?" he said. "I just left her. She seemed all right, but please tell me exactly what it is."

"Anything can happen, Rock," the doctor said.

"You mean she's *not* recovering?" Rock said. "We talked a minute or two and she seemed fine."

"I'm delighted, Rock," Dr. Lowell said. "The next twenty-hour hours will tell. It's one of those things. We can only wait and hope. Will you ask the family not to go in there from now on?"

"Shouldn't I have gone in?" Rock said.

"Yes, of course," the doctor said, "but she must rest and stay calm, Rock. Please let's all of us let her rest during the next twenty-four hours."

"My sister wants to spend the night on the couch," Rock said.

"I *want* her to," Dr. Lowell said. "That's important. Your mother speaks in Armenian frequently and it's important for the nurse or myself to know what she says, and your mother needs to know that Vava's there."

He talked with the doctor a half hour, asking every kind of question the answer of which he believed might be helpful, but there were no answers. Something had happened. They would know in twenty-four hours the meaning of what had happened. They would have to wait.

It had happened inside her skull, without warning, something that might *not* have happened, something that had not happened to her own mother. It was a secret thing, and it could have a swift and terrible meaning, but she was still breathing. She could still see and talk and touch and remember and think and tell her son the things she believed to be the truth. Another secret thing, a hundred thousand more secret things would be happening to her in the next twenty-four hours, and after they had all happened, he would know if she would go on breathing ten or twenty years longer. His mother was still herself, still his mother, still Araxi, still his girl, and she was still breathing. He believed she would get up from her hospital bed and go home and mix flour and warm water and salt and yeast and melted butter into a dough and bake bread, and he would sit at the table and eat the bread. She was still breathing, and he believed she would go on breathing.

A man's coming and going is lonely and secret, and yet all of his going and coming seems to have been with companions, strangers who fell in beside him because they were coming or going, too, strangers he knew instantly, with whom communication began without reference to who spoke or who listened, and yet a man was always alone, and the stranger who was an instantaneous friend was also alone.

A man has no years. He is instantly and continuously himself and that flash of time which is the moment coming to him, reaching him, and leaving him. He has no years, for a man cannot cease to be who he is until he is dead and who he is is who he is instantly, standing there, holding the hands of his dying mother, looking into her eyes, saying something to her without words, saying something with words, something that means something more than what the words say, saying to her, "Hang on, Mama, there's nothing better to do if you can do it. There's nothing better than to read the Armenian papers that come every morning. But if you can't hang on, don't regret anything. Don't regret the deterioration of each of us. It happens, Mama. The Armenian papers are going to accumulate if you're not there, and there's not going to be anybody to read them. The postman's going to bring them every morning with your name on them, so if you can do it hang on, and read them a few years longer. See the boy in New York when he's a man. See the girl when she's a woman. See Ann again, listen to her talking and laughing again, listen to a lovely girl who is a liar and be delighted with one of your kind, one of the best of your kind. If you can hang on, Mama, and love her, let her know you love her, let her know again. There's bread to bake, Mama, so if you can, hang on."

A man has no years. He is a coming and going thing, arriving and departing at the same time all his life, alone and speechless and full of secret wisdom and ignorance in the suspended instant when the coming is almost but not quite the going, and the best that he has ever said is without words, with the mute but living flesh of himself, with the hands and eyes, speaking no language better than the language of the speechless animals.

THE SON AND THE DAUGHTER

HE went alone to St. Anne's of the Sunset four hours after he reached San Francisco, knelt there, and prayed as an animal must pray. "I have this woman, this girl, who is my mother, who carried me inside her flesh, and a secret thing has happened to her that I know must happen to every woman, every girl, every man's mother. I would rather this thing did not finish this woman now, for I believe she does not wish it, and there is more for her to read. I would rather, I would rather she were here this summer, for it is fine then, not cold and gray as it is now, in February. We have spoken to one another from time to time, but there is more to be said, and I would rather it were said."

He drove from St. Anne's to the St. Francis Hospital and went to his mother's room. His sister was there, standing over her mother, watching her sleeping face. The nurse was not there. She was out for a cup of coffee.

"She's in a coma again," his sister said. "It happened a couple of hours ago. Is Mama dying, Rock?"

"No," he said.

"Rock, is she dying?"

"No, this is part of what we're waiting for."

"Do you understand these things, Rock?"

"No."

"Old Lula lived to be almost ninety, Rock," his sister said. "Mama's a strong woman. There's never been a stronger woman than Mama. Does she look as if she's going to come home, Rock? Does her face look like the face of somebody who's going to stay?"

Her face did not look like the face of somebody who was going to stay. He remembered his son Haig's face when his son had just been born. That was an angry face, the face of a man who was going to stay. He remembered his daughter's face

239

when his daughter had just been born. That was a petulant face, all twisted out of shape because she was a woman just out of a woman, and it was a face of a woman who was going to stay. His mother's face did not look like the face of somebody who was going to stay. Her face said one thing, "Now I am *altogether* alone. I have seen it all. It was all unfortunate. I regret it, I pity it. I sleep. I am alone. I am going."

"Does Mama look all right, Rock?"

"I never saw her when she didn't look as she looks now," he said.

"Mama's a serious woman," his sister said. "Mama's proud. She's the proudest woman I know. Is Mama going to stay, Rock?"

"I don't know, Vava."

"I'm sorry about Sark in the car," his sister said. "I'm sorry about that, Rock."

"He only wanted Mama to see me looking well," Rock said.

"What did Mama say?" his sister said. "What did she say to you, Rock?"

"The things she has always said," he said. "Listen, Vava. I want to have another talk with the doctor. Where is he?"

"He was here an hour ago," Vava said. "He's done everything he can do. We've just got to wait, he said. He's home."

"I'll telephone him," Rock said. "I'll be back in a minute."

He went downstairs because he didn't want to use the telephone in the room, didn't want his sister to hear his questions.

"What is it?" he said.

"I wouldn't tell any other member of the family," the doctor said, "but it isn't good, Rock. She went into a coma soon after she spoke to you. We decided not to tell her you were coming. It was my idea."

240

"Is it fifty-fifty?" Rock said.

"No, Rock," the doctor said, "but we don't know very much about dying, about who dies, and when, and how. It's different each time. From what we *do* know it isn't fifty-fifty. I'm hoping she'll come out of it. Her temperature isn't down. It's up. I'm hoping the next twenty-four hours will see a miracle happen."

"A miracle?"

"Yes, Rock. She's still bleeding. It may have stopped for a few hours. She may be bleeding from another part of the vein now, or even from another vein. I think she knew you would be coming and was waiting for you. I've been her doctor almost ten years, Rock. I know her nature. I wish there was something wonderful I could say that you could pass along to the rest of the family. I'm coming by again in an hour or so."

"What *is* her temperature?" Rock said.

"It's never been lower than a hundred and four," the doctor said.

"Was it a hundred and four when she spoke to me?" Rock said.

"Yes, or higher," the doctor said. "I think she was waiting to see you and speak to you. She herself may not have known it. I can't otherwise account for her not having gone into a coma earlier."

"Is she in pain? *Herself?*"

"Well, she's in a coma, and she's supposed to be insensitive to pain, but we don't know about that, either. I don't know, Rock."

"What about surgery?" Rock said.

"I had one of the best men in early in the day," the doctor said. "No. Surgery can't help. Will you be there?"

"Yes," Rock said.

He was there when the doctor took some more fluid from her spine.

"I don't know," the doctor said. "There's no telling."

They went out into the hall and talked, then into the street. The doctor went home. Rock went back upstairs and stood over the bed and watched his mother's face.

"What's he say, Rock?" his sister said. "What's the doctor say?"

"We have to wait," Rock said.

At two in the morning he went out into the street, then drove to the house he'd built for her. There were three Armenian papers on the table in the hall: *The Asbarez* from Fresno, *The Hairenik* from Boston, and *Nor Giyonk* from Paris: Horizon, Homeland, and New Life. There would be other papers, too, from other cities. The print would not stop. The language would not stop. He took *The Asbarez*, sat in the chair in the hall, and read it for half an hour, as if he were able to read. He looked at the print of each word as if he were reading. He then went downstairs to his apartment and wandered around there among his junk. There beside the fireplace was the pianola he'd bought years ago because he had heard pianolas in Fresno, at three weddings of members of his family, and she had always liked that music. There were the shelves filled with the books he had accumulated over the years. There was the framed picture of his father, thirty-three years old, the ends of his moustache curved upward, his eyes intense. There was the framed picture of all of them together: Vahan, Araxi, Arak, Vava, and Haig.

He put a match to the paper of the waiting fire in the fireplace, turned off the light, sat in the chair that had been his father's, and watched the fire until it was almost finished. He then went upstairs and took the cloth from the tubful of dough and smelled the dough. He stood over the mass of fermenting dough and breathed the odor of it.

What does a man think? What does he think of himself? What does he think of his father, his mother, his sister, his brother, his family, his race, his religion, his birthplace, his nationality, his class, his profession? What does he think of his life, his own life, the going and coming of life in his own head and hide? What does he think of his own breathing? What does he think he wants? What does he think he can get? What does he think there is to be got? (Bread. There's bread. Water. There's water. Shoes. There's shoes to put the feet into, to stand upon, to walk in. They're thoughtful, clever things, a man's own shoes. Peace. There's peace to stand in as if they were shoes, to walk in, to kick at things with. There's kicking. There's kicking about the peace that's hardly worth the standing in. Death. There's death to get, to get like new shoes, to get like peace, to put the feet in, to stand in, to walk in, to walk off in.)

What does a man think when he isn't thinking? What does he think when he is thinking, when he thinks he's thinking? What does he think when he is being thought, when all of him, when all of his body and life and time is being thought by the one who gave birth to him, lying in a bed in a hospital, in a coma, dying? What does he think when he's being thought by the dying one who, not so long ago, made him? What does he think then, at three o'clock in the morning, wandering around the house he made for her?

What does he think when the coma of death in his mother

thinks him, thinks him whole, thinks him from long before she met his father, from long before his mother and his father were together for themselves and for whoever it might be, and it turned out to be himself? What does he think when he is being thought alive and real by the one who once, young and alive and beautiful then, rubbed him into a flame within the secret of herself, burned with him, and put him forth to burn alone, to put the fire into one of her kind, for another of his kind? What does he think when the keeper of the flame lies dying, with the secret of the flame dying in her, and thinks him whole?

MY girl's dead, he thought. She's gone. She'll not come here again. She'll not come here to bake the bread again.

He slept on the couch across from the fireplace in his study, his own sleep a coma. He got up after a couple of hours, shaved and showered and put on fresh clothes—clothes he hadn't worn in years, still hanging in the closet of his bedroom.

It was half past seven when he got to her room. His sister sat up in bed, still asleep.

"She awoke twice during the night," she said, "but I don't know, I don't know, Rock."

"What did she say?" Rock said.

"Well, once she said, 'Shame,' " his sister said.

"That's the fight I had with Papa that time," Rock said. "I didn't *want* to fight him. I'm sorry, Vava."

"Oh, Rock," his sister said. "That wasn't your fault. She said some other things, too. Names, I mean. Names I don't know. I guess they're people she knew in the old country. Ahlkhatoon. Who's Ahlkhatoon?"

"That's Mama's aunt," Rock said, "that she used to know when she was a little girl, that she loved so much."

"She said the names of some places, too, I think," his sister said. "Tsopper-Gore."

"That's the name of the spring," Rock said, "where they used to get their water."

"She said our names," his sister said, "all of them, and the second time, Rock, Mama almost cried. Mama's a proud woman. Mama doesn't cry. There were tears in her eyes, though, and I cried. I talked to her, but she didn't know what I was saying. Her eyes were open, Rock, but I don't think Mama knew it was me. I don't think she *saw* me. I'm sick, Rock. I'm scared."

She began to sob softly.

"I want to go home," she said. "I want to see my damn kids."

"I'll take you home," Rock said.

"Oh, Rock," his sister said. "What is it? Did you ever see such kids as my kids? All big and smiling, all good?" She pointed at the woman on the bed. "What is it, Rock? For God's sake, Rock, is *that* Mama? Mama's proud, Mama's the proudest woman I ever saw. Is this something to happen to Mama, lying there that way? This stupid room. The stupid dark of this room. These stupid walls."

She suddenly burst into terrible sobbing.

"I want to take Mama home," she said. "For God's sake, Rock, let Mama die in her own bed, in her own house."

She stopped suddenly, ashamed and angry at herself.

"I'll go out until you get dressed," Rock said. "I'll take you home."

"No," his sister said. "I'll take a taxi. You stay here. I'll send Dovey. Mama loves Dovey."

He went out into the hall and stood at the window looking down at the hospital parking lot, where the doctors left their cars. There was only one car in the whole lot, space for twenty-four. Further off, hanging on a clothesline, were two pairs of a man's winter underwear, three shirts, four pairs of socks, and a woman's skirt and blouse. There were other lines, but without things hanging on them.

His sister came out of the room.

"I thought I'd telephone the priest, Zadik," she said. "You remember him. He was at the engagement party the other night that Mama had such a fine time at. I thought I'd telephone him to get his cross and robe and cap and book and come here."

"Yes," Rock said.

"I'll ask him to take a taxi," she said.

"No," Rock said. "You tell him to wait for me, and when Dovey comes, I'll go get him. I know where the church is."

"I ought to come back for that, Rock," his sister said, "but I'm so sick."

"You don't have to come back," Rock said. "I'll stand with him. I'll ask the nurse to leave, but if Dovey wants to stand, too, she can."

"All right, Rock," his sister said, and went.

Rock went back into the room and looked at her face again. It was another face altogether now. The pride, the regret, the compassion, the resignation, the pity were all gone. They had been driven out of her face by the pain of death, by the secret struggle of a woman with death.

Still, he believed she might come to the miracle the doctor had spoken of. She might struggle through the pain and away from the death.

The nurse now was the German one, the deaf one, a woman older than his mother.

"She's the same," the nurse said, even though he hadn't asked. "She's not in pain."

His niece came, a big girl with a sweet face, now bewildered and hurt. Rock went off to the church and found the priest Zadik inside, waiting. They spoke in English, then in Armenian, the priest explaining that in the Armenian church there was no hell, but not saying there was also no heaven. He explained the difference between what he would soon do and what a Roman Catholic priest would do. They went upstairs and Rock's niece got the nurse out of the room, then came back and stood at the foot of the bed. Rock stood at his mother's head, opposite the priest, now in robe and cap, the open book in one hand, the cross in the other.

"Araxi Vagramian," the priest began softly, then went on in classic Armenian, a language Rock only half-understood, the *written language*, as it was called, the language of the church.

He drove the priest back to the church, then returned to the hospital. The doctor was there then.

"I don't know, Rock," he said. "I can't say. I *won't* say."

The next day Sark telephoned Rock early in the morning to tell him that Vava was sick and Dr. Lowell was coming to see her. He went over and saw his sister come downstairs in a robe. She was pale and stunned, and seemed to be shivering. She went to him and he embraced her.

"Rock," she said. "Something terrible happened in my sleep. I woke up and hollered, 'No. No.' I *had* to. Poor Sark. My poor kids. I scared them all."

"Mama's going to get better," Sark said. "You wait and see."

"Oh, Sark," his sister said. "For God's sake, Sark."

"Mama's a strong woman," Rock's brother-in-law said.

"She's not going to let a little thing like this stop her. She'll be home in a week, bawling everybody out, especially Rock."

"You don't know what's happened to Mama," Vava said.

"I don't care what's happened," Sark said. "I don't care what the doctor says. I don't care what anybody says. Mama's going to get better, that's all."

The doctor came and told Rock and Sark what it was. Rock understood what it was. It was supposed to be oxygen now, dextrose and water through the veins, but he knew.

When the doctor had gone Sark said, "See, Rock? This oxygen and all that other stuff means Mama's getting better."

Rock got in his car with Joe and drove back to the hospital. The hours, the days, and the nights went by one by one.

The rubber tube from the oxygen tank was taped to his mother's face, the end of it into a nostril.

Her veins were pierced again and again for the dripping of water and dextrose into her burning body.

Members of the family came from Fresno to San Francisco one by one to visit Vava, to speak to Rock, to eat and drink, the ones who had been young when Rock had last seen them now grown to manhood or womanhood, the old gone along to new illnesses, their faces and eyes older now and more confused, their voices loving and lonely.

He went out in his car with his cousins, his nephews, and his uncles to saloons, to stand and drink, to talk, to wait. He had watched his mother's face travel from pity and beauty to desperate violence. Her breathing became filled with noises. Her eyes fell half-open, and his sister believed her mother could still see and hear. He heard her speak to her mother. "Mama? It's Vava. I didn't bake the bread, because only you can bake the bread. It's waiting there for you. I know you can hear me,

Mama. I know you can see me, too. I know what a terrible thing's happened to you, Mama, all these things they're doing to you, a proud woman like you. It's Vava, Mama. I'm waiting for you to come home, so I can come and visit you every morning again."

He saw the color of her skin change from the color of life to the color of death. He listened to her breathing, and wanted to know why a man had to be nonsense all his life, asking death not to be death, asking the ugly not to be ugly, asking pain not to be pain, asking the end not to be the end, asking the alone not to be alone. And he went out two or three times a day and night with the men of his family, his anger suddenly flaring up at them because they had deteriorated or had grown to manhood nonsensically, because there was nothing he could do to help the poor woman go. Nothing he could do about the swollen lump of pain she had become.

The night before she died he stood over the violence she had become. He was alone in the room at two o'clock in the morning. He took her burning hands and held them tightly at first, then tenderly, kissed them, and then her tortured face, each cheek, as her half-open eyes stared at nothing. He spoke in Armenian to her.

"Mother," he said in Armenian. "Araxi. Try no more."

An hour later he spoke to her again, saying only one word again and again: "Rest." Saying it slowly, softly, gently.

He was there the next day at noon when she stopped at last, nine days after death had come to her. He left the room so that the nurse and the intern could go to work on another corpse. He drove to Vava's, and when she saw him she knew. She ran to him, trying not to sob, and he said, "Before we take her to Ararat I'd like you to bake the bread."

"No, Rock," his sister said. "Only Mama can bake that bread. Throw it away. Bury it. That's Mama's bread."

He put the white porcelain tubful of dough on the table in the storage area off the garage. He dug his fingers through the surface that was now dry and brittle to the gummy moist dough underneath. He pulled out a handful of the stuff, rolled it into a ball, put some wax paper around it, and put it into his coat pocket.

They put her in Ararat beside her son Haig, her husband Vahan on the other side of Haig, and then Rock went alone to the house on Winery Street which had been sold to a family named Clayburn. He asked if they wanted to sell it.

"Well," the man said, "we hadn't thought of it because it's a good house, old but solid and good. We'd sell it if we got a good offer. Come on in. I'll show it to you."

The man showed Rock the house Rock was born in. "We paid three thousand dollars for the place three years ago," the man said, "but real estate's gone up since then."

"How much do you want for it?" Rock said.

"Oh, five, six thousand, I guess," the man said. "That's fair, the way real estate's shot up."

"Let me think about it," Rock said.

"Five, at least," the man said. "It's a good house. Solid, not like the houses they're building these days. It's got a good fifteen, twenty years to go. Maybe more. I'd have to have five, at least."

He went out to the sidewalk for another look at the house, then got in his car and drove back to Ararat. He wandered around there, looking at the tombstones, reading them, saving for the last his mother's new grave.

He came to the drowned boy's grave, and remembered Dick

Cracker trying with the rest of them to swim across the San Joaquin River at Skaggs Bridge and not being able to make it, turning to the others and saying, "I can't make it, boys. So long."

That was a long time ago. That was thirty years ago now. He read the tombstone.

> Dikran Kirakjian 1909–1919
> Drowned in the San Joaquin River
> September 7, 1919
> Body Not Recovered
> Goodbye, Cracker
> Papa & Mama

He looked at the stones on either side of the boy, the stones of Papa and Mama, all of the stones standing in dry weeds.

"Well," Rock said to the boy's monument, "they'll never know what a great man you were, will they, Cracker?"

He wandered away, wandering as he had wandered twenty-five years ago with Murphy, glancing at one stone, stopping to read another, to look at the Armenian print on some of them, not a word or letter in English, an angel with wings, a lamb, a cross. One stone had an arm with a clenched fist held high from jagged rock. Who was *he?*

Murphy said, "This is the only city, Rock. This is the capital of the world. This is where Christians and Jews and Moslems and all the others say to each other, 'Make way for a pal.' This is where we've got to go, boy, but I still say a hole in the ground is a hell of a place for a soul. Let's go see your brother."

"It's over here," Rock said.

Haig's grave was alone then in the family plot, but only a

year later the soul of the father was put in the hole in the ground beside the soul of the son, and now the soul of the boy's mother had been put beside him there.

When Rock came back to the fresh grave, it was covered with flowers. He brought the ball of dough out of his pocket, broke off a piece, put it into his mouth, chewed and swallowed it. The rest he buried in the fresh dirt.

"Goodbye, old girl," he said. He turned to go, and saw his sister Vava hurrying to the grave, her son Joe walking slowly behind her, saying, "Now, Ma! Ah, Ma!"

His sister flung herself on the flowers, sobbing, and the boy said to Rock, "She *made* me drive her back, Rock. She didn't let anybody know, and she made me keep quiet about it. Everybody's looking for you. They're all drinking and eating and talking and asking for you."

"We'll go back in a minute," Rock said.

"Ma's taking it bad," Joe said. "I don't know what to do."

"We'll wait a minute," Rock said.

"What did *you* come back for?" Joe said.

"You've got to bury your mother yourself, *alone*," Rock said. "The family's got to bury her, the church has got to bury her, and then you've got to bury her yourself, alone, because she's not the same to you that she is to the family. You've got to bury her alone where they put the body, and you've got to bury her alone everywhere else she ever was. It takes time. It takes the rest of your life."

"I want to go young," Joe said.

"You do?" Rock said.

"I want to go quick," Joe said. "I can't wait to get in the new war. I don't want to hang around."

"How old are you *now?*" Rock said.

"Nineteen."

"How many girls you got?"

"One steady," Joe said. "Six or seven part-time. I don't know. Ma's having a rough time. Living stinks, doesn't it, Rock?"

"Yes, it does," Rock said. "We love it, though. Every one of us loves it."

"I don't," Joe said. "I hate it. Always have. Always will. I have a little fun with the girls, that's all. What's the use kidding? It stinks."

"How much do you weigh?" Rock said.

"Two hundred and forty," Joe said.

"How tall are you?" Rock said. "Six feet two?"

"Three," Joe said.

"Get your weight down to two hundred," Rock said. "Take it easy. You're having a hell of a time."

"It's not fat," Joe said. "It's all muscle and bone."

"You weren't any two hundred and forty when you played high school football," Rock said.

"That was two years ago," Joe said. "I've grown."

"You've grown fat."

"No, I'm as hard as nails."

"No," Rock said. "A man ought to be lean and hard until he's thirty at least, and he ought to look hot and hungry. You look round and soft."

"I can get twenty pounds off in a month."

"How?"

"Lay off eating and drinking, get to the gym twice a week."

"A man ought to be in shape who wants to get himself killed quick, in the new war," Rock said.

"Ah, you know what I mean," Joe said.

253

"A fellow who knows living stinks ought to be in perfect shape," Rock said.

"I mean, look at Mama," Joe said. "She worked hard for us kids, to get us grown up healthy and O.K. and all that, and then just when we're all halfway grown up and not the kind of trouble we used to be, her own mother dies. If that isn't stinking, I don't know what is. Ma believed Grandma was going to be alive at least twenty more years. I'm worried about her. I haven't taken my girl out since Grandma went to the hospital. I've been taking care of Ma."

"Of course you have," Rock said. "You just take care of her a few days more. She'll be O.K."

His sister came to them, her eyes dry now, and she said, "Well, Rock, Mama's gone."

"Yes, Vava, but you've got your kids, and I've got mine." He turned to the boy. "Joe," he said, "I'll drive Mama back to the party."

"I'll say it's a party," Joe said. "Is that the way the Armenians do it?"

"It's not a bad way," Rock said. "I'll see you there."

He drove back to the party at his uncle Krikor's house, the big new house by the high school, and he began to drink and eat. One by one the members of the family got up and went home. He saw his sister and her husband and children go off on the two-hundred-mile drive back to San Francisco.

"We'll be home around eleven," Sark said. "Joe drives fast but he drives good."

"What are you going to do, Rock?" his sister said.

"I'll drive up soon," Rock said.

"You take care of yourself now," Vava said.

He drove to Fat Aram's and drank there until the place

254

closed, sitting alone. Then he drank with Fat Aram. At four in the morning he got up and had two cups of black coffee. Then he began to drive back to San Francisco, knowing the enormity of a man's nonsense, knowing it mile after mile, and now, with one more of his girls gone, he felt himself falling into humorlessness, apathy, indifference, fat, and everything else that is not hard and good, but *is* also nonsense.

Every man is afraid and fearless. A man is a game fellow all his life, and never less than half scared to death. There is a good deal within a man by which to be unafraid of anything, and a good deal outside of him by which to have the fear of God thrown into him every instant. Outside is a woman who was for many years his wife. Outside is his son. Outside is his daughter. Outside is taxes. Outside is debts. Inside is only the wink.

ONE day Ann telephoned and said, "What are you doing?"

"What do you want?" Rock said.

"Money," Ann said. "I owe rent for two months. The bills are piling up. I've got to have money."

"I haven't any," Rock said.

"You've got to get some," Ann said.

"You're home," Rock said. "Borrow some from your mother, or her husband, until I get some."

"I can't," Ann said. "They won't lend me any."

"Why not?"

"They don't want to pay for the upbringing of your kids."

"Send the kids out here," Rock said.

"I'll never give up my kids," Ann said.

"Well," Rock said, "I haven't any money and if your family

won't help, I don't know what you're going to do. I could sell the car, but it's eight years old and I couldn't get very much for it. It's falling to pieces, too, but I'm fond of it. I'll sell it if you want me to, though."

"I've got to have money, that's all," Ann said.

"You need too much money for a girl who hasn't got a dime of her own and can't get more than the equivalent of a tip from her mother once in a while," Rock said. "I'll sell the car and send you the money."

"If you haven't got any money, what are *you* living on?" Ann said.

"I don't need much," Rock said. "I've got everything I need."

"What about all those San Francisco society girls you're entertaining all the time?" Ann said. "It's in all the columns in New York. You've got to pay money to entertain *them*, don't you?"

"I don't know any society girls, except you," Rock said. "You *were* a society girl, weren't you? Café society or something like that? Or was it *high* society?"

"High," Ann said. "The *highest*, from Second Avenue to Park Avenue in one jump. What are you doing, Rock?"

"I'm learning to read Armenian," Rock said. "The priest who buried my mother is helping me. I look at the papers that come every day."

"The Armenian papers?"

"Yes."

"What else?"

"I'm trying to write in Armenian."

"Why don't you try to write in Turkish?" Ann said.

"I don't like the mother of my kids to be a smart aleck

about Armenians and Turks," Rock said. "They're people who are pathetic enough without any help from anybody else."

"What's the matter with you, Rock?" Ann said. "Don't you enjoy my jokes any more? You *used* to."

"I'm tired of jokes," Rock said. "You made me very tired of jokes, even good ones, Ann. You made a joke of my son and my daughter, and the others that were to have been born. You made a joke of love and marriage, of yourself and myself. I guess I've laughed as much as I'm ever going to about the joke you made of these things. I can't laugh any more. I haven't got any money, Ann. I've got taxes to pay for two years, and a lot of debts. I'll sell the car and send you the money, though. Is there anything else?"

"Well, yes, there is," Ann said. "The money from the car won't be enough. You agreed to send a thousand dollars a month. A thousand isn't enough, but I agreed to it. I'm trying to give the children a nice home and a good life. It would be monstrous if you didn't send money for the support of your children."

"I don't have any money, Ann."

"You could sell the house, couldn't you?" Ann said.

"I thought I'd keep the house," Rock said. "I built it for my mother. I don't like the idea of selling it. Besides, I wouldn't have anywhere to go. It's the only home I have."

"Well, I've got to have money," Ann said. "Where you get it or how you get it is your problem."

"When I talked to your lawyer just before I left New York a month ago I had three thousand dollars," Rock said. "I planned to go to work, but I had to spend the money, and the work I was going to do fell through. The production of the play was abandoned."

"You could get work if you wanted to."

"On a vineyard or tending bar maybe."

"You know very well you could get work that pays big money if you wanted to," Ann said.

"Is that so?" Rock said. "Where?"

"At your old studio. U.S. Pictures," Ann said.

"How do you know?" Rock said.

"Oh, I just happened to find out," Ann said. "I have friends in Hollywood. I happen to know Schwartz offered you a contract."

"Do you happen to know the kind it was?" Rock said.

"Well, it's not the best, but so what?" Ann said. "Who are you? Are you too good to take a test again? After all, you've been a bum for eight years. He's got a right to find out if you're worth anything, hasn't he?"

"Is there anything else?" Rock said. "I have to pay for this call, and I don't want them to take the phone out."

"I happen to know he'll give you a contract for a year at five hundred a week," Ann said. "I could use that money."

"I'll sell the car, Ann, and send you the money," Rock said.

"Aren't you going to ask about the children?" Ann said.

"Is somebody there who knows something about them?" Rock said.

"I know all about the children," Ann said. "I adore them, and they adore me. Sell the car and send me the money, though, if you don't want to talk about your own children."

"How are they?" Rock said.

"A lot you care," Ann said.

"How's Haig? How's Lula?"

"If you cared for your children you'd send them money."

258

"I'd like to talk to them, Ann, if I may, please."

"They're asleep and I'm not going to wake them up. Goodbye."

He hung up, got in his car, and drove to the ocean. He went out to the edge of the water and stood there a half hour, listening to the sea, then drove home, trying to drive out of himself the fear of God that had been thrown into him about his children by their mother.

He drove to town the next day to sell his car, but before trying to do so, he went to Harry Klein's and bet a thousand on the Yanks to beat the Red Sox, and they did. They did it in the bottom of the ninth, but they did it. His friend, the betting commissioner, counted out eight hundred and twenty dollars in currency, so Rock had at least a little money to send her, and he still had the car, too. He filled the car with groceries, enough for a month or two, kept a few dollars for himself, and sent Ann $750, asking her to please have the nurse drop him a word or two about the children every couple of weeks.

There was no word from the nurse, though, or from Ann, and then one night she telephoned again, reversing the charges, as she always did.

"What are you doing?" she said.

"I thought perhaps the nurse would write and tell me about the children," Rock said. "I thought you'd tell me about the eviction. All I know is what I saw in the papers. They served me with a summons, but I telephoned the lawyers and told them I owe them the rent money all right. I told them I'd pay them as soon as I get some money. It's three thousand, including court costs. I'm sorry that happened. I thought your parents would help you. I didn't think they'd let somebody else help you. Somebody must be helping you. I thought you'd answer my letters and tell me about it."

"What else?" Ann said.

"Well, I even thought you might want to tell me——"

"Tell you *what*, Rock?"

"Well," he said, "I thought you might want to tell me you're sorry for making a joke of so many things, and then maybe——" He stopped again suddenly, for he was sick of the joke, and never felt the sickness so much as when he spoke to her, even by telephone, even with three thousand miles between them.

"Listen," he said suddenly. "I'm sorry. That's all. What do you want, Ann?"

"I want money, Rock."

"I haven't got any."

"You could gamble again," she said. "That betting commissioner owes you plenty. Gambling owes you plenty."

"I don't like to gamble," Rock said. "I haven't any money to cover a loss with. I took a chance last time because I hated the idea of losing my car. They won't give me more than eight or nine hundred dollars for it, anyway."

"I happen to know Schwartz's offer still goes," Ann said. "All you've got to do is get in your car and drive down there and let them shoot a test in a couple of hours, and then go to work a year at five hundred dollars a week. That's twenty-six thousand dollars a year. I can use that money. I happen to know he's pretty sure he's going to like the test."

"I happen to know he knows I'm broke, and is trying to take advantage of that," Rock said. "I have his telegrams and letters."

"Well, what are you doing about it?" Ann said. "Reading the Armenian papers?"

"I told you I don't like the mother of my kids to be a smart aleck about their family," Rock said. "They're also *my* kids. They're not yours alone."

"All right, Rock," Ann said. "I just think it would be monstrous if you didn't send money for the upbringing of your children."

"Is there anything else, Ann?"

"No. I just need money."

"Is there anything you want to tell me about yourself?" he said. "What you're doing? What your plans are? Why you keep using the word monstrous all the time? What you're thinking of for the future, for yourself and for the kids?"

"We're divorced, Rock. Those things are none of your business."

"Well, goodbye, Ann."

"What about the money?"

"I haven't got any. If I get some I'll send it. *All* of it."

"What are you doing about getting some?" Ann said.

"Well, I won't say that that's none of *your* business," Rock said. "I don't like Schwartz's offer. I don't have any other. I've spoken to a number of good agents in New York and Hollywood. They haven't come up with anything yet. Goodbye, Ann."

He went to the betting commissioner's a month later when he was broke again and took a flyer on a two-team parley, and won. The betting commissioner counted out eighteen hundred dollars, knowing Rock was broke (since Rock had told him so), and even though he hadn't had any word from Ann about the children he sent her fifteen hundred dollars. It was late June then and the children were out of school. He asked if she would please think about having the nurse bring the children out to San Francisco to spend a month with him. She did not answer his letter, but a month later telephoned again.

"What are you doing?" she said.

"What do you want, Ann?"

"I want money, Rock."

"Is there anything you want to tell me about anything?" Rock said.

"About what, Rock?"

"Anything," Rock said. "Anything you think I might be interested in."

"I can't *think* of anything," Ann said.

"I'll send you some money as soon as I get some," Rock said. "Goodbye, Ann."

"Is there anything *you* want to tell *me* about anything?" Ann said quickly. "Why don't we put it that way, Rock?"

"The kids aren't with me," Rock said. "There isn't much for me to tell. Oh yes. I forgot. Your mother telephoned a couple of weeks ago and said that if I would go back to work and make some money you and the children would come back to me."

"What did you tell her?" Ann said.

"I told her you ought to marry a man with a lot of money," Rock said.

"You mean if you could afford it, you wouldn't *want* me back?" Ann said.

"No, Ann."

"Why not?"

"I can *afford* it now," Rock said.

"You haven't got a dime," Ann said.

"No, but I can afford it," Rock said. "If I had a job and a lot of money put away and a steady income, I couldn't afford it. I don't need a lot to live on, and kids don't, either, except love. An imitation of love is purchasable only from whores, Ann. Good men sometimes need to make this transaction with whores, but only whore-makers make it with the mothers of children. Goodbye, Ann."

One day in September David Key came to the house in San Francisco and said, "Schwartz sent me, Rock, but I came for reasons of my own, too."

"What are they?" Rock said.

"Well, I know you've been having a rough time," David said. "I mean, everybody knows. Well, I thought maybe I could——"

"You could *what*, David?"

"Well, I think you know what I mean," David said. "I'm pretty sure you don't like the idea, so maybe I'd better skip it."

"Yes," Rock said, "but I want you to know I think it's kind of you. What's Schwartz up to?"

"Well, you know how he can't do anything except in imitation of my father," David said. "He's got his heart set on getting you back to U.S. Pictures."

"His offer's a poor one," Rock said.

"It is," David said, "but things have changed in Hollywood, Rock. The test is nothing. He's just doing that to look important."

"I don't mind the test," Rock said. "I don't mind his being important, either. Maybe he *is* important, David. He doesn't offer enough money, that's all. I'm supposed to send a thousand a month to my kids and their mother. I've got to pay taxes on that money. I've got two years back taxes to pay, and around sixty thousand in debts. A year at five hundred dollars a week wouldn't do me much good. I've got an agent hustling around in Hollywood, and another in New York."

"The public's forgotten you, Rock," David said. "They've forgotten so many others, too. It's not the worst offer in the world, because if you do one good picture in the year that you work, when the year's over you can make a much better deal. The idea of limiting the contract to one year wasn't Schwartz's idea, Rock. It was mine. I told him you might not turn out the way you did the first time. I told him that because I know you'll be better than ever, and you won't have a bad long-term contract to keep you from getting your debts paid. I hope you don't mind, Rock."

"I don't mind," Rock said, "but a year's a long time to spend in Hollywood at five hundred dollars a week, more than half of which has to go to New York. Tell Schwartz to make it a thousand a week, and I'll drive down and take the test. If he doesn't like the test, nobody's lost anything. I want to work again all right, but I can't get into something that's only going to get me deeper into debt."

"I'll fly back and tell him," David said, "but I don't think he'll take you up, Rock. He's sure you're going to accept his offer sooner or later. He happens to know your agent hasn't had any luck with any of the other studios. I'll tell him, though, Rock. I'll try to get him to——"

"No," Rock said, "don't try anything. Just tell him what I told you. I don't like things to get too much help. You don't seem as troubled as you were when we talked in New York. I hope things are working out all right."

"Sam says I'll be producing soon," David said. "I know that

only means *he'll* still be producing. But I'll get my name up as the producer, anyway, and more money. They'll be the same pictures, though."

"They're not bad pictures," Rock said.

"The photography's pretty good," David said. "The pictures are bad all right. I've seen all of my father's pictures again. I made a point of seeing every one of them again after our talk in New York. I saw them in order, one a day, and I thought about each of them, forty-five pictures. They're very bad, Rock. There's something in every one of them that is very bad. It's in the fourteen pictures you were in, too, Rock."

"Was I in that many?" Rock said.

"Yes," David said, "and every one of them's bad. I've thought about it a lot, and I think I know what's the matter."

"What is it?" Rock said.

"We're liars, Rock, and don't need to be," David said. "Don't need to be at all. Every place in every picture that is false could just as easily have been true, but wasn't. I was terribly disappointed in my father at first, but I'm not any more."

"I wonder if you know about the play he wrote?" Rock said.

"Yes," David said. "Myra Clewes told me the day after we talked in New York. I meant to write you about it, but I didn't know what to say. I found *all* of his writing. It's *all* bad, worse than the movies, except that one, and that's not very good, either, Rock."

"No?" Rock said.

"The play itself is almost something," David said, "but it isn't my father, and the reason it isn't is very simple. He'd already changed his name from Keesler to Key. That's O.K. But you can't change Paul Key to Patrick Kerry, too, and expect what you do to be O.K. You can't hide, and expect *anything* to be O.K. I didn't think my father was that kind of a man. I can't imagine how it happened that he became such a man."

"Can't you, actually?" Rock said.

"No, I can't, Rock," David said, "and I know what you're thinking. No man has a right to fool with something that goes out to people who is not himself true, who is not proudly himself. If he is justified in not being proud of himself, then he has got to live in such a way that will compel him to be proud of himself, even if he sells neckties out of a satchel on a street corner. He has no right to hide from himself and from the world that he is not proud of himself, and that's what my father did. He was unhappy about being a Jew, about being Paul Keesler, about being himself. Why? Who the hell else did he expect to be? Who the hell is the man who *is* happy about who he is? Is he somebody better than my father?"

"No," Rock said. "What is it *you're* going to do about it?"

"Well, Rock," David said. He went to the door, opened it, then stopped and turned. "I guess I'm going to work as well as I know how to put across the superiority of truth to anything else: convenience, effectiveness, expediency, profit. Schwartz sent me about his offer, but I came for reasons of my own, too, one of which was to tell you these things. I love my father more than ever. I'm not sorry, though, that I don't admire him so much any more. I think he could have been almost a great man, perhaps even a great writer. Well, I'll tell Schwartz what you told me to tell him, Rock."

Every man is afraid and fearless. He is fearless about his

father turning out to be his son, but fearful about his son living long enough to turn out to be his father.

Every man needs his family, whether his family is his father and mother, sister and brother, or the brothers and sisters of his father and mother, and their children. He needs his children, or the people who are supposed to be of his own nationality, the Americans, for instance, or the people of that part of the world in which he was born and spent his boyhood and early manhood, the people of California, for instance, or people like himself in other things, in things of the spirit and mind, in humor or velocity, for instance.

A man needs his family, whoever or whatever his family is. He needs them whether he loves or hates them. He may not need a great deal of them, but he needs a little of them, he needs at least a moment of them now and then, he needs to have another look at them, he needs to be among them again, he needs to be astonished by them. Why not? Isn't it a fine thing to see them? To see the faces of them again? Isn't it an amazing thing to see so many of them still alive, still working hard, still trying to make both ends meet, as they put it, still trying to keep body and soul together, as they say, still asking tenderly if old acquaintance should be forgot, still standing around and talking things over? Why shouldn't a man have another look at his family? Isn't it better than looking at print in books all the time? Isn't it better than nothing? Isn't it a little something or other to get out among one's own family and holler to them and see their terrible faces?

ONE morning he telephoned Zadik.

"Zadik," he said, "I would like you to come to the house

some evening for some food and drink and talk. Could you make it tonight?"

"I will come gladly, by streetcar, Rock," the priest said. "At what hour?"

"I'll come and get you at the church at seven," Rock said.

"Very good, Rock."

They had Scotch before dinner, which was broiled steaks, and brandy after dinner.

Rock brought out the sheet of lined paper he had kept for twenty-five years.

"Will you read this handwriting to me, please?" he said.

"Very good," Zadik said. "I will if I can. Let me put on my glasses."

The dark little man with the black beard, happy and half-drunk, put on his glasses and studied the handwriting a moment, then began to read. When he had read the entire poem aloud he looked at Rock and said, "What is this, Rock?"

"I want *you* to tell *me*," Rock said.

"Do you understand this poem?" Zadik said.

"Not altogether," Rock said. "What does it say?"

"It says several strange things," Zadik said. "Who is the writer?"

"I will tell you in a moment," Rock said. "What does the poem say? As far as you are able to tell me in English and in Armenian, what does it say?"

"It says several things at once in the words," Zadik said, "and at the same time it says several other things at once, but not in words."

"Yes," Rock said. "Well, let's have another drink, please take all the time you need, and tell me each of the things it says in words, and each that it says without words."

"It says things we all say in our hearts, now and then, perhaps once in a lifetime, to somebody we love, or somebody we hate, or somebody we love at whom we are very angry," Zadik said.

"Yes," Rock said. "Now, here's this drink. Drink, and then drink more. What does the writer of the poem say? What does he say?"

Zadik swallowed his drink and said, "He says, Rock, it is to God he wishes to speak. He says he speaks to God with pity but without love. He says he loves not God but man, and especially the enemy, the Turk. The Turk, Rock, in his own father, in himself, and in his own son. He says he must pity God because God is the Father, and His children love Him like fools or hate Him like fools or mock Him like fools. He says he has breathed a long time, from beneath the mulberry tree on the hillside of Baghesht—which is the ancient name of Bitlis—halfway across the world, to the fig tree in the garden of *The Asbarez*, just beyond the Armenian printing presses of Fresno."

Zadik stopped. Rock filled Zadik's glass with brandy, and his own as well. They swallowed their drinks, and the priest said, "He says, Rock, that he has a son, no better than any Turk's son, but a man in whom his own heart beats with terrible hope for love between all the children of the Father. He says if he is to live he is to live in this son, for the other one, the better one, died as a child. If he is to go on breathing, he says, this son must restore to him the breath of life. If he is awakened from the sleep of death by this son, he will live and he will love. If he is not awakened, he will never know that he was never awakened, he will not remember that he breathed the mulberry-scented air of Baghesht once, he will neither know nor care that he hated the Turk until the last moment when he loved him more deeply than he loved the sons of Haig themselves, he will not remember his father, himself, or his sons. If he is not awakened by this son, he will never know the gladness with which he stopped breathing, stopped loving, and stopped hating."

The priest looked from the sheet of paper to Rock, and said, "That is what he says, Rock."

"Yes," Rock said.

"What do you want to tell me about this poem, Rock?" Zadik said.

"My father wrote those lines the day I came home and found him dead at the kitchen table," Rock said. "He had closed the doors and shut the windows, and he had opened the gas of the stove."

"Could you not have reached home a little earlier, Rock?"

"No."

"Had you reached home perhaps only a half hour earlier you would have given him the breath he wanted."

"I reached home when I did," Rock said.

"Where *were* you?" Zadik said.

"What's the difference where I was?" Rock said. "Where was *he?*"

"It is not said in the words," Zadik said, "but it is deeply felt that he believed you would awaken him."

"He was dead," Rock said. "He had stopped breathing. It might have been my mother to find him."

"Did you stop somewhere on the way home?" Zadik said. "Perhaps to visit a friend?"

"I had just driven Murphy back from Bakersfield," Rock said. "I put the car in the garage and started walking home, walking down Eye to Ventura. I ran into a friend talking to a couple of girls. I stood and talked with them a half hour, and then I walked home."

"Was it necessary to stand and talk with them?" Zadik said.

"Yes," Rock said. "Yes, it was. It was certainly as necessary as it was for my father to do what he did. I don't say it wasn't necessary for him to do what he did. Why should anybody feel it wasn't necessary for me to do what I did?"

"A pity, Rock," the priest said. "A pitiful accident."

"What he did was no accident," Rock said.

"You meant a great deal to your father, Rock," the priest said.

"My son means a great deal to me," Rock said, "but already he's lost to me, a stranger in a strange city, his own mother, whom he loves, a stranger to me. I'm not going to kill myself about that, Zadik."

"Of course not, Rock."

"I'm not going to kill myself about anything," Rock said, "or anybody, and I'll tell you why. I want my son to know that his father is somewhere in the world, demanding nothing of his son, offering nothing to him, so that if ever his son wishes to speak to a friend, his father will be there to speak to. I am not angry at my father for what he did. I am not sorry I stopped on my way home to talk to my friends. I do not pity the Father. I love Him, because my son will soon have a son of his own. I have waited twenty-five years to learn what my father wrote before he died. I waited until my mother was dead, so that I could go on pretending that he had died of a heart attack, as our family doctor and I agreed to pretend."

"It is a great poem, Rock," the priest said.

"No," Rock said. "He did not live long enough to write a great poem."

"He lived a long time, Rock," Zadik said. "It takes a long time to write a poem like that."

"It takes a longer time to live a life," Rock said. "At the end of that time the going is not easy, it is not at the table of your own house on a summer's day. It is not ended in an hour of dreaming. The breathing doesn't stop in one hour. The departure is in a terrible room, in a fearful bed, in which hundreds of others have suffered pain and died. The breathing doesn't stop in an hour, it doesn't even begin to stop for days and nights of feverish, frightful sleep, sleep involving hundreds of thousands of dreams and details, from which there is no awakening. The arrival of the son on time cannot stay the going, cannot make it easy: the arrival in time to give the news of wife and children, to receive the instructions of life and manners, cannot stay the going, cannot restore the traveler to health and home, to the kitchen, to the stove, to the bread to be baked. I came home on a happy summer's day and saw my father dead. I came home again on a winter's day and saw my mother alive. I saw her for nine days and nights, alive every moment, but dying. I saw her die. I saw a life end. There's no poetry in it. It's ugly. There is nothing uglier than a life dying. It has no beauty at all, no dignity, no form, and there is no art in it. I adore women, all of them, good and bad, for their rejection of art in favor of life, for their beauty, for their patience, for their wisdom. Will you read the whole thing again, please?"

The priest read the poem again, slower this time, with better timing, and when he was finished Rock said, "Well, at any rate, you forgot to mention that he *does* speak with love of his wife. I didn't notice that the first time, either."

"It is *altogether* a poem of love, Rock," the priest said.

"May I borrow it? I would like to write it out and read it from time to time."

"Why?" Rock said.

"Rock," the priest said, "I am one who must not hate, each of us is such a one, yet I hate. I hate the Turk."

"Hate him," Rock said. "Don't worry about it."

"No, Rock, it is no good," the priest said. "It is no good to hate."

"Hate the Turk a little," Rock said. "You were born in the old country. Let it go. Hate him. Don't worry about it."

"It is no good to hate, Rock," Zadik said. "It is bad for the soul."

"Let a little of the soul be bad," Rock said. "Hate the Turk a little. Give him the happiness of your hatred. Let him always feel that Armenians born six thousand miles away from Armenia hate him. Let him always feel that Armenians who cannot speak a word of Armenian hate him. Let him feel that Armenians whose mothers or fathers are Russian or French or Italian or Scotch or Irish hate him. Let the Turk heal himself in the hatred of the Armenian."

"You will let me keep this a few days?" the priest said.

"Of course," Rock said. "I had thought I would translate it into English, but I do not want to do that now."

"Could you not have gotten home perhaps a half hour earlier, Rock?" the priest said.

"Zadik, you're drunk," Rock said. "My father has been dead twenty-five years. If he was dead twenty-five seconds when I got home it was forever. Take good care of the poem. I'll drive you home."

They went out, after last drinks, loitered along the walk to the gate, stood a moment on the small patch of lawn, then stepped to the car, speaking of hate and love, fathers and sons. They got into the car and began to drive to the church, the driver of the car saying to his friend, the member of his family, "A man needs his family. He needs the Turk of his family, to hate, to think he hates, to love, to think he loves, to hate and love, to think he hates and loves. I have seen only half a dozen Turks in my whole lifetime. They *are* members of the family, Zadik. They are entitled to a little decent hatred."

No man knows what a man is, but every man tries to guess. No man knows what a woman is, but no man tires of getting near enough to one more of them to try again to find out. A man is a lone thing and a woman is a lone thing, except when she is with child. Even a man and a woman together are a lone thing, a new lone thing, their togetherness a lone thing. Men and women are lone things needing one another, and needing men and women come out of their need. Having come from women, men must return to women. They must return again and again. Having been made unalone by men, having become with children by them, women must return to men, they must return again and again, as each of them knows. If not to husband, then to father, to son. There is no other way for man, which is man-and-woman-forever-separate-and-forever-inseparable to live, to love, to give life, and finally to give it up. There is no other way to love God, truth, art, beauty, science, money, roses, clothes, automobiles, houses, soap, or Saturday nights.

ONE day in December Ann telephoned again.

"What are you doing?" she said.

"How are you, Ann?" Rock said. "How are the children?"

Is it snowing in New York? Are you having fun? I hope you're well. Put Haig on the phone. I want to hear Haig's voice."

"What's happened to *you*, Rock?" Ann said.

"Put Lula on the phone, Ann," Rock said. "I want to hear Lula's voice."

"Have you made a lot of money?" Ann said. "You sound like a man who's made a lot of money."

"No, Ann," Rock said. "I haven't made a lot of money, but I've still got my car."

"Have you still got your debts?" Ann said.

"Yes," Rock said, "I've still got my debts, too, Ann. Let me speak to Haig, will you, Ann?"

"He's asleep, Rock."

"Wake Haig up for me, Ann. He'll understand."

"I need money, Rock."

"I know you do, Ann. Wake Lula up. Put her on the phone. I want to hear Lula's voice."

"You've got to send me money, Rock."

"I know I do, Ann. Let me speak to Haig, please."

"Hold on a minute."

He waited a moment and then began to hear their voices as they came to the phone. He heard Ann say, "You talk first, Haig. Then you, Lula."

"Is it Papa?" he heard the boy say. "Where *is* Papa?"

"He's in San Francisco," he heard Ann say.

"San Francisco?" he heard the boy say, laughing. "*I* was in San Francisco. That's not so far away." The boy got on the phone.

"Papa?" he said.

"Yes, Haig," Rock said.

"How are you, Papa?" Haig said. "I haven't talked to you in a long time, Papa. A long, long time, Papa."

"How are you, Haig?"

"I'm fine, Papa. I'm in school. I go to school. Of course it's vacation now. Christmas vacation, Papa, but I guess you know."

"No, Haig, I didn't know. Christmas vacation must be very nice."

"Yes, it is, Papa. Is it Christmas vacation in San Francisco, too?"

"Yes, it is, Haig."

"Papa, Lula's bothering me. She wants to talk to you. She's *always* bothering me. Now, wait a minute, Lula, I want to tell Papa something. Papa? Do you think it's right for ghosts to come back and haunt houses the way they do on television?"

"Well, what do *you* think, Haig?"

"Well, Papa, some of the ghosts haunt easy and funny, but *some* of them haunt the way that scares you, Papa. Do you believe in them, Papa?"

"I don't look at television," Rock said. "I don't have a set. Do *you* believe in them, Haig?"

"Well, Papa, I suppose there are no ghosts, but I've seen them on television, and there they are, Papa—ghosts!"

"They must be good things to see on television, Haig."

"Yes, they are, Papa. Are you coming home, Papa?"

"No, I can't come home, Haig."

"Lula!" Haig shouted suddenly. "Papa? She wants to talk to you. Thank you for telephoning, Papa."

"Goodbye, Haig."

"Goodbye, Papa."

"Papa?" he heard the little girl say. Then he heard her giggle with excitement.

"Papa? You know what?" she cried.

"What, Lula?"

"When Mama woke me up and told me you wanted to talk to me you know what I thought?"

"What, Lula?"

"I thought, 'Mama's fooling, Mama's fooling me,' but when I heard Haig talking to you, Papa, you know what I thought?"

"What, darling?"

"I thought, 'Mama's *not* fooling. She's *not* fooling me.' Papa, oh Papa, Haig hits me, Haig *always* hits me!"

"He loves you, darling," Rock said. "He's your brother. Brothers always hit their sisters."

"There's a brother, Papa, who doesn't hit his sister," Lula said. "He was at Haig's birthday party. He didn't hit nobody. He didn't even hit *me*. He didn't hit me, Papa, when I hit *him*. Isn't he a funny brother, Papa?"

"Yes, he is, darling."

"I was so surprised, Papa, when he didn't hit me. His name is Robert Moss, so when he didn't hit me, I hugged him. He's a *good* boy, Papa. He let me hug him three times. He didn't move or anything. He just stood there. First I hugged him once. Then I hugged him twice. Then I hugged him three times. Then I went and hit Haig, and you know what he did, Papa?"

"What did he do, darling?"

"He hit me, Papa!"

"He's your brother, darling. He loves you."

"I know, Papa. He loves me very much. But Robert Moss, he doesn't hit when you hit him or move when you hug him or anything. Papa, oh Papa?"

"Yes, darling?"

"I hugged him three times. Mama, please! I want to tell Papa something. Haig told Papa something and I want to tell him something, too. Papa? Do you think it's right for ghosts—— Do you think it's right, Papa? Do you think it's right? Do you think it's right——?"

"Lula," he heard Ann say, "tell Papa what you want to say. Don't just keep saying, 'Do you think it's right?'"

"Oh, Mama," Lula said, "can't you let me just talk to Papa? Papa, I know what I want to tell you. It's this. When I'm a big girl and get my money I'm going to give it *all* to you."

"What money, darling?"

"From the piggy bank, Papa. I've got money in there." He heard his son roar with laughter, and shout, "She's got eighteen cents, Mama! She's going to give it to Papa!"

"You shut up, Haig!" he heard his daughter say to her brother. "Papa, oh Papa! Can't you come to New York, Papa? Haven't you got any money, Papa?"

"Lula," Rock said. "I've got more money than any man in the world."

"Papa's got more money than any man in the world," he heard her say. "Papa, oh Papa! Mama says I got to say goodbye! Papa?"

"Yes, darling?"

"Goodbye, Papa! Goodbye!"

"Goodbye, darling."

Ann came to the phone.

"Hold on, Rock," she said. "I'll get them back in their beds and come right back."

She was back in a moment.

"Rock?" she said.

"Yes, Ann."

"What are you doing?"

"I'm not doing anything," Rock said. "They sound fine. Thanks, Ann. Thanks very much."

"What are you going to do about money?" Ann said.

"I'll get some," Rock said.

"They need all sorts of things for Christmas," she said. "I don't mean foolish things. I mean clothes."

"Are you having their teeth looked after?" Rock said.

"Their teeth are fine," Ann said. "I haven't paid the dentist, though. You've got to get money, Rock."

"I'll get money, Ann. Are you all right?"

"I need money."

"For God's sake, Ann, I know you need money."

"I don't need anything else."

"I know, Ann. I'm going to get money. Thanks for letting me speak to the kids. Goodbye, Ann."

He couldn't sleep all night, remembering the voices of the kids. He got up at five and drove to his sister's. She couldn't have been much asleep herself, for she came to the door almost instantly.

"I knew it was you, Rock," she said. "The minute I heard the bell I knew it was you. I can tell who it is from the way the bell rings. You always ring it loud but quick and just once, and I always know it's you. Come on, I'll make you some coffee."

He went into the kitchen and walked around while his sister got coffee going.

"What's the matter, Rock?" she said.

"Ann telephoned again last night," Rock said.

"How is she?"

"She's fine."

"Why don't you go back, Rock?"

"I talked to the kids," Rock said. "This is what I'm going to do. I'm driving to Hollywood. I'm going to stop in Fresno first. I'm going to buy the house."

"What house, Rock?"

"Our house," Rock said. "The house on Winery Street. I want to talk to the people and let them know I want to buy it. Then I'm going to drive to Hollywood and go to work. I'm not going to be making very much money, and I'll have to send most of it to Ann, but I'm going to buy our house."

"Rock," his sister said, "there's no house on Winery Street any more. I got a letter from Alice, Popken's girl, about a month ago. It's burned down."

"Is the coffee ready?" Rock said.

"I'll fix you some eggs, too," his sister said. "Four, or six?"

"Well, six, then," Rock said. "The white porcelain tub with the dough in it is on the table in the storage space off the garage. Throw it out. Look after the place for me."

"You'll come here for Christmas, won't you?" his sister said. "For God's sake, Rock, fly up for Christmas, anyway."

"No, Vava," Rock said. "I'm going to work. I couldn't sleep last night. I couldn't sleep the way I couldn't as a kid, from gladness, because I'd heard the voices of my kids. How are yours, Vava?"

"Oh, you know my kids, Rock," Vava said. "All big. All nice. I never saw such innocent kids. They don't know anything about the world. Only Joe knows a little. They're all fine, Rock. I've got to get those girls married, though. How about a steak now?"

"No," Rock said. "Take care of yourself."

He embraced his sister, went out to his car, and was soon

plunging down the highway. He was at the house on Winery Street in four hours. He walked among the black ruins to where the table had been in the kitchen. He kicked at some charred timber there and got to the earth under it. The earth was clean there, and green weeds were growing in it. He loved weeds. He loved weeds more than he loved anything else, certainly more than stars. His kids were weeds.

He went back to his car and began the last half of the journey, knowing no man knows himself, or his father, or his son, but each man lives his life the best he knows how, and tries to speak, in speaking of ghosts and the rightness of them on television, of all of the things between fathers and sons which kindness, charity, manners, and love keep a man from saying.

What does a man mean? What is the meaning of a man? What is he supposed to be? How is he supposed to be what he is supposed to be? What is the purpose of him? What is he supposed to do? How is he supposed to do it? Does he mean anything? Does his birth mean anything, his boyhood, his early manhood, his manhood, his work, his failure, his humor, his anger, his despair, his death, his actual death in his body? What does it mean for a man to live, to go on living? What does it mean for him to get up from his bed in the morning, shave, shower, put on fresh clothes, drink coffee, eat bread and cheese, step forth among his kind, among the occupations of his kind, work, become tired, rest, read, sleep, dream? What does it mean for him to look upon a woman with love, to take her with love, to fill her with love, to get her with child with love, to behold the child with love, to dwell with her and the child with love, to speak with her to the child with love?

What does the end of himself mean in his own body? What is the purpose of a man? What is the secret of his indestructibility? Is he an immortal thing? If he is immortal, what good is it? What good is it to be immortal? If a man comes to nobility of soul, what good is it? What is a man?

A MAN is a captured thing, captured by living matter, by the habits, customs, compulsions, and dreams of this matter. A man means nothing. Two thousand million of him living and dying at the same time mean nothing, but no man lives who does not mean more than the sum of everything in books, for a man is a terrified jackrabbit running between capture and capture. He is a tiger in the circus, a lion in the zoo, a worm in the flower pot, a bat in the barn. All of him together mean nothing, but one at a time a man means the sum of evergrowing meaning. A man means business. He means doing, though there is nothing good to do, or bad to do, or fair to middling to do, except one thing, to love his wife, to love her hair, to love her feet, to love her teeth, to love the nails of her fingers, to love her tonsils, to love her nose, her ears, her eyes, her cheeks, her neck, her shoulders, her arms, her elbows, the soft hair of her skin, her breasts, her nipples, her underarms, her navel, her flanks, her thighs, the geography and topography of her, her legs, her knees, her shins, her ankles, her speech, her laughter, her anger, her tears, her petulance, her imbecilities, her mother, her father, her son, her daughter. A man is a family thing. His meaning is a family meaning. A man comes from a long time ago and is on his way to a long time hence, walking with his family, loitering along the way, looking for the daughter of a stranger walking in the opposite direction with *her* family, falling back a little as she falls back, looking at the flowers she's looking at as she waits for him to fall upon her, waits to bite him with love, to be bitten with love by him.

His secret is *being*, and his being is most truly being when he falls upon her to be bitten and to bite, to hold fast, to kiss, to put in her all of his family, from long ago, all of his time, to have her grow their families together in a new man, to capture the unknown one, the one long gone, to bring him back to the grass and green of being.

What good is it? (It's fun, brother. It *is* better than nothing. To be, to be trying, to be at love, to be on the way with the family, to be going, to be dying, to breathe, to be angry, to be mad with astonishment, to be running at the capturer, to be wrestling with the capturer, to be killing the capturer, to be walking with the capturer in comradeship, is better than nothing, brother.)

What good is it? (It's no good at all, sister, but it *is* better than nothing. Sandwiches are good. Thin sandwiches. A bath is a good thing. To scratch the nose is better than nothing. For God's sake, woman, to be *rotting* is better than nothing.)

What about philosophy? Will that help? (No. The best philosophy is to open a can and if there is anything good in it to eat it. A can of something good to eat is a good thing. A tree with fruit growing on it has a certain wisdom to it. The thing to do is to pick the cherries and eat them, the apricots, the peaches, the figs, apples, pears, plums, or whatever the philosophy of the tree happens to have put it to bearing.)

What about religion? Will that help? (No, but if it's time to sing hosanna, sing it and let it *not* help, for it is better than nothing. If there is a red rose on a rose tree, pluck it, give it to a loitering girl, fall upon her, for that is better than nothing, that is much the best of the variations of better than nothing.

It is religious and will not help, but it is much the best of the little that is better than nothing.)

Is there anything at all to art? Will art help? (No, but if it seems like a good idea to look at things carefully, though this will help nothing, look at things carefully, for that is art, that is what art is, and it is often a good idea to look at things carefully, and to see them. This also is better than nothing. To see an eye clearly is art, but it does not help. It's just that it's better than nothing.)

What about being great? Wouldn't it be great to be great? Wouldn't being great be a great help? (No, but it is better than nothing, although it *is* no different, the same as not being great, the same as being a fool, for a man is a jackass with the heart of a lion, as he himself knows. This, too, is better than nothing.)

What about music? (Music is fine. A man ought to listen to music. A man ought to listen. He ought to listen to the music in everything, including the music of orchestras, although it will not help, for this also is better than nothing. Music is fine. It will not help.)

What about jokes? Will the telling of jokes or the listening to the telling of them help? (No, but this will come nearest to seeming to be something that will help. It will not help, but it is better than nothing.)

What about money? Will money help? (No, but it's all right, and every man should collect Indian-head pennies. Every man should have at least two or three of them carefully collected.)

Is there something to be said for shoes? (Yes, a man should wear shoes except in the bath. This will not help, but it is also better than nothing. A prosperous man, a spendthrift, should have a pair of black shoes and a pair of brown shoes, the black for his feet, the brown for his hands if that's what he wants to do.)

Is penmanship nice? (Penmanship is one of the nicest things there is. A man with a flair for it can sit down and write a letter to somebody, or his name, with flourishes. Penmanship is a very nice thing. Many great men have had it, and their signatures are to be seen here and there, though they are dead. There is a certain innocent confusion and absurdity in penmanship, but it is better than nothing, too.)

Would swifter airplanes come in handy? (No.)

Is there anything at all to the dropping of bombs more destructive than atomic or H or I or J or K or L or M or N or O bombs? (These should be dropped, especially the I and O ones, but this is *not* better than nothing. It's just pure. Dropping them will not help and is not better than nothing, but not dropping them would be to waste them, and as they are expensive, they ought to be dropped. Their dropping should be pin-point, on the head of whoever spoke so clearly.)

Wouldn't it be better if people were different? Wouldn't it be better if Russians were more Americanized and Americans were more Russianized? (No. The theory that people should be different from apes is a false theory. There is nothing for apes and people to be different from. This also is better than nothing.)

Are eggs good? (Yes, with salt and pepper.)

Do you like it in Hollywood? (Drop dead.)

He drove the old Cadillac into the old parking lot across the street from U.S. Pictures and got out. The policeman with the pistol on his belt who parked the cars for the U.S. boys said, "Rock Wagram! Tell me, Rock, is Yale a good school to send my boy to?"

"I'm glad you asked me that, George," Rock said. "It *is* George, isn't it?"

"Yes, Rock," the man said. "George Warrington. I've been here twenty-five years now."

"Yes," Rock said. "Now, about Yale. It just happens I've been giving a good deal of thought to questions like Yale. You've got a boy to send to school, is that it?"

"Yes, a fine boy," the man said. "I've heard about Yale. Is that the school to send my boy to?"

"Now, let me think about this a minute, George," Rock said. "I don't want to make a careless answer."

"Take your time, Rock," the man said.

"Yale," Rock said. "That's in New Haven. Well, this is my answer, George. Yale's the place to send your boy. It's a fine place. They *teach* at Yale, George. Philosophy, law, medicine, poetry."

"Is that where you went, Rock?"

"Yes." Rock smiled. "Majored in Armenian, animal husbandry, and meaning. You're going to be very happy about your boy at Yale."

The policeman roared with laughter because he hadn't seen Rock in years.

"Shall I wash the car?" he said.

"No," Rock said. "Get it painted. It's been gray for eight years, and I'm tired of it. Get it painted bright yellow-green. That was the color of Murphy's Cadillac."

"There's a place down the road about a mile that does a complete job for twenty-nine dollars and ninety-five cents," George Warrington said. "It takes them three hours."

"Take care of it for me, will you?" Rock said. "I'll be in there at least four hours."

"Bright yellow-green, is that right, Rock?"

"Yes."

When he came out four hours later he saw the tired old car looking like sad sin itself. The sun was going down and Sam Schwartz was saying, "It's about time you came home, Rock. I know the test is going to be great. We'll sign the papers immediately afterwards."

Rock stopped on the broad brick walk to look at the sinking sun.

"Look over there," he said.

"What is it, Rock?" Schwartz said.

"The sun," Rock said. "Look at it. Did you ever see it so bright and hot in December before? Did you ever see it so alone before?"

"Rock, does the sun travel in groups?" Schwartz said. "Did I ever see it so alone before? It's always been alone. Let's go to Romanoff's and talk. This is like old times, Rock. Paul Key is a happy man in his grave."

Rock stood and looked at the sun.

"Look over there again," he said.

"What's the matter *now?*" Schwartz said.

"It's red, Sam," Rock said. "It's red now. Bright, hot, alone, and red, Sam."

He began to walk suddenly, moving swiftly, the heavy man taking after him.

"We've got a lot to talk about, Rock," Schwartz said. "We've come a long way, the both of us, and we're in better shape than ever. I knew you'd come home, Rock. The past is past and the pictures of the past are nothing to what the pictures of the future are going to be."

They went across the street to the parking lot. Rock walked

around the car slowly, examining it and the new paint job while George Warrington and Sam Schwartz walked behind him, Sam talking steadily about Paul Key's happiness in the grave and George Warrington saying nothing because Sam was U.S. Pictures itself. Rock opened the door for Sam, who got in and settled himself on the blue leather seats. Rock then lifted the hood of the car and had a long look at the motor, black and greasy now, while George Warrington said very softly, "He ain't no Paul Key, Rock, but they say he gets them out, they say he gets them out fast and cheap, they say they make a lot of money. They say he's a human dynamo. I remember when he was a half-wit. He runs the place, Rock."

"He went to Yale, too," Rock said. "That's the place to send your boy all right."

He got into the car and drove off. The old piece of junk had a lot of power still. It was quick to start, quick to go, and it still plunged, it plunged the instant Rock asked it to.

"What's that old smell I smell, Rock?" Schwartz said. "What's *that?*"

"It's me and the leather of the seats," Rock said.

"Is this the same car you drove me to the hotel in Fresno in, Rock?"

"Yes, it is."

"I thought it was a brand-new car," Schwartz said.

"No," Rock said. "I had it painted this afternoon."

The sun was almost gone now. The car plunged toward it, on the way to Romanoff's, each passenger of the car meaning just about all there is for a man to mean.

A man lives in ignorance all his life. He is a fool, a crook, and a hoodlum all his life. He counts his money all the time. He thinks it has something to do with the soul he's losing or

288

gaining. If he spends or wastes or loses some of his money, he feels vaguely that he's lost some of his soul. If he accumulates a great deal of it, he feels vaguely that he has neglected his soul, but he doesn't mind so much because he has the money. If he has no money to count, spend, waste, or lose he feels vague, and gets a haircut.

AT Romanoff's Eddie Lucas came to the table and said, "Rock, I want to talk to you the minute you're free."

"Right now," Rock said.

"No, I don't want to bust in," Eddie said. "Besides, I've got this girl at the table."

"Which one is this one?" Rock said.

"This one's not a wife," Eddie said.

"Which *wife* is it now?" Rock said.

"It's the sixth," Eddie said, "but I'm divorced, Rock. We just didn't see eye to eye."

"Sit down," Rock said. "You know Sam."

"I've met Mr. Schwartz," Eddie said.

"Hi," Sam said, and went back to his eating.

"When can we talk?" the song-writer said. "It's important."

"Any time," Rock said. "Call me at the Beverly Wilshire."

"In a couple of hours?"

"Sure."

"O.K., Rock," Eddie said, and went off.

"That no-good," Sam said.

"You know him?" Rock said.

"That sneak," Sam said.

"What did he do?" Rock said.

"I can buy and sell him a dozen times," Schwartz said, "and a dozen more like him. *Dreamy Arabia!*"

"Did he write *that?*" Rock said.

"I *paid* him to write it," Sam said. "I tried to keep all of P.K.'s people at U.S., so I kept this one, too."

"Wasn't *Dreamy Arabia* at the top of the hit parade, as they say?" Rock said.

"Sure it was, and the film made a lot of money, too," Schwartz said.

"Isn't that good, Sam?"

"He can write songs all right," Sam said. "I'm not saying he can't, but songs aren't everything."

"No, I guess not," Rock said. "I've always liked songs, though, even bad ones, and there was never one worse than *Dreamy Arabia*."

"*Dreamy Arabia* was fine," Sam said. "It had a nice lilt. It *should* have had. It was swiped from the *Blue Danube*. The guy that wrote it is a son of a bitch, though. He'll never work for me again."

"He can be liquidated," Rock said. "You can get him bumped off."

"Why should I waste my money?" Schwartz said. "Two or three hundred dollars of my good money. I'll just sit back and wait for him to commit suicide."

"What'd he do?" Rock said.

"I had this girl in a picture," Sam said. "He comes along, a married man, a man with his sixth wife at home. He gives her that fast, nervous, excited, intellectual talk all these dumb stars go for."

"What happened?"

"I suspended her," Sam said. "She's at Fox now, playing drunks."

"What happened between her and him, I mean?"

THE SON AND THE DAUGHTER

"The usual," Sam said. "What else? Moves me out, moves himself in."

"You didn't mean to *marry* the girl, did you?" Rock said.

"I haven't time to get married," Sam said. "Marriage is for suckers."

"What'd you suspend her for?" Rock said.

"I took her out of the star part," Sam said. "Had the writers change the character. Brought in a girl from Italy who spoke with an accent. Gave the American girl the part of the chambermaid at a cheap hotel. She refused to play the part. I suspended her. Finished her."

"Who is the girl?" Rock said.

"Maybe you've heard of her," Sam said. "Marcy Miller."

"I was in a picture with her once," Rock said. "She seemed like a nice girl. Married to a cameraman, wasn't she? Had a couple of kids."

"She threw him out years ago," Sam said. "Married a director. Threw him out when he couldn't make a good picture any more."

"How are the kids?" Rock said.

"How should I know how the kids are?" Sam said. "What kind of kids can they *be* with a mother like her?"

"They can be fine kids," Rock said. "I hope Paul's sister's all right."

"Who?" Sam said. "My *mother?*"

"Yes. Is she well?"

"The same as ever."

"I'm glad to hear that, Sam."

"I don't think any son in the world has taken the kind of care of his mother that I have," Sam said, "but she's the same as ever. All she says is, if Paul had lived, this, if Paul had lived,

291

that. Well, Paul didn't live. I think she thinks he was Lincoln, and she's Lincoln's mother, not mine."

"She sounds wonderful, Sam."

"Don't think I'm not crazy about her," Sam said. "I've been crazy about her all my life, but isn't there a limit? She was seventy-five her last birthday. All she does is order the servants around, eat chocolates, and tell everybody she meets she's Paul Key's sister. 'I'm Paul Key's big sister,' she says. What a woman, Rock. Bosses me around as if I was eight years old. I came home with a girl once that I wanted to marry. It was during the war. She thinks the girl's Irish or something, I guess, so she talks to the girl in Yiddish, and the girl talks back to her in the sweetest Yiddish you ever heard. I think she's going to love the girl, but the first thing she tells me is, 'That girl's a crook, Sammy. She's taking lessons. She speaks Yiddish with an accent. She's after your money. Don't trust that girl. She's no good.' She keeps it up day after day. I'm afraid to bring the girl home again. So the girl marries a Christian millionaire. They've got three kids. So my mother says, 'See, Sammy? What did I tell you? A phony.' That's Mama. But I love her. She bets the horses all day, by telephone, and do you want to hear the pay-off? She wins. She bets them twenty on the nose, every race, every track, and she wins. She sits there by the radio and the phone, waiting for the results, phoning and eating chocolates. She came home with a new mink coat the other day. I've bought her two already, but this one's different, it's got more style, it's cut different. Three thousand wholesale, horse winnings. I've got to take her to Las Vegas at least once a month, to the Flamingo. She sits at the wheel all day and all night, betting ten-cent chips, and comes home with a profit of anywhere from two hundred to two thousand dollars.

Once she lost two hundred dollars and was so upset I thought I was going to lose her. I talked to her for hours, but it didn't do any good. The next day she went back and lost another hundred. I didn't know what to do."

"What did you do?" Rock said.

"Well," Sam said, "I talked to her again. 'Mama,' I said, 'don't you understand? You don't have to worry about two hundred dollars. You don't have to worry about two hundred *thousand* dollars, Mama. Don't you understand? *I am U.S. Pictures now!* I make a fortune every year, Mama! Here,' I said. 'Here's two hundred dollars out of my own pocket.' Listen to this, Rock. 'I lost two hundred *twenty-two* dollars,' she says. 'So all right, Mama,' I tell her. 'Here's a hundred more. Now, will you stop being unhappy?'"

"Did she stop?" Rock said.

"My mother?" Sam said. "Hell no. She didn't stop being unhappy and she didn't stop playing. A half hour later she was back at the wheel. It turned out all right, though. It always does for Mama. She finally won it all back, and eleven dollars besides. Those eleven dollars—in silver—she keeps stacked in a pile on her dresser with the perfume bottles—about a hundred expensive perfume bottles she's got, I guess—and looks at them all the time. She loves money, perfume, furs, and food."

"And her son," Rock said.

"No," Sam said. "Her brother. I'd like her to take a look at the books sometime, though. I've made twice as much money in half as much time as Paul Key ever made for U.S. Pictures. I've got great plans for you, Rock. I've got two writers working on a story right now that is going to be perfect for you. Listen to this, Rock. A man does everything in the world for his mother. She turns around and nearly wrecks his life. So what happens? The man goes right on being a good son. At last she dies and everybody says the man would never have amounted to anything except for her. The man keeps the secret all his life. Do you like it, Rock?"

"It's great," Rock said.

"You're not just saying that, are you?" Sam said.

"No," Rock said. "It's great, that's all."

"I want you to do the son," Sam said.

"Yes," Rock said.

"You've known me a long time," Sam said. "You know the kind of man I really am. This one's going to be a *class* picture. At the same time it's going to make a lot of money, too. I've done everything but win the Academy Award. Well, now I'm going to do that, too, and you're going to help me, Rock."

Rock was thinking about his son and his daughter. He was remembering their voices on the telephone.

"Yes, I am," he said. "Yes, I am, Sam."

"Now, here's an episode from the time when I was four years old," Sam said. "I want to tell you a lot of these episodes. We'll meet every day. We'll drop in on the writers at least once a day and throw some of these episodes at them. Listen to this, Rock."

Rock listened to Sam Schwartz, but all he could hear was his son saying, "How are you, Papa?" And his daughter saying, "Papa, oh Papa."

He listened to Sam Schwartz and heard the voices of his children all through dinner and for an hour and a half afterwards. His eyes smiled the whole time, and just before they got up to go Sam said, "Rock, I knew you'd be excited about this story. I've never seen you so excited about a story."

Rock drove Sam Schwartz to his mansion high up in the

hills overlooking Hollywood, then turned around and drove back to Beverly Hills, knowing how a man lives in ignorance all his life, but at the same time is some sort of an angel, overweight or underweight, who is involved in the matter of the mother and the money.

It was after eleven when he reached his room. He sat down to wait for Eddie Lucas to telephone.

Every man is a good man in a bad world. No man changes the world. Every man himself changes from good to bad or from bad to good, back and forth, all his life, and then dies. But no matter how or why or when a man changes, he remains a good man in a bad world, as he himself knows. All his life a man fights death, and then at last loses the fight, always having known he would. Loneliness is every man's portion, and failure. The man who seeks to escape from loneliness is a lunatic. The man who does not know that all *is failure is a fool. The man who does not laugh at these things is a bore. But the lunatic is a good man, and so is the fool, and so is the bore, as each of them knows. Every man is innocent, and in the end a lonely lunatic, a lonely fool, or a lonely bore.*

But there is meaning to a man. There is meaning to the life every man lives. It is a secret meaning, and pathetic were it not for the lies of art, for which every man must be grateful, as he himself knows. For the lies tell him to wait. They tell him to hang on. The lies wink and tell him he is the one, and a man winks back, and goes about his business.

ROCK'S business was to sit and wait, and he attended to this business. He sat in the absurd room and waited. He knew he was not waiting for Eddie Lucas to telephone, although that was supposed to be what he was waiting for. He was waiting for anything, as he had waited on Saturday afternoons when he was a small boy, sitting in the big tree in the backyard of the house on Winery Street. He was waiting for time. He was waiting for the present to disengage itself from the past and from the future and come home. He was waiting for the figs to ripen, for wealth and importance and meaning to come to him, but most of all for love, which he waited for now in the absurd room, sitting on the writing table as if it were a branch of the fig tree.

He waited for love as if he were his seven-year-old son waiting for it. He remembered saying a year ago to his son's mother while his son and daughter stood by, "Listen, Ann, nothing is more important in this life than a father and a mother and a son and a daughter together. We're divorced. I haven't seen you or the children in almost a year. Even so, there's nothing anywhere for you or for me except these two, and the others we were going to have. You don't want to go on with this affair with a married man, do you? I'm home. You come home, too. You don't want to go on, do you? You *can't* want to go on. Come home, Ann." Rock saw his son turn and watch his mother's face. "Come home, Ann," Rock said, "because I love you."

The boy waited at the end of the room for his mother to speak.

"But I don't love you," he heard his mother say.

"Are you sure, Ann?" Rock said.

"Yes, I'm sure," the boy heard his mother say. "I don't love you."

The boy walked between the two of them to the window overlooking the street. On his way, moving slowly, he looked from one to the other. He stood at the window a moment, then walked back to his father and stood in front of him, looking into his eyes. He was trying not to give way. He laid himself down across his father's knees. When Rock heard him stifling sobs he burst into laughter and hugged the boy. The boy's mother, and his sister, ran to him.

"Why, what's the matter, Haig?" Ann said. "What's the matter?"

"I'm unhappy," Haig said. "I'm unhappy."

"Why?" Ann said. "Why are you unhappy?"

"Because you said you don't love my father," Haig said.

"Listen," Rock said. "That's not so at all. Your father and your mother weren't speaking about themselves."

"No," Ann said. "They were speaking about some friends of theirs."

Rock lifted the boy and handed him to his mother. The boy was deeply ashamed of having given way, and soon the father and the mother heard him laughing again. But he knew, Haig Vagramian knew, as every man knows. Your mother and your father—even your own mother and your own father cannot love one another. Then, how can others love one another? How can there be love? How can anything mean anything without love? How can anything be worth anything when your own mother and father cannot love one another?

When Eddie Lucas telephoned Rock said, "Tell me something about Marcy Miller, will you?"

"She's no good," Eddie said. "She's a tramp."

"How many kids has she got?" Rock said.

"Three, I think," Eddie said. "They're nearly grown up by now, though. What's Marcy Miller got to do with anything, Rock?"

"I had a cousin, got killed in the war," Rock said, "wanted to meet her. Everybody's got something to do with every-thing, Eddie. If she's got three kids, she's got a lot to do with everything. Is she finished? Is that it? Has she had it? Did she have bad luck? Does she look bad? Is she drinking?"

"She's still got *something*," Eddie said. "But how long can any of them last? She's nearly forty. I want to talk to you, Rock. It's very important. How about Dirty Dan's in a half hour?"

"Is that place still there?" Rock said.

"It's got another name," Eddie said, "but I still call it Dirty Dan's."

"Who *was* Dan?" Rock said.

"Nobody ever knew," Eddie said. "Half hour O.K.?"

"O.K.," Rock said. "Give me her phone number, will you?"

He wrote the number on a sheet of hotel paper, then called her. They talked as people who don't know one another very well and who are talking over the telephone talk and then Rock said, "How are your kids, Marcy? I remember you showed me pictures of them. How are they?"

"They're just fine, Rock," Marcy Miller said. "The oldest's almost twenty, in the Marines. The other boy's eighteen. He's going into the Navy soon. The girl's sixteen. Good God, my own kids, grown up already."

"Marcy?" Rock said. "Come to Dirty Dan's and have a drink with me."

"No, Rock," Marcy said. "I've gone to bed. You know, Rock, when you're finished and don't want to be, you've got to behave. I didn't think you even remembered me. What made you call? Don't tell me you had a yen for me back there in the old days?"

298

"Of course I did," Rock said.

"You did?" Marcy said. "Why didn't you let me know?"

"I couldn't," Rock said. "I couldn't because I believe in marriages and families, even bad ones. I called to ask about your children, Marcy."

"You're kidding."

"No, it's the truth."

"I've had a rough time with them," Marcy said, "but they're O.K. now. Why don't you come and have dinner with us next week?"

"I'd love to," Rock said.

She gave him the address, the day and the hour, and then they said goodbye.

He went downstairs, got into his car, and drove to Dirty Dan's on the Strip. He found Eddie Lucas at the same corner table, and sat down across from him, his back to the rest of the room.

"This time it's about *you*, Rock," Eddie said.

"I don't mind hearing you talk about yourself," Rock said. "Let's have it."

"Ann phoned this afternoon," Eddie said. "It's hard to believe I still have the same number, but I do. It's even harder to believe she kept it, but she did. I never knew Ann well, Rock, but she remembers that I was the one who introduced you two to each other, so I guess that's why she phoned."

"I talked to her last night," Rock said.

"She told me," Eddie said. "She tried to reach you in San Francisco. She tried for hours. She didn't think you'd be in Hollywood, but in case you were, and in case I ran into you somewhere—which I did, Rock—it was an accident—I could have taken the girl to any number of other places instead of

Romanoff's—would I talk to you? I told her I would. What did she want me to say? Well, she didn't know. I told her I'd tell you *that*. The point is, Rock, she telephoned and asked me to speak to you, that's all. So that's what I'm doing."

"Thanks," Rock said.

"Don't you think you two ought to go back together again?" Eddie said.

"No," Rock said. "I *want* to. Maybe she wants to, too. I know the kids want us to. We *can't*, though. I love her more than I love anybody else in the world, and she's a liar and a crook. I'll always love her more than I love anybody else in the world, and she's a cheap, conniving, giddy, stupid girl. Bring me a girl who is all truth and virtue and beauty, and she'll scare me to death. Why? Because *this* girl is the mother of my kids. I've got to love the mother of my kids because *they* love her. I talked to *them* last night, too. That's why I'm down here. I can't have them to live with me on a vineyard, or I'd have them there. I'd have her there with them, too, if a week of it wouldn't drive her crazy, only it would. I'm down here to work. For money. I don't like to work for money, but I'm going to try to do it. I'm a father, and I haven't any choice any more, that's all."

"Don't you think you ought to phone her and talk about it?" Eddie said.

"No," Rock said. "She breaks my heart. Her lies break my heart. Her crookedness breaks my heart. They break my heart because I know she ought to be the truest woman of them all, the one we are all looking for. Look at this," he said suddenly. "She gave it to me." Rock examined an aluminum coin about the size of a half dollar, and remembered when and how he had gotten it. It was at the Amusement Center at

52nd and Broadway in New York, in September, 1942. Ann Ford asked him for a dime to put in the machine. He watched her work the machine, and then she handed him the coin. He now read, as he'd done a thousand times before, what she had stamped on the coin:

—I—LOVEA—YOU—ROCK—ANN—

Rock handed the coin to Eddie Lucas.

"The machine got every word right but LOVE," Eddie said.

"Yes," Rock said.

They finished their drinks and got up. Rock dropped Eddie Lucas off at his apartment, then began to drive back to Beverly Hills. On the way, though, he decided against it, and found his way to Highway 101. He put the top of the car down, and began to drive south. It was after three now, and the night was clear and cold. He drove along easily, not speeding, stopping at Oceanside for coffee, and again in San Diego.

He was on his way to Tia Juana when he saw the sun come up. He stopped the car on the side of the highway, got out, and watched the sun. He watched it until he could feel the heat coming from it. Then he got back into the car, turned it around, and began to drive back, altogether alone now, without wife, without son, without daughter, without home, without hope, but not yet altogether without humor, for he knew he had driven all night to the sun, as if the sun might be nearer a little farther south, to see it come up once more, and wink, for a man *is* nonsense all his life, as he himself knows. All his life a man knows, he knows, he knows forever and forever, but all he knows is, I am alone, I am unhappy, but I've still got my car, and I've still got my ten-cent coin that says I lovea you.